UNDER THE LIGHTS

USA TODAY BESTSELLING AUTHOR

TIA LOUISE

This book is a work of fiction. Names, characters, places, and incidents are products of the author's imagination or are used fictitiously. Any resemblance to actual events or locales or persons, living or dead, is entirely coincidental.

Printed in the United States of America.

For the heroes.

Contents

Chapter 1	7
Chapter 2	19
Chapter 3	35
Chapter 4	47
Chapter 5	55
Chapter 6	69
Chapter 7	77
Chapter 8	97
Chapter 9	113
Chapter 10	129
Chapter 11	137
Chapter 12	145
Chapter 13	161
Chapter 14	167
Chapter 15	181
Chapter 16	189
Chapter 17	203
Chapter 18	213
Chapter 19	223
Chapter 20	231
Chapter 21	249
Chapter 22	261
Chapter 23	273

Chapter 24 285
Epilogue 293
Acknowledgments 321
About the Author 323

CHAPTER 1

"Show me a hero, and I'll write you a tragedy."
-F. Scott Fitzgerald

Mark

The first thing I see is the gun on the floor.

Fear tightens my neck, and I'm frozen in the doorway. My backpack slides from my shoulder down my arm as ice trickles into my veins. The room smells like the fourth of July, firecrackers mixed with the musty odor of smoke and damp.

It's hot.

The air barely moves in New Orleans at this time of year.

The dog days.

"Uncle Rick?" My voice is low and even.

My closest living relative, a man I barely know, is hunched in the fetal position on the couch. Eyes closed, both his hands are between his knees, and his lips have disappeared in his teeth.

He could be sleeping, napping while watching a television show. Only the screen is black, and he's not responding.

Fuck. The ice in my veins melts into panic. My eyes dart around the room assessing the scene. Drawers open. Papers spread across the hardwood floor. The corner of the rug is curled under… Signs of a struggle?

I should slowly leave the room, go downstairs, and call 911 to report a crime.

I don't.

I swallow the fear and pick my way forward, across the small apartment to where my few possessions are stashed. I've been here less than a week, long enough to grow suspicious of his late-night errands, the jerk of surprise when the phone rings after hours, the presence of a .44 Magnum at the dinner table.

Uncle Rick was annoyed when I showed up on his doorstep last week, looking for a place to crash. My plan was to come here, study hard, and get into the police academy.

"You can crash until you've found a place to live," he growled. "By the end of the week."

He was my father's only sibling, and I'd taken a gamble coming here. Then, when he found out my plans, he was even more pissed.

"Why the fuck you wanna be a pig?"

He said I was "part of the problem."

Naturally, I disagreed.

"I want to fight crime, find men like the ones who ruined my dad and bring them to justice," I'd say.

The ones who run the off-track betting rings. The ones who own the prostitutes. The ones who take everything men have and ruin them.

I wanted to be a hero.

He said I was a fool.

Now who's the fool…

My eyes fix on the handgun on the floor. *Don't touch anything.*

Covering my hand with my sleeve, I open the closet door and scoop my few hanging clothes off the rack. A fatigue-green army-surplus bag is in the corner. I shove my extra pair of boots, shirts, underwear… everything I brought with me in it, then

I do my best to retrace my steps to the door.

Out on the street, I don't pause before heading up the damp sidewalk. Light mist fills the heavy air, and it's after nine on a Wednesday. Nobody's walking the dark streets. Nobody sees me walking away from a crime scene.

My gut twists, and I feel sick thinking about him dead on the couch. Even if I didn't really know him, he's kin. I have to let the cops know... Leave an anonymous tip or something.

For now, I've got to find a place to go. It helps that I've been searching for my own place since I arrived. Crossing the street, I head toward the river. I remember reading about a few hostels and rooms for rent closer to the shipyards. At worst, I could get a room at the YMCA.

Six more blocks, and I start to encounter the stragglers coming off Bourbon Street. It's the street that never sleeps in the city of excess.

A block away, I stand and watch the bodies slowly passing like a drunk parade in the middle of the night, always moving. Making my way around the perimeter, I read the street signs, looking for the place from memory.

The Marigny is a single door squeezed between a daiquiri shop and a wig and souvenir store. If you're not looking for it, you'll walk right past and never even see it. A skinny guy who looks about ten years older than me sits on the front stoop smoking a cigarette, watching the herd of tourists slowly pass.

"Any rooms available?" I pull my cap lower on my brow. I'm tall, and if I play my cards right, I can look older.

As the guy glances at me, a tendril of smoke curls into his eye and makes him squint. He's dark, Italian or Acadian, and when he pushes off his knees to stand, his head only reaches the top of my shoulder. I dwarf him with my pack on my back.

Black eyes assess my frame. "Where that accent from?"

I've only just gotten used to people swapping *d* for *th* in the Quarter. *Where dat accent from?*

"Evergreen."

"Where that?"

"Avoyelles Parish."

He takes another long drag before he nods. "Are you strong?"

"Who wants to know?" My response is sharp. The shock of the night is wearing off, and unless this guy is the manager, I don't feel like small talk.

"Terrence Price." Cigarette in mouth, he sticks out a hand.

I pause before giving it a shake. "Mark Fitzhugh." His eyebrows rise and my brow lowers. "Family name. You got a problem?"

"No. Fitz. I like it." Cigarette out. "Got a burlesque show at the corner of Royal and Orleans looking for a crew. Go with me tomorrow, and you can have a job."

"What makes you think I need a job?"

"Why you here?"

"I don't know." I don't know if I want to stay in this city. The bad luck of my family feels like it's already found me. At the same time, I have nowhere else to go.

"Come on, you kidding? Pretty ladies showing their tits." He leans closer. "Play your cards right, and you get a private show."

He grins and drives an elbow into my arm. The memory of Rick dead on the couch creeps at the corners of my thoughts, and I shake my head, shake them away.

"Not into girls?" Terrence draws back. "I could see if they need anybody at Oz—"

"No." Clearing my throat, I wave my hand. "I like girls. I'm just... Rough day."

"In that case." He opens the front door. "Get some rest. Take Room 12. I leave in the morning at nine. Meet me here, and you can see what you think."

I leave him on the stoop and enter the narrow building. Two yellow lamps spaced evenly down the length of the passage light the dim hall, and a staircase leading up is at the very back. The hall is lined with doors, and each has a small brass plaque engraved with a number. Number 12 is the first on the left.

Inside, it can't be more than ninety square feet, shallow and wide with no windows. A bed is against the back wall, and a small table and lamp are centered to the left. On the opposite wall is a narrow armoire. I catch the faint whiff of hospital grade ammonia under the stale smell of dust. At least it's clean.

Setting my duffel and backpack in the middle of the floor, I pull the skinny mattress back and check the corners for signs of bed bugs. Going to the head, I pull it back. Not seeing anything, I reach over and kill the lamp before dropping fully clothed onto the blue-striped mattress.

If I decide to stay, I'll have to buy sheets... and food, which means I need money. The muffled roar of street noise filters through the walls, and I consider Terrence's offer. It would tide me over until I make a decision.

Until then...

Reaching into my pocket, I pull out the small burner phone I picked up last week. It's untraceable, which is probably perfect for this. My thumb wavers as I hold it over the numbers. I take a deep breath and slowly dial, 9… 1… 1…

Dread tightens in my chest as I wait for the answer.

"911, what is your emergency?" The voice is robotic, bored.

"Uh, I need to report a noise." *Shit!* I didn't plan this before I dialed.

"A noise?"

"Sorry." Scrubbing my fingers against my eyelids, I try to think of words that don't sound incriminating. "I thought I heard a car backfire, but—"

"Modern cars don't backfire. You heard a gunshot." Again, bored robot. "Give me your address. Are you in a safe location?"

"Yes… I'm fine. I—it's 216 Evangeline, second floor. Maybe my neighbor?"

"Don't go in or out of your apartment until police arrive. Keep your door locked. Police are on their way. I—"

"Thanks." I press the pad of my thumb against the red *end call* button and drop the small phone onto the bed.

A chill skates over my skin, and I curl my knees into my chest, covering my ears with my palms. The sight of Rick that way unearthed memories of my dad, and that old pain radiates through my spine. I don't cry, but the fist of grief tightens my shoulders. It's oppressive and relentless, demanding action.

Sliding my hands to the back of my neck, I hold on, waiting for sleep to come. Waiting for answers I'll never have.

Terrence is on the stoop holding a paper cup of coffee in his hand when I emerge the next morning. A cigarette is in his mouth, and he smiles when he sees me.

"Good call," he says.

I pause in the entryway and consider my stuff. I don't have much worth stealing, still, it's all I have. "No lock?"

He pulls a key out of his pocket and motions me outside, locking the front door behind me. "Reopens after six."

Key in his pocket, he takes off, headed northeast on Bourbon. I jog after him up the littered sidewalk. It's far less crowded than at midnight, but even at this hour, people still roam, drinks in hand and beads around their necks.

"So you own the place?"

"My aunt does." He takes a drink of coffee. "She lives in Chalmette. I run it for her."

We cut across the street when we reach Orleans in the direction of Royal. Rounding the corner, we're on a narrow lane of wrought iron balconies over narrow doors. Archways blocked off by wooden barriers. It's Pirate Alley.

We're half a block away when Terrence hits my chest with the back of his hand. "Let me do the talking."

A man who looks like the classic dockworker stands in front of a group of similar men giving orders. He's my height, but he outweighs me by at least fifty pounds, with thick hands and cords of muscle.

"Shipment arrives at ten," he growls. "New set design requires a catwalk and series of cranes and pulleys. They'll be mechanically operated, but I need extra men to work late as safety backup during the shows." A trickle of laughter filters through the crowd. "Now get busy. First show rehearses at three o'clock."

He turns, and he's facing Terrence and me. "Who is this, Price?"

"New tenant looking for work. I'll vouch for him." Stepping back, he gestures between us. "Mark, this is Darby Stamp. Darby, Mark Fitzhugh."

"Fitzhugh..." Darby's eyes narrow, and I stand straighter. "You do drugs?"

"No," I answer fast.

"Good. Half these guys do, which means half won't be back, and if they are, they're late." He starts walking and Terrence nods for me to follow. "If I catch you with any of the dancers, you're fired."

"Got it." After all that's happened, romance is not on my mind, and I've never been into drugs. Not that I could afford them.

"Those two rules mean I have to find a new crew about once a week."

He stops at a table holding a coffee dispenser and a large platter of assorted bagels, and dispenses what looks like liquid tar into a paper cup. Then he picks up a bagel and takes a bite, frowns, and tosses it in the trash.

"Pay's seventeen-fifty an hour. Stop by the office to fill out the paperwork before the end of the day."

"Thanks." I hesitate by the table as he heads to the auditorium.

"Help yourself to the food."

I reach over and quickly take a bagel. As soon as I pick it up, I realize it's hard as a rock, but beggars can't be choosers.

Darby keeps talking. "No breaks. You eat while you work. Follow me, and I'll show you the safety backup."

He pulls a metal door open, and we enter the side of a large backstage area. Ropes and boxes are scattered among long strips of red velvet curtain. Metal ladders lead up into the rafters, and squinting overhead, I see a narrow catwalk.

"We'll install two more of them for the performance tonight. The girls wear these belts that are attached to these mechanical pulleys." He motions to an ancient-looking switchboard. "You'll be up there holding the safety rope. It's attached to one dancer, so I need you and a few other guys I can trust to agree to take turns..."

While he speaks, movement catches my eye from the backstage area. Two women dressed in tight black pants and cutoff shirts approach. They're both blonde and stacked. One looks up at me and smiles. Her dark brow arches, and her pink tongue slips out to touch her upper lip. My skin heats at the invitation, and I cut my eyes back to Darby.

He nods in their direction. "Some of the girls live here. Don't go in their rooms unless Gavin or me tells you to. I'd hate to fire you so soon."

"Right."

"Now get back outside and help unload the truck."

I step back as he continues forward and turn on my heel to exit through the metal side door opposite the way the two dancers went. I'm not looking for trouble.

Out of nowhere a small, dark form collides with my chest. She starts to fall, and instinctively, I grab her by the upper arms, pulling her to me.

"Oh!" It's a breathless cry.

"I'm sorry. I—" My voice trails off as bright blue eyes framed by thick lashes capture mine.

I quickly take in full, pink lips and long, glossy waves swishing down her back. She smells fresh like flowers after rain, and as I hold her, I can feel she's slim but strong. She's fucking beautiful.

"I'm okay." Her voice is confident, and... annoyed? Amused?

I let her go. "I'm sorry," I repeat. "I didn't see you in the dark."

She glances down. "I am wearing all black."

I quickly scan the tight halter-top and workout pants she's wearing. It's the same as the other two girls' outfits, but her exposed torso is lined with muscle, not soft like theirs. Her expression is playful as well. I can tell she's younger, more innocent.

"No worries." She starts to go, but I can't help myself.

"Hey... What's your name?"

Her head tilts, and blue eyes meet mine. "Larissa. But everyone calls me Lara. You?"

"Mark." I put a hand in my pocket. "I'm just Mark."

She nods and a smile curls her lips. "Nice to meet you, just Mark."

At that, she takes off toward the food table, and I try to go. Everything in me says don't let my thoughts wander about this girl, follow the rules, turn around and get out of here... but my eyes linger on her slender back, slipping down to her cute little ass. *Larissa.*

"Hey!" The sharp, male growl grabs my attention. "New guy. Get out here and help unload these trucks."

Snapping out of it, I hustle to the door feeling lighter than I have in weeks.

CHAPTER 2

"When it's dark, look for stars."

Lara

Tanya finishes in a split.

Center stage, arms raised in a *V*, breasts completely bare.

Cheers and catcalls explode at us from the predominately male audience, and we're all frozen on our marks as the lights go out. The curtain falls, sending the odor of musty velvet swirling around us, and all arms drop.

The applause continues in front of the heavy fabric, but behind it is the swift *click* of stilettoes on hardwoods, the whisper of tights brushing thighs, fishnets and feathers. I exit stage right and catch the small hand waiting for me in the wings as I pass.

The glare of the spotlight dazzled my vision, but I've done this so many times, I could find my way blind. We navigate the maze of boxes and discarded scenery to my dressing room, surrounded by the odor of talc, cigarette smoke, cheap perfume, and sweat. Rosin crackles beneath my feet with every step, and we pass dancers speaking in low voices about what worked and what didn't and whose fault it was.

"These fucking pasties are for shit. Mine almost fell off twice," Vanessa growls, slamming the red-sequined tassels on a box.

"Just paint them on." Bea holds her hair up, inspecting her full breasts with bright-red tips. "You can't even tell the difference."

"I can tell," Vanessa says. "No tassels."

"Piercing?"

We keep moving.

The dark passage turns into a dimly lit hall lined with tiny dressing rooms where many of us live. Secretly, of course, since this old theater isn't zoned for residents. I lift the handle on our tiny door, and we push inside, both speaking at once.

"Oh, Lara!" Molly's voice is breathless. "Tanya was like a feather, floating and drifting—"

"Help me get this thing off," I interrupt, easing into the chair and trying to hold my shoulders still as I unfasten the enormous feathered wings. "They must weigh fifty pounds."

She hurries over, her small fingers searching my back for the remaining hooks.

"She was more like a pipe cleaner the way she bent over backwards," she continues as she lifts the enormous mélange of cut glass and feathers from my back. "She's so flexible. I wish I could move that way."

"Great." I rub my neck, rolling my head side to side. "You aspire to be a stripper."

"Exotic dancer!"

I straighten and peel off my fake eyelashes as Molly pulls my dark brown hair behind my shoulders and down my back.

"You can do better."

"At least you can sing," she says. "Your voice is the best of all of them."

My chest tightens at the idea of my dream. "Nobody cares about that. They just want our bodies."

I glance up at her bright blue eyes. Her blonde

hair is streaked with auburn highlights, and every day she grows more beautiful, her breasts rounder, her hips more narrow. It makes my head hurt. I have to get us out of here before she's pulled into this world.

"I'll go back to the library tomorrow."

"I don't know why you're so determined to find a new job." She turns to my mirror and places the feathers on her shoulders. "I love it here. Everyone's so nice, and the girls are so pretty. Some of them make a lot of money!"

"It's pretty average for burlesque."

In my dressing mirror, I watch as she blows kisses, wondering for the thousandth time if I made a mistake begging Rosa to let Molly stay that night I found her starving in the alley.

For a year, we've shared my bed, shared my food, and she's worn my old clothes. She's never cost the show a penny. Still, she's catching up with me in size, and with a body like hers, Gavin's going to notice soon.

A gentle knock interrupts our conversation. "Lara?"

My heart jumps, and I'm out of the chair and crossing to unlock the door for Roland. Our show is unique for its original music, composed and directed by the most talented man in the Crescent City... Standing right here in front of me.

"Hey," I say breathlessly, trying to sound mature.

Roland is a little taller than me with sexy brown eyes and glossy dark hair he tucks behind his ears. He smokes too much, but his white smile still dazzles. He leans against the doorjamb, taking the cigarette from between his lips, and his elegant hands distract me.

I remember a time when I had the most enormous crush on him, imagining him sliding those long fingers along my neck, making my pulse tick higher with every touch... playing my body like he plays the piano...

And then he told me he's gay.

And I grew up and learned not fall in love here.

"Some rich guy wants to meet you." He smooths my hair around my head, licks his finger and scrubs mascara off my cheek. "He asked specifically for the young brunette who kept her clothes on."

"He must've had binoculars to see me. I was all the way in the back—covered in feathers."

"I want you to give him a chance."

I inspect the tiny pink-feathered cups covering my small breasts. A pink silk corset is drawn tight around my waist, and my legs are covered in pink fishnets that stop mid-thigh. My sky-high pink stilettoes put me almost at his eye-level. Even without the nudity, this get-up is still pretty sexy.

"I don't know." My nose wrinkles. "Those guys in the audience make my skin crawl."

Molly pulls my arm. "But a rich guy... Maybe he'll buy you expensive gifts or take you to New York. You could be a rap star!"

Air snorts through my nose. "I don't rap."

"One rapping stripper is quite enough." Roland gives her a wink. "This one would most likely take you to Paris. He's French. Freddie Lovel."

"What's a Frenchman doing in New Orleans?" I pull out a makeup remover wipe and remove my blue-red lipstick.

"He works in shipping—coffee, souvenirs. Parisians love Louisiana merch."

"I couldn't be less interested."

He steps back and returns the cigarette to his lips. "Still, guys like him can be good for your career. Turn on the charm, keep him coming back for more."

My throat tightens. "Are you saying I should... do whatever he wants?"

"No." The sharp tone in Roland's voice is a relief. "Just encourage him. Molly, hide behind the screen. I'll be back in a second."

The door closes, and I only have a moment to grab my red velvet robe. It's loose and flowing with short sleeves and a V-neck that closes tightly with a large button in the center of my chest.

Soft knocking begins, and I fake a smile as I open the door with a flourish. "Mr. Lovel?"

"Ms. Hale." He turns and hands me a huge bouquet of red roses.

"Oh my goodness! Are these for me?" I cradle the flowers in my arms like a baby. "You're so sweet!"

"You're so beautiful." He leans in and kisses my cheek. "Beautiful roses for a beautiful lady."

"I'm not a lady, Mr. Lovel." I gaze at the velvet buds.

"Call me Freddie." He smiles, revealing straight white teeth.

He's tall, dressed in a tux with a thick, stainless steel watch on his wrist. Dark hair that's a little too long curls around his ears, but he's still elegant and not bad looking.

"Then you must call me Lara." I look around for something large enough to hold the bouquet. "I'll have to borrow a vase..."

"I'll buy you one. I can buy you anything you need. Just say the word."

Okay, I have to admit *that* is an intriguing proposition. I've had admirers before, but they've only ever sent notes or candy. They've never come backstage to meet me, and they've never been rich.

I blink slowly up at him. "What brought you to the Pussycat Angels, Freddie?"

Again his lips curl into a smile. I try to decide if it's sexy…

"I wanted something exotic but beautiful… like the runway show on television. The concierge suggested I come here."

"You know, we have nothing to do with that show."

"I know. Your show is more interesting."

I scan his features looking for any signs he's a creep. Nothing about him sets off my alarm bells. Freddie Lovel is not the usual star-struck douche wanting to screw a stripper—or *burlesque dancer*.

Leaning closer, his voice drops. "Can I walk you home?"

Then again, I could be wrong.

"I, umm…" A tiny bead of perspiration tickles down my spine as I search for a good excuse. Roland said to keep him coming back for more, but we're not supposed to tell anyone we live in the theater. "I actually have to stay late tonight. They're changing one of the numbers. I'm sorry."

"I can wait?"

"It's probably going to run long."

He straightens, and his dark brows pull together. "And you're tired, I'm sure."

My chest tightens. I'm losing him. He thinks I'm blowing him off…

"I'm not always tired." Sliding my tongue over my lips, I tilt my head to the side and blink slowly like I've seen Vanessa do a million times. "Some nights I'm so full of energy, I simply lie awake in bed."

It works. He moves closer. "I guess I'll have to come back, then."

"Are you sure? It's just the same show every night."

His eyes move to my mouth and slowly back. "But not entirely the same."

I hold out my hand, and he catches it. I'm not sure what's about to happen, but he gives it a squeeze, sliding his thumb over my fingers before kissing it lightly. "I'll say goodnight, then."

"Au revoir?"

"Au revoir." He backs away and gives me a wink before turning to go.

I wait, watching as he walks down the narrow hallway. A definite bounce is in his step, and I close the door, breathing a sigh of relief.

Molly comes out from behind the screen and picks up one of my roses as I unbutton my robe and toss it aside.

"That was close." I reach for a pair of jeans and a faded navy tee.

She lies back on the bed, holding the rose to her nose. "He is very interesting!"

"Meh," I pull the shirt over my head. "He barely held my attention."

"It must be amazing to be a dancer," she sighs. "Men just dying to meet you, dreaming of kissing you... I can't wait for my first kiss."

"They're dreaming of more than kissing." My gaze meets hers in the mirror. "And I'd better not catch you kissing anybody. You're too young."

"I know," she sighs, putting the flower behind her ear. "But one day..."

I walk over and sit beside her on the bed, sliding a strawberry curl off her cheek. "One day, we'll be in a better place. We'll be able to do what we want and see who we want, and we won't have to deal with… men's expectations."

Her eyes flicker to mine. "You seemed to like Freddie—"

"Because I'm a great actress." I stand and go to the door. "He's probably the least creepy guy I've met, but do not fall in love in a place like this. Everything is fake."

"I can't wait to fall in love." Her eyes go dreamy again.

"Well, you'd better keep that on a short leash." I jerk my pants over my hips and button them. "Most men who hang around here are assholes. Now get ready for bed."

A light knock on my door tells me Roland is back, and I pull open the door.

"Good job. He said he'll be back tomorrow."

I do a little bow. "I aim to please!"

"Come on—we're all upstairs."

I follow him to the stairs leading to the roof, but as we pass certain doors, I hear moans and the occasional rhythmic tapping. My stomach sinks, because I know what those noises mean. Some girls are allowed to supplement their earnings by offering special "private performances" for a few extra thousand dollars.

Of course, Gavin, the theater owner, keeps a percentage of these arranged meetings. He's the pimp, which makes us high-class hookers. The thought turns my stomach. I'm old enough to take a John, and I've heard some of the girls complaining because I never have. It's why I thought Freddie had come to my room tonight. Until I realize…

"You found him, didn't you?" My voice is quiet,

and we stop halfway up the stairs. "You're looking out for me again."

He pauses and steps down. "I have to take care of my muse." His face is serious, which is rare, and he touches my cheek with his thumb. "No one sings my songs the way you do, Lar. You've got real talent. And now Gavin's given us a chance..."

My heart swells at his words, and I take a step up, putting us closer together. "What are you saying?"

"Gavin wants more variety. I told him I'd write some new songs, and I asked if you could sing them. He's been promising you a part for a while. He owes it to you. He owes it to your mother." He gives me a warm smile and takes off up the stairs ahead of me, calling back over his shoulder. "If you're interested."

"I'm interested!" I chase after him, and we push through the metal door together.

A small group of us are celebrating Evie's birthday on the roof tonight. She's pretty much the weakest member of the group, but so far, it hasn't seemed to matter. Her face is plain, but she's got full breasts. She's also willing to go totally nude if Gavin asks her, which I guess keeps her in the show.

And she's my best friend.

Besides Roland, of course.

He grabs my hand, and we go to where Evie is perched among our friends. Bea sits to her right. She's sexy and petite and one of our best dancers. Bea's best friend Vanessa sits on the other side of her sipping champagne. She's a total bitch to me. Roland says it's because Vanessa thought she'd be Tanya's understudy until I came to live here after graduating from boarding school with the nuns. He says she took one look at me and knew her chances of becoming the lead were over.

Tanya, the star of our burlesque show, isn't here. I'm not surprised, as she's been losing weight, being late to practices, and seeming lethargic in her moves. She's a contortionist, so she can hide a lot of fuck ups, but Roland said she'd better get her shit together before Gavin demotes her.

Although, if she goes down, it means I go up, and as excited as I might be about singing Roland's songs, being out front means all the male attention is focused on me.

"Lara!" Evie jumps up gives me a big hug. "I'm so glad you're here."

I hug her back. "Happy birthday."

Evie's a runaway from some podunk farming community in Memphis. She left home and became a New Orleans showgirl—not that it's necessarily a step up.

A glass of champagne is placed in my hand, and we all raise a toast to Evie.

Roland takes my arm and we step over to the balcony. The city is spread out far below in a mixture of thick oak trees, rainbow neon lights, and yellow street lamps. Off in the distance, I hear the noise of a train whistle.

"What'd you think of him?"

"He's okay, but I know how it goes. If I don't put out, he'll lose interest."

Roland lights a cigarette and exhales a long puff of blue smoke. "Not necessarily. I talked to him, and this guy's different."

"He's gay?" I give him a pointed look, and he laughs.

"No—he's an entrepreneur." Another pull, another long exhale. "He's interested in trying new things, putting his money behind unique investments."

"So I'm an investment?"

He nods. "You could be. Singers can do very well if they have the right backer, and if you get him emotionally invested as well as financially—"

"Then I'd be prostitute in every sense of the word."

Roland's growl is interrupted by a loud laugh from Evie. I glance at her still sitting among our strange family, and my mind travels back to the first night I saw what really went on after hours in our theater home.

Vanessa's door had been open, and when I looked inside, she was on her knees, her fingers splayed over a man's naked ass. Her head was pressed all the way to his pelvis, and he fisted her blonde hair, groaning loudly. His knees wobbled, and she coughed and gagged. He released her, shoving her back, and I watched him come all over her face, white liquid spilling down to her breasts.

I thought he was done, but he grabbed her head again, jerking his cock rapidly, milking the final drops as he finished. Then he threw her back on the floor and pulled up his pants.

I couldn't tell if she enjoyed what happened.

Evie told me she was earning her keep.

Pushing the ugly memory aside, I look up at Roland watching Evie's birthday group with a smile. "How long can I keep this up?" I ask him quietly.

"Keep what up?"

"Hiding, pretending like one day Gavin will actually make good on his promise. Staying away from those men."

He shrugs. "I've been able to keep you away from them, and Gavin just gave me the go-ahead to write a new show. This could be it."

My stomach tightens, and I want to believe him. I want to believe that my time has come, that Gavin's promise to let me sing, to make me a real star and not a prostitute, might actually happen… It's the one thing that keeps me from taking Molly and running away—well, in addition to free room and board and the fact I have no other job skills or prospects.

Another low horn sounds in the distance, three notes played together, one a half-step off. I try to place it. "Barge?"

Roland looks out across the dark city rooftops. Then he frowns. "Train. Headed north to Chicago, I bet."

In his voice is a sound I seldom hear, one he never allows anyone to hear. It's somewhere between longing and regret, and I glance up at him. He's only a few years my senior, but in that moment he could be as young as Molly, wishing for something just out of reach.

It's gone in an instant. He exhales a laugh, breaking the spell, and wraps his arm across my shoulders. "Relax. Gavin's practical, but he never forgets a promise."

My lips press together, and I don't share my other fear—that Gavin's promise doesn't cover Molly, and the older she gets, the closer she gets to earning her keep.

"It also helps that your voice is smoky silk laced with heartbreak." He squeezes me. "I can't wait to get started writing. Come on."

We return to the group where Evie is retelling how she stepped on Vanessa's feather tail during the third number and ripped it off her ass.

"Good thing it wasn't a butt plug," Vanessa deadpans, and Evie screams.

"I blew champagne through my nose!" They're getting a little tipsy. "At least it was funny!"

"Fiona didn't laugh," Roland says. "Our Mistress of the Dance was livid. You should've seen her backstage."

"I'm such a menace." Evie drapes a hand across her face, but my stomach sinks.

The clock is ticking on her days of staying in the show, and she's my best friend. I reach for another glass of champagne to calm the anxiety pulsing in my chest, and as I lower it, I see the metal door slowly open and Gavin step into the night. Our owner is tall with light brown hair and calculating blue eyes.

Tonight his expression is grim. "Tanya said Evie is up here..."

The glass slips from my hand and shatters at my feet. His eyes flicker to mine, and he frowns. I'm silent, afraid of what he might say, but Roland crosses the space between us and takes hold of my wrist.

"Here to celebrate?" he asks, standing so his body blocks mine. "I was just discussing the new format with Lara."

Gavin grunts. "Sound good to you?"

My throat is tight, but I manage to answer. "Yes, sir. Thank you."

He nods then walks over to Evie, standing in front of her with his hands on his hips. He seems to grow taller in that instant, more sinister.

"Gavin?" Her eyes slowly rise to meet his. "Come to wish me a happy birthday?" She smiles, but I hear the tremor in her voice.

"Walk with me," he says. "I've had a few queries about you. One is willing to pay top dollar..."

Roland pulls me through the exit and down the stairs. I follow him almost tripping to keep up with his fast pace.

We reach my door, and he shoves me toward it. "Go to bed."

My heart is hammering, and fear radiates through my chest with every beat. "Will she… tonight?"

He pauses, sliding the backs of his fingers across my cheek and nodding slightly.

She's out of the show, but Gavin has other ways of making money off our bodies. A breath hiccups in my throat, and the pain moves from my heart to my stomach as I imagine the things she might have to do. I imagine men hurting her, pushing her on the floor like Vanessa.

Roland pulls me into a hug, and my fingers clutch his sleeve as tears heat my eyes. "I'll help her if I can," he whispers.

But I know there's nothing he can do. If she chooses to stay here, she'll be a sex worker. She'll be pulled into Gavin's ring of darkness until she's convinced it's all she's worth doing. It's the same lie that keeps them all here. It's a lie I refuse to believe about myself. I have talent. I have options, and I'm giving him one last chance to keep his promise.

"Go to bed," Roland says, releasing me. "You'll feel better in the morning. We'll start our new project."

Nodding, I go inside and slide the lock on my door. I always lock it against those men. We're not humans to them. We're a means to an end, and they're dangerous, unpredictable. They don't always wait for permission.

The lamp is still on, and Molly's copper curls are spread over the pillow. With a sigh, I gaze down at her sleeping face, so placid. So trusting.

At thirteen, she's way more interested in boys than I ever was. I have to double down on finding a backup plan, a new job that will get us out of here. Just in case anything goes wrong. Just in case Gavin tries to go back on his word.

Shoving off my jeans, I climb into the bed beside my little friend. "Because he'll never pass up the chance to make more money," I say to myself.

I turn off the light, and Molly snuggles closer to me like she's done since that first night when I found her dirty and starving. I'm no better, a lonely orphan who managed to sing my way to a spot in the show, but I have no family, no one to love.

"Who won't?" Her voice is sleepy.

I wrap my arm around her shoulders. "You're still awake?"

"A little," she whispers. "Tell me who."

"It doesn't matter." I've never wanted her to know about what happens here. I don't want her to be afraid—not as long as I've got us covered.

She's quiet and just when I think she's asleep, she says, "Then tell me how I came here."

"You want to hear that old story again?"

"Yes." She burrows closer into my side, and I stare into the darkness trying to remember how it goes.

It's a silly made-up story I used to distract her when she'd wake up crying in the night those first days after I rescued her. Even though the minor details change every time I tell it, she doesn't seem to care.

"Let's see," I begin. "Oh, yes, your mother was a gorgeous dancer. And when she met your dad, she couldn't help but love him." I smooth a curl. "He played beautiful music on the guitar, and she danced for him."

"But he couldn't marry her," Molly says. "Because he had no money, and she was a rich man's fiancée."

"So he went away to find his fortune, but before he could return, your mother married the rich man. Still, he came back, and she went to him. Then nine months later—"

"Tell me about our future," she interrupts. "I like that story better."

My eyes are heavy, but I take a deep breath and shift gears. This story is *not* pretend; it's a promise I've made to both of us. "One day we'll leave this place. I'll find a better job, something legit. Maybe Freddie will help me."

"Will he take us to Paris?"

"He might." I kiss the top of her head. "And if he does, we'll fly right out of New Orleans and never look back. We'll live on the Avenue Montaigne."

"The richest street in Paris!" she adds. "And we'll ride in a limo, and you'll have diamonds and a little dog."

I squeeze her closer as my throat grows tight. "And we'll never think about being here. Ever again." I trace my fingers along her upper arm until I feel her relax. "Now go to sleep."

CHAPTER 3

"Every moment of light and dark is a miracle."
-Walt Whitman

Mark

Darby is shouting as Terrence and I enter the theater.

Even though we worked solid from the time I got here, yesterday ended before we could test the new machinery for last night's show.

"Priority one is getting that pulley system operating and the safety backups tested *today*," he yells. "Don't let me catch you fucking around or flirting with the dancers. Gavin wants it ready to go tonight."

One glance tells me only half the crew is back to work. "What happened to all the men?"

"Eh, it's pretty common." Terrence taps a fresh cigarette out of his pack. "They get a few bucks, spend them on screwing some pretty girls, and they're gone."

That makes me frown. "How does anything get done around here?"

He only shrugs. "Maybe it does, maybe it doesn't. They don't pay enough for loyalty in this business. And Darby's an asshole."

I look over at the stocky man shouting at a truck driver. My lips tighten. Terrence has a point.

"Why did you come back?" I glance at my new friend.

"I need the money, and I don't like sitting around. You?"

"Same." It's a good enough reason, and I'm not about to say the grueling labor keeps my mind off the shitstorm my life has become. That it quiets the nagging voices wanting revenge for my uncle's death. I feel pretty confident Terrence wouldn't be impressed.

I definitely don't say a part of me hopes to see a certain dancer again. The last thing I have time for is a girl, no matter what my dick says.

"You need the money?" Terrence chuckles. "How old are you, boy?"

His tone irritates me. "Twenty-one."

"Youth is wasted on the young. If I was twenty-one, I wouldn't be here either—unless I was waking up in one of those back rooms."

Lowering his chin, he gives me a pointed look before going to join the other men. I stand by the coffee and day-old beignets, bruised fruit, and water. I grab a bagel just as the dancers start filtering in.

I don't want to look for Lara, but I can't help it. She pirouetted through the few dreams I had last night with her silky dark hair and crystal blue eyes. I woke up with a hard-on, the image of her lean body, gorgeous and lined, slim hips rocking rhythmically on my cock taunting me to come. Both hands on my face, I scrubbed that vision away. I know from last night's show, she doesn't strip. I wonder why…

Loud clapping breaks through my thoughts. A dark-haired guy about my age strides across the stage shouting, "Eat fast, ladies. We need to get moving."

He goes to the piano and stacks sheet music on it. As soon as he sits, he begins to play, but I don't recognize the tune. A few of the girls go to the center to stretch or warm up and I linger, watching them. Two nights of lost sleep caught up with me last night, but I plan to stick around for the full show tonight.

One of the blondes from yesterday looks over her shoulder at me and winks before bending forward in a stretch. With her ass pointing right at me, she blows a kiss through her legs, and I decide I'd better join Terrence and the other guys when I see *her*.

She walks slowly across the stage, seeming distracted. Her long hair is looped up in a high ponytail, and she's wearing black dance pants and a black tank.

Lara.

She moves so gracefully, she's like the ocean swaying out at sea or the movement of tree limbs in a thunderstorm. I wonder what I'd give to have my dream come true, her slim body naked in my arms.

She doesn't stop until she's standing next to me inspecting the contents of the table. She chooses a small blueberry muffin, and for a moment she only holds it, lost somewhere else in her thoughts.

"Not a fan of blueberries?" I give her a friendly smile.

She blinks as if coming out of a dream and lifts those crystal blue eyes to mine. "What?"

"Sorry. You seemed sad."

"Oh," she exhales a small laugh. "I'm sad to be out of bed. We don't usually start this early."

"Late night?"

"Hmm, no later than any other night." Her voice is soft and faintly melodic, and she doesn't walk away.

I should walk away, but I don't. "Did you go out after the show?"

"No." She shakes her head, and her dark hair swishes around her cheeks. "Did you?"

"Nah. They worked our asses off yesterday. I got back to my place at nine and crashed."

Her cute little nose scrunches. "You didn't stay for the show? I thought it was one of the perks of the job."

"I stayed for a few minutes." *Long enough to see you...*

Images of last night's performance filter through my memory. Tanya's performance is primarily backbends and splits with scraps of clothing tossed off as the show progresses, until the only thing she's left wearing is a jeweled thong.

The rest of the girls saunter around like models on a catwalk in sky-high heels, thongs, and drippy, jeweled straps. Their legs are lean, their breasts are round, and they're hot.

Sure, I'm a red-blooded American male and their bodies got my dick going, but I was only interested in one of them... This one right here. And when she waltzed onto the stage in an elaborate feathered costume complete with enormous, white wings, I was unexpectedly relieved to see she wasn't nude.

She showed the least skin on stage, and still, she was the sexiest one out there.

"It was interesting," I say. She makes a sound of disbelief, and I smile. "What does that mean?"

"Interesting? What made it so *interesting*, just Mark?"

"You remember my name."

"You just told it to me yesterday." She lifts the coffee cup to her pink lips and takes a sip.

I want to ask her if she has a boyfriend. I want to know everything about her. "Maybe I could take you out one night after the show. If you're not too tired."

Her body stiffens, but it's too late to take it back—not that I want to take it back, but I don't want to seem like an asshole only interested in her for her body. I really want to know her better. She's pretty and thoughtful and I can tell she's smart...

"I don't like to go out in the city," she says. "I don't want anyone to recognize me." Worried eyes meet mine. "You probably think I'm silly."

"I think you're smart. New Orleans can be pretty rough." As I know too well. "I could bring a disguise? Black glasses with fake noses and mustaches attached?"

She smiles, but the distance remains. "Isn't it against the rules for you boys to be mixing with the dancers?"

"I was told not to go into your room, but otherwise..."

"Fitz! Get your ass over here," Terrence shouts.

My mouth pulls into a frown, and her head tilts. "I guess that's you? Nice chatting with you, Mark Fitz. Take care of yourself."

That makes me smile. "I will. And I'll be sure this thing is safe for you."

"I appreciate your commitment." She does a little nod.

You have no idea. "See you at the top."

* * *

Lara

Molly appears at my elbow as Mark, the friendly new guy, walks away. He's cute, tall with bright blue eyes and a friendly smile. I like talking to him, and I'd probably take him up on his offer if I weren't focused on more important things.

"I've been looking for you," Molly says.

"I've been right here getting coffee." I catch Roland's eye. He's sitting at the piano playing "The Very Thought of You," and we exchange a smile. He knows it's one of my favorites.

Last night, I lay awake thinking about what he'd said for so long. The first time he'd called me his muse, I'd instantly fallen in love with him. I was eighteen, and a silly, lovesick puppy. It was the first time I'd ever felt appreciated for my talent.

I felt seen.

I felt safe.

I threw myself at him and tried to make out with him. My cheeks heat at the memory of me French kissing him. He took my arms and gently removed them, so gracious. I was so blind.

Roland only ever leaves the theater with other men.

Molly's eyes are glued to my face. "That's why you don't care about Freddie," she says. "You're in love with Roland."

"No," I shake my head. "I'm not."

"I'm not blind. There's clearly something between you two."

"It's called *friendship*." I grab a mug and slide it under the coffee machine. "Anyway, why are you so obsessed with love all of a sudden?"

She picks up a shriveled orange. "It's not so sudden. Rosa's new book is full of it."

"Rosa and her books."

Our wardrobe director is a matronly former dancer who keeps us stocked with reading materials, and she has a weakness for romance—the dirtier the better.

"Besides," Molly continues. "You're way overdue for a lover."

"*A lover?* You sound like someone's grandma."

She takes my arm, eyes sparkling. "So, am I right? Are you and Roland secretly lovers?"

"No." I sip my coffee, the warm liquid sending a tingle down my spine as it wakes me.

I sniff the bitter-chocolate aroma mixing with sugary beignets, rosin, talc, and stale cigarette smoke—the smells of home.

"I think you're lying," she says.

I shake my head as I clutch my cup in both hands. "I'm not."

"Lara, come try this for me," Roland calls from where he sits at the piano, erasing and rewriting notes. I walk over. "See if you can sing this."

He plays the introductory chords as I scan the sheet music.

You're in my arms and it feels so right;

but it's simply aaaan illusion…

He joins me in harmony on *illusion,* and our voices hold the chord perfectly for eight beats. I close my eyes, letting the beauty of it relax the pressure in my chest. That's why I fell in love with him—for his sheer, raw talent.

When I stop, he's smiling at me, and backstage has fallen silent. I smile back at him. "Perfect."

He immediately returns to scribbling notes on the score, and everyone else returns to their conversations. I lean on the back of the piano as he writes; his brow furrowed as he silently composes.

Molly frowns. "And *that's* supposed to convince me?"

Roland looks up at her and grins. "What's on your mind, shortcake?"

"Love," I answer for her.

His eyebrows rise. "You've fallen in love, Mol?"

"More like Lara has, and she refuses to confess."

"Again?" He shakes his head. "So fickle."

I narrow my eyes at him. Even if I've accepted his truth, it's not nice to tease me about it. I walk around to sit beside him on the bench. He slides over to make room for me as he continues to play. Molly leans on the back of the piano and watches us.

"And *who* is the incredibly lucky fellow this time?" He tilts his head toward me.

"It's you, of course. Don't you remember?"

His hands still over the chords for a split second, then he glances up at Molly. "Of course. Silly me."

"I knew it!" She bounces on her toes clapping. "Oh, it's so romantic! Do you write all your songs for Lara?"

"Yes," he says quickly, resuming his play.

Shaking my head, I stand and take Molly's hand so she'll stop clutching her chest. "Stop swooning and come on."

We're halfway across the stage when Gavin appears, and everyone stops what they're doing.

"Roland, Darby, Fiona," he says their names as if reading off a list. "I need to speak with you."

Roland stands and walks toward the theater owner. Darby emerges from behind a set, and Fiona, our dance coach, scampers with perfect poise from where she was working with Bea and Tanya.

"Lara," Gavin says, noticing me. "Is this little Molly?"

My mouth goes dry, but she smiles at him all innocence. "I'm not so little!"

"No?" Bloodshot eyes move up and down her body, and my throat closes. *Shut up, Molly.* "Let me see those legs."

She puts her hands on her hips and starts to turn, but I quickly catch her arm and jerk her behind me. "She's just teasing."

Gavin glances at me. "Roland mentioned something new. You up for leading a show?"

"O-of course."

"Good. Now back to work," he barks. "I want the new blocking ready for tonight."

From far away, it seems, I hear Evie and Tanya do a *stomp-stomp!* My eyes meet Vanessa's, and hers are shooting daggers at me. I can only imagine what's bugging her ass, and I don't have time for it.

"Don't *ever* do that," I say through clenched teeth at Molly. "Don't you know anything?"

Roland's pencil is in her hand, and she sketches on a blank staff. "You're always so panicky. I think Gavin's nice, and he treats you like you're the next big thing."

The thought makes my stomach roil. "Gavin is only interested in money."

"Because he cares about us. If the show fails, we all fail with it."

"Not all of us. Gavin will survive, even if we don't." Once we're at the back of the stage, I push her in the direction of our room. "Go back and see if you can help Rosa."

She makes a complaining noise, but she leaves. I go to my spot at upstage right and follow the lead of the other girls with warming up. I spend some time going over the steps from last night, repeating and reworking my entrance.

Burlesque is not complicated stuff, and my part

is pretty insignificant. All of the eyes are focused on the girls taking off their clothes. I'm starting to get bored and annoyed that I had to get out of bed early for this when Roland joins me.

"How are you feeling today?" Real concern is in his expression.

Lowering my arms, I face him. "I'm okay. I'm worried about her."

He knows I'm thinking about Evie, the one person who always made rehearsals fun.

"Don't worry. I'm working on a way to help her."

"How?"

I've never known how he does it—his connections and ways of getting things done. I'm only sure half, if not all of it is illegal.

His lips tighten, but he smiles, sliding a dark curl behind my ear. "It's not something for you to worry about. Anyway, I was sent to find you." He takes my elbow. "We need to test out this new contraption they've built."

I follow him to where Darby stands by the piano facing the back wall. He's looking up into the rafters, but when we appear, he turns to me.

"The idea is you'll float in like a bird… or a cloud or something." The confusion in his gravelly voice almost makes me laugh.

"Or an angel?" I tease. "You haven't watched the show much this season."

"Seen one set of tits, you've seen 'em all. You're not afraid of heights, are you?"

My eyebrows rise. "What exactly am I doing?"

"Sit on the bench, don't fall off, and we lower you slowly down to the stage."

"What do you think, Lara?" Gavin's baritone is full of authority, asking me what I think as if I have a choice. "How does our newest angel feel about flying?"

"I'm sure it'll be… interesting." I peer up… up… up into the darkness high above the stage, and while I'm not afraid of heights, the skinny catwalk so far above makes my stomach turn.

"It's time you show more skin. Tell Rosa you'll be topless tonight."

"I don't see why that's necessary," Roland argues. "Lara's just a kid."

"She's a woman," Gavin says, pinching my cheek. "No more hiding it. Give me a little shimmy on the way down. The men will eat it up."

I try to smile, but it dies on my lips. I knew this day was coming. What the hell am I doing here if I don't intend to strip? I just wasn't ready for it to be tonight.

Roland's steely gaze meets mine, but I shake it away. If I'm going to lead the show, his days of sheltering me are over. I don't have the right to feel betrayed.

Still, a sense of dread creeps across my stomach. I've been around here long enough to know what comes next. First I'm topless, then I'm on my knees.

This is how it starts.

CHAPTER 4

"Survival is an inside job."

Mark

My place is fifty feet above the stage, in the dark, on a narrow catwalk. A thick rope hangs beside me, and I wait for Lara to arrive and take her seat.

This afternoon we rehearsed it, and the new props worked perfectly. She sat on the wooden swing with the flesh-toned belt around her waist, and the machinery lowered her smoothly down to the stage where the girls sashay below.

"It's sophisticated enough we can time it to match the beats of music in the score," Darby had said, beaming with pride.

I didn't respond, but when he asked who wanted to be up here holding the safety rope, I was the first to volunteer.

The music barely reaches me all the way up here in the dark. Only the lights on the dancers below are visible. Everything else in the house is black. The second song begins, and I feel the vibration of another body climbing the metal ladder.

I can't see her, but my muscles tense knowing she'll be with me in this lonely place in just a few minutes. I look across the ceiling at the wires and canned lights. The air isn't as smoky; it's almost like a different world.

She's at the top, and our eyes meet. She takes a step back, clutching the red robe over her costume. I don't know if it's the shadows or her exaggerated makeup, but her eyes are so round, something in my chest pulls.

"What's wrong?" I whisper. "Did I scare you?"

"I didn't know you'd be up here tonight."

"I'm just the backup." I try to be reassuring, but she still seems uneasy. "Don't worry. We tested everything this afternoon. It's all working fine."

Her bottom lip disappears under her teeth and she looks out over the dark house, still clutching her robe. "I can't see anything. It's like they're not even out there."

My eyes follow hers and a cheer rises from the darkness. "They're out there." She nods, and for a moment, I think I've said the wrong thing. "If there's a glitch, no one will ever know."

"Roland will know. Fiona will know. Tanya... and trust me, Vanessa will know." Her voice is even, and her eyes don't meet mine.

I'm surprised by her nervousness, but I don't know much about theater work. Perhaps she feels this way before every show.

"Like they've never missed a step."

"It's time for me to take my place." She blinks up at me, and just as fast her eyes cut away.

Is she embarrassed?

"I'll hold the bench for you." Her hands tremble unfastening the button on her robe. "I'll be here the whole time."

Without a word, she lets the robe fall away.

"Shit!" I hiss, and my grip falters.

Her legs are wrapped in pink fishnets that stop thigh-high, and her waist is covered in a feathered corset that stops right below her breasts...

And her breasts, her beautiful breasts are completely bare.

They're small but full, perched high and pointing straight at me. A line of jewels traces the curve under each and another line follows between and up the center of her chest. They meet at a sparkling collar around her neck, and her nipples are dark pink and hard, sprinkled with glitter.

I see it all so fast, like the sexiest centerfold come to life and standing in front of me, and all the blood rushes from my head straight to my cock. When I'm finally able to tear my eyes off her, I realize my interest isn't only visible on my face. I slide my hand over my semi.

"Sorry," I clear my throat. "I wasn't expecting that—"

"I guess it has the desired effect." Her voice is small, and she seems so young all of a sudden. Round eyes flicker below my waist and up. "That is exactly what Gavin hopes will happen. To every man in the audience."

Her fingers tremble as she reaches for the swing, and a surge of protectiveness tightens my chest. In that moment I understand.

"It's your first time?"

Her gaze is fixed on the stage below, but she nods slowly. "No going back now."

I swallow the tightness in my throat. I don't understand her reasons for being here or why she seems to hate it. I only know one thing.

"You're beautiful," I whisper. "You'll be the most beautiful one out there."

As I say the words, it hits me... Once the audience sees her, she'll be a star.

"Not the most experienced."

"Experience doesn't matter. You could stand in one place and have them eating out of your hand."

That gets me the tiniest smile. Her chin drops, and I can tell from her expression her cheeks are pink. She takes her place on the bench. Her dark hair is swept up in a large feathered pin, and as much as I try not to, my eyes keep returning to her soft breasts. *Fuck*, she's so beautiful. Her skin is smooth as silk, and my fingers curl wanting to touch her. I won't touch her… unless she lets me, but Jesus. I'll dream about her tonight. Again.

I distract myself by securing the safety harness at her waist and making sure it's connected to the cables. We're so close I can feel the warmth radiating off her skin. I can smell the faintest hint of her perfume. It's sweet like springtime. The light glistens off her glossy lips. They're full and pink.

"Listen," she whispers, and her head tilts to the side. "That's my cue."

Stepping back, I take my place holding the rope. "Break a leg."

Our eyes meet, and my muscles are tight. I can see it in her eyes—she knows everything is about to change. The machinery makes a clatching sound just like earlier, and I hear her breathe as she glides out, away from the catwalk and over the open stage.

The music rises from below, and she leans into it like it's the most wonderful thing she's ever done. She starts to descend, and the spotlight rises to meet her. Her voice rises with the lyrics to the final song floating up in the velvet curtains.

You reach for me, and I disappear.

My heart is what you long to share…

Far below, the other dancers open in a semicircle for her to land. It's all going exactly the way we rehearsed it. She sparkles and the effect is dazzling…

Until a sickening, metallic groan blasts right at my ear.

I step back, searching the network of wheels and cables above me.

A loud *Pop!* and the larger wheel drops so fast I have to duck to avoid being hit in the head.

The metal line holding the swing goes slack, and with a loud *Zzzzz*, the rope in front of me flies past as the bench goes into a free fall.

"NO!" I shout, as Lara's body hurtles to the stage floor. Her arms splay out like a starfish, and she's grabbing at anything to stop the fall.

Collective screams resound throughout the theater, and I don't have time to think.

Every muscle in my body tenses, and I reach out to grab the zipping rope with my bare hands.

"AHH!" My cry echoes across the top of the theater as the rope slices through my palms like a hot knife through butter.

Warm blood runs down my forearms, but I grip it tighter, slinging my leg around the length for added resistance. My eyes squeeze shut to block out the intense pain, and I drop my weight against it.

I step once, twice, trying to get the remainder under my boot. Finally, it catches, and tugs like I've caught a big fish. I shout again as the violent jerk of Lara's weight slices the rope deeper into my palms.

The pain cuts through my mind like a white-hot poker, but it's nothing compared to my fear of seeing that beautiful girl broken on the stage floor below.

"Mark!" The scaffolding shakes, and through the haze I know someone is climbing the ladder. "Hold on, Mark! You've got her!"

I'm holding on blind, my eyes closed. The rope is

around my leg and under my boot, and warm blood is on my hands and arms. The line is buried in my palms, but I'm not letting it go for anything.

Two hands join mine. Darby is right in my ear. "Ease up if you can. We're going to lower her the rest of the way to the stage. She's almost there. Roland has her."

I loosen my grip, but the minute the rope moves, I yell out again. "Fuck!"

The scaffolding shakes, and another person is climbing the ladder.

"Step back and let her go. I've got her," Darby says.

"No," I growl through gritted teeth.

"It's okay, son, I've got her." My eyes flinch open, and I see he's wearing leather gloves and holding the rope above and below me.

Terrence is at my side. "Step back. Give me your hands."

My muscles shake with adrenaline and force. It took everything in my power to stop her falling, and now I have to let her go.

"I won't let it move," Darby says. "Open your hands and pull them straight off the line."

With a groan, I do as he says. The cable smacks out of my grip and tightens around my leg. Just as fast, Terrence wraps cloths over my shredded palms.

"Squeeze these," he says. "I'll unwrap your leg."

I do as he says, closing my fists over the cloths to stop the bleeding as he unties me. I stagger to the ladder, looking down as best as I can.

They've got her. She's wrapped in a white blanket, and Roland is carrying her in his arms. Her head moves limply against his shoulders, but her eyes are closed.

I have to know she's okay.

* * *

Lara

Everything is a blur.

I can't focus on anything except getting air into my lungs.

I'm not dead.

I feel like I've been cut in half, but I'm not dead.

Chaos is all around me, and I'm lying on my side. The pain in my middle is mind numbing, and my arms and legs feel paralyzed.

I slowly realize I'm covered in something soft and Roland is at my side, lifting me in his arms.

"Lara?" His voice breaks with panic as someone unfastens the belt. "Can you hear me?"

I try to nod, but I'm not sure if I'm successful. I'm still dazed. The belt is off, and we rise as Roland stands, carrying me. My cheek is against his chest, but I see movement in the wings. I try to lean forward, but it shoots pain through my stomach. Still, straining my eyes, I see Mark at the bottom of the ladder. Someone is with him, but he pushes through the crowd and jogs to where Roland is passing. He's holding his hands awkwardly, and I see dark red... *Is he bleeding?*

"Is she hurt?" His voice is desperate. "Lara?"

"You need to come with me," Terrence touches his arm, but he jerks away.

"Is she going to be okay? I held her. I caught her as fast as I could." His voice comforts me. I remember how he tried to encourage me before.

"Step back." Roland's voice is icy. "This had better not be your fault, boy."

I look into his dark eyes wanting to make him stop. *Stop talking to Mark that way…* But I can't seem to make my voice work.

"What is it?" Roland asks. Then inhales raggedly and clears his throat. "I'll take you to your room."

Terrence leads Mark away, and I look back in time to see Fiona unwrapping his hands. Inch-thick bloody lines tear down both his palms.

"Shredded your hands all right, but it's lucky you caught her," Terrence says. "She'd be dead otherwise."

I shudder and press my head against Roland's shoulder. His grip around me tightens. "This will not happen again," he says through clenched teeth as he carries me to my dressing room.

We follow the dark, narrow corridor fast, past dancers hanging in the hallway looking curious, past the closed doors. He places me on my small bed. "I'll get Rosa to come and check you over." Someone hands him a small bottle. "Here, take this."

I stare for a moment at the white pill in his palm before he puts it to my mouth and I take it, swallowing it down with a sip of water. The medicine works fast, and I roll onto my side, closing my eyes, overcome by exhaustion and shock.

CHAPTER 5

"The universe loves a stubborn heart."

Mark

"Who built that fucking thing?" Roland paces from Darby to where I'm sitting. "Who worked on it? I want to know which one of you imbeciles nearly killed her!"

My insides are humming, and I want to go back there and see her. I need to know she's all right for myself. Instead, we're all being held here to meet with Gavin.

"Calm down, Roland," Darby growls. "Nobody wanted to hurt Lara."

"I don't give a fuck what you want. I want to know which idiot I'm going to kill."

My bandaged hands are clutched tight under my arms as I walk. My insides are shaking, and the panic of almost witnessing another death has my stomach in knots. As much as I tried to believe what happened to my uncle didn't matter to me, I can't deny the shock I'm feeling.

Terrence sits on a box staring at his fingernails while he smokes his third cigarette in a row. "What's taking Gavin so fucking long," he mutters under his breath.

"He'll be here," Roland says through tight lips as he lights his own cigarette.

I cut my eyes at him trying to understand his interest in Lara. Are they lovers? Their features are similar enough that they could be related. Only her bright blue eyes are different. I'm about to ask when a man dressed in a tuxedo and carrying a bouquet of roses strides in the middle of the group.

"Roland." His voice is breathless. "There you are. What's happening? Is Lara okay?"

The pianist's expression changes. He actually smiles and holds out his hand. "Mr. Lovel, you're here. She's actually with the doctor now. They've given her pain medication, so I'm afraid you can't see her."

Straining my ears, I get the information I've been aching to know while we've been held back here. She's okay. They're taking care of her.

"I understand… I just—I have to return to Paris in the morning. I had hoped to let her know, to tell her I was worried, and to give her these."

"I'll make sure she gets them." Roland takes the bouquet. "If you'll come with me."

He leads the rich guy away, and I lean against a concrete pillar.

"What? You didn't think a girl like that would have a boyfriend?" Terrence squints up at me, and I straighten, clearing my throat.

"I don't know what you're talking about."

He only laughs and shakes his head. "Don't go down that road, my friend. You'll only get your ass handed to you."

I'm about to argue when Gavin finally joins us. He goes straight to Darby.

"Any idea what went wrong?"

Our boss shakes his head. "I inspected the machinery myself this afternoon. Everything was working fine when we tested it after lunch."

"So it just broke somehow?"

Darby shrugs. "I don't know what else to say. It was working fine. We all went home after five and came back at seven. For two hours anything could have happened."

"You're saying you think someone tampered with it?" Roland is with us again, eyes flashing.

"I'm not accusing anyone of anything." Darby's gruff voice is solemn. "I'm only saying what happened."

Gavin is quiet a moment. His hand is over his mouth, under his rust-colored mustache, which matches his ginger hair. He's a stocky, well-dressed man, and he takes a few steps to the side.

Finally, he turns and makes a pronouncement. "Lara needs to recover. She can take a few days off. In the meantime, we'll repair the damage and get that swing working for tomorrow night's show. Use a different girl until Lara's able to resume her role."

Roland jumps in at that. "Another girl can't sing my songs—"

"You're not the one who gets to decide, are you?" Gavin's eyes level on him, and the younger man backs down. "It was an accident. I'm glad she wasn't hurt... now let's make the best of this. We're the talk of the Quarter. Make it count."

My stomach turns at the idea he wants to capitalize on Lara's near-death experience, but from what I understand this place runs on a deficit. I don't understand why, since the audience is always full, and he isn't spending much on salaries. I suspect mismanagement of funds, but I haven't been here long enough to know anything.

"You!" I look up and realize Gavin is walking to me. "What's your name?"

I stand a little straighter, putting us at eye level with one another. "Mark Fitzhugh."

That stops him, his brow clutches and his pale eyes look me up and down. "Fitzhugh?" I watch as he thinks. "That's an unusual name. You related to Rick?"

Unease tightens my chest. "He was my uncle."

"Was?"

"He's no longer—he passed away."

Gavin's gaze holds mine, but I can't tell what he's thinking. "I'm sorry."

"We weren't very close."

A brief pause, and he continues. "Darby tells me you're a dependable worker. How would you like a better job? Something inside, that requires more… confidence."

The unease in my chest grows stronger. Everything I've seen about this place tells me to beware, especially since Gavin clearly knew my uncle. "I don't mind construction."

"What I'm offering will double your pay."

"I don't have time to spend what I make now."

"It's steady work. Not seasonal."

I don't understand what he means by seasonal. Hell, I don't know what he means by requiring confidence, but my instincts tell me to be careful. I don't want to arouse any suspicion I might have been involved in my uncle's dealings.

I shove my hands in my pockets and look down at my boots. "I don't know what my plans are just yet."

His eyes narrow a moment, then he nods. "You think about it and get back to me. I'll hold a place on Monday."

He takes a step back, and Terrence nudges my arm. "You ready?"

I glance to the back passage one last time wishing I could see her. "Yeah, let's get out of here."

We slam out the back door and trudge down to the flagstone sidewalk. Terrence trots ahead with both hands in his pockets, but I take a slower pace, allowing my eyes to trace the side of the building, counting the windows and wondering which one might be hers. We take a quick right onto Royal, then we're heading up Orleans in the direction of Bourbon Street and the Marigny.

"Stop in here for a drink."

I glance up just in time to see him duck into a small bar with a flashing *Jazz* sign and a pair of legs swinging out. We go to the shiny wooden bar, and he slaps a twenty in between us. "Two car bombs straight up!"

I climb onto a red vinyl-covered stool and glance at the women in booths behind the bar. They're wearing beaded bras and panties, and they're twisting and shaking their hips and shoulders in time to the house music. Their expressions are bored, and my eyes return to my hands. My mind returns to what I saw tonight high above the stage floor. The most beautiful thing...

The drinks are shoved in front of us—two pints of Bass with whiskey shots on the side. Terrence raises his shot glass and drops it into the beer then lifts the whole thing to his mouth and shoots it, drinking for several seconds.

"Ahh!" he growls, slamming the pint onto the bar. "Now bring me a Guinness!"

I lift the whiskey and sip it. It burns my throat, but the heat eases the adrenaline still buzzing in my chest. Too many fucking flashbacks for one night.

"To the hero!" Terrence raises his pint and gives me a nod.

"I'm not a hero." I finish off the whiskey and move to the pint. "I did what you'd have done. What we're paid to do."

My bandaged hand is around the pint of beer, and I wince when I remember the slice of the rope cutting into my palms.

"I would not have done what you did." He shudders into his drink and mutters. "Fuck."

I lean back, scowling at him. "You'd have let her fall? You'd have stood there and let her hit the stage without even trying to stop it?"

His lips poke out, and he takes a moment to light up. "I don't know."

"That's more like it." Leaning against the bar again, I take a drink. I'm leaning on my elbows, looking into the amber, but my vision is far away on her silky skin, her bright blue eyes, her shiny brown hair.

"Don't fall in love with a stripper," Terrence growls in my ear. "It will end. Badly."

"What the fuck? I hardly even know her."

"Shit. You're already gone for her. Admit it!"

Shaking my head, I lift the pint glass and take a long pull. Then I slam it on the bar. "Thanks for the drink."

I'm out the door and headed back to our place with him yelling after me not to be mad. Whatever. I don't know how the fuck I expect to get inside. Terrence has the only key, but I'll be damned if I sit there and let him ride me.

I'm still trying to figure my shit out. I'm not in love with anybody, and I'm not a hero. At least not yet. He's full of shit when he says he wouldn't have tried to catch her. He'd have grabbed the rope same as I did, or he'd have done something else.

I reach the apartment, and I sit on the stoop like he was the first night I came here. People are herding up and down Bourbon like always, like nothing ever changes and nothing happens outside this short strip of real estate.

Tonight I'm not being hounded by ghosts. I'm waiting for a bed, then I'll get up and do it all again tomorrow.

* * *

Lara

When I open my eyes, it's dark. My lamp is lit, and my breath catches at the sight of my nurse. Evie sits with her back leaned against the bedside holding one of Rosa's books.

I haven't seen her since her birthday, and I've been so worried.

"Hey, she's awake." Her voice is warm, and her smile kind. It breaks my heart. "How are you feeling now?"

I ease myself into a sitting position. "How long have I been asleep?"

"Oh, since yesterday. Doc gave you more Vicodin for the pain and said you should sleep it off."

I pull up the thin white tank I'm wearing to reveal a hideous purple and black band around my torso.

Evie gasps. "Oh, Lara!"

"Better than being dead, I guess," I try to joke.

"Are you in pain?"

"Only when I move." I lean gingerly against the pillows, trying to be still.

My old friend slides her fingers under my hand. With her other she pats the top of it. We're quiet several minutes, and all I can think about is not asking where she's been or what happened to her. She doesn't meet my gaze, and I wonder if she knows what I'm thinking. A tap at the door breaks the silence, and Roland peeks his head in.

"How is she?" he whispers.

"Ask her yourself." Evie stands and moves to the head of my bed.

He enters and kneels at my bedside. His hand goes where Evie's had been around mine. "I could kill those apes... But I'm glad to see you're awake. Moving around some?"

"As little as possible," I say. "I'm really sore."

He sits on the side of my bed. "I'll never get the image of you falling out of my head. Jesus!"

I look at his hand holding mine.

"We're investigating what happened," he continues. "Darby insists they checked the mechanics and made sure it was working." He pauses, and I watch his jaw clench. "He's trying to imply someone might have tampered with it."

My heart beats a little faster. "Tampered—like someone wanted to... hurt me?" I can't even say the word *kill*.

Black eyes meet mine. "If he's right, I'll find out who and handle it."

Closing my eyes, I remember the blood on Mark's hands. "I'm so glad Mark was there."

"The girls are all calling him a hero," Evie says quickly. "They're taking dibs on who's going to help him change those bandages."

"The girls are idiots," Roland says. "They should save their tricks for men with money."

"He was brave," she insists. "He reached right out and grabbed that rope. It was flying by, and he just grabbed it. Shredded his hands, but he caught you."

I shudder at the memory. "I need to thank him."

"You need to take it easy," Roland says. "Gavin expects you back in the saddle by Sunday, so you only have a few days to recover."

"He's going to make me do it again?" I try to sit up, but a sharp pain in my torso halts me. "I can't go back up there. Not if someone's trying to hurt me!"

Roland catches my shoulders. "Easy."

"No one's trying to hurt you," Evie's voice is soothing. "Mark said he'll be at the top of the ladder every night you go on. Sounds like he's committed."

Commitment… I remember his words.

Still, my worried eyes find Roland's, and he shrugs. "We'll make it work." He stands and then leans down to kiss my head. "Sleep."

Evie follows him to the door and he stops. He speaks to her in a low voice, but I can only hear part of what he says.

"Will that work for you?" he asks. I watch Evie nod and look down.

"They'll pay you extra for your silence," he says.

She doesn't look up at him. "If Gavin says it's okay."

Roland gently pats her cheek. "Gavin only cares about the money, not where you get it."

Fear tightens my chest. Is it possible Roland is working with Gavin to pimp out Evie? Why would he do that? I thought he was on our side…

She shuts the door and walks back to where I lie. "Just you and me tonight," she says, sitting and picking up her book. "Want me to read to you? This one's a panty-melter!"

I try to smile, but my throat is tight.

"I think I'll try and sleep if I'm actually being ordered to." Then a flash of panic hits me. "Where's Molly?"

"In the wings watching. Vanessa's taking your place as the dark angel, and Molly's convinced she'll suck at it. I'm actually a little curious myself."

I think about what Roland said, about Vanessa taking my place. "You don't think…" But I shake my head. It's a huge leap from disliking someone to trying to kill them.

Her green eyes flicker to mine. "Don't think what?"

"I just…" I look down at my lap. "I think being cooped up in this theater makes people start imagining all kinds of sinister things."

"The girls are bitchy," she says, seeming to read my mind. "But I don't think any of them are smart enough to sabotage Darby's equipment. They're certainly not strong enough."

"You're right." I nod, sliding down into the blankets. "I'm glad you're back. You left without saying goodbye, and I was afraid I'd never see you again."

"I wasn't given much time to say anything to anyone." Her voice trails off and her eyes look past me at some memory.

I'm quiet a moment, but I have to know. "So you're not dancing at all now?"

"No need for that." She tries to laugh. "And Fiona's glad to have me gone, I'm sure."

I nod and study my hands. I've known Evie so long, I don't want to make her feel ashamed, but I remember how proud she'd been to be a dancer. I wonder if she'll leave now that her fate has changed. Now that she's selling herself for money.

Our eyes meet, and she sees the question in mine. "He was an older man. He wasn't very attractive, but his rooms were in the penthouse suite of the W… and he was gentle."

"Oh, Evie." I swallow the knot in my throat.

She stands and walks over to my makeup mirror, lifting the brushes and arranging the tubes of lipstick and eyeliners. "Don't get all big eyed and scared. We all know what happens here. I could have found another job. I could have left this place."

"You wanted to be a dancer."

"But I wasn't good enough to be legit." She studies her reflection, lifting her chin. "Admit it. We're attracted to the darkness, the tease and the thrill of what might happen. It's why we stay."

It's not why I stay. I stay because I'm holding onto a promise. "I'm so sorry."

She gives me a wink. "Well, don't you worry about me. Roland's found something that could be very enjoyable… and lucrative."

I'm afraid to ask what, still, I know curiosity is in my eyes. She crosses the room to sit at the foot of my bed.

"He has these friends. They're young, hot, and very wealthy, and they want to see me together."

I realize even though I live in a strip club, I'm still the girl who grew up surrounded by nuns. "I don't know what that means."

Her cheeks flush, and she chews her lip. "I'm pretty new to the whole thing myself. I'm really not much more than a beard, but I know a good thing when I hear it."

I realize I'm leaning forward and stop. "A beard? Wait… They're gay? I don't understand. Why do gay guys want you?"

"Well, for the most part, Roland says I'll be Phillip's date to major events. Phillip's father is the leader of some mega-church, and he's heavily involved in politics. Phillip doesn't want to embarrass the man. Can you imagine?"

My head shakes slowly no. "So you won't actually have sex with them?"

I'm holding onto the hope that Roland hasn't betrayed us.

"I guess I'll find out… But a girl can hope, right?"

I manage a smile as I slide down into the bed. I know some girls like to watch gay guys having sex. Looks like my friend Evie is one of them. "Then I guess this is a good thing?"

"Damn straight," she laughs. "They're rich, gay, and paying me to hang out with them. I win!"

Is this a win? I can't help wondering for how long, and why? Why doesn't she just go back to Podunk, Tennessee, and start over…

Okay, I know.

I understand the drive to be in this city, the hope that a break might come. Even when all around us is darkness and night, it's the tiniest flicker of a promise, the smallest hope that *it* might happen.

The dream might come true.

Pulling the blanket over my shoulder, I close my eyes. "I hope it works out for you."

I really do.

She picks up the book again and takes her seat at my bedside. As my eyes close, the danger of life in this place presses on my mind. The days are counting down until I return to the spotlight, the freshest face in the Pussycat Angels lineup, and once I'm there, it'll be my turn to see what happens. Will Gavin keep his promise? Will he give me a pass from the sex trade in return for the increase in revenue from my performances? Will the demands of the bidders grow too loud? Will their offer of money exceed my earnings?

A long time passes before I drift into an anxious sleep, and when I open my eyes again much later Evie is gone. Molly is curled up beside me. Her head is beside mine on the pillow, and I curl with my arms around her. She whispers words in her sleep, and my eyes go to the enormous bouquet of red roses on my dresser.

I made the bargain to be here. I have no money, no family, nowhere to go. My fall might have bought me more time, but it's only borrowed time.

I can't escape why I'm here. I can only find an insurance policy in case I fail.

CHAPTER 6

"Where there's authenticity, there's escape."

Lara

My fall dominates the morning chatter. I walk slowly to the coffee, trying not to make eye contact with anyone. I don't feel like talking.

"She's alive!" Roland calls as he crosses the stage to where I stand. I don't meet his eyes. "Feeling better?"

I nod, focusing on my cup.

"This came for you last night. Mr. Lovel, I presume." He hands me a small box with a card, and I take it quickly. "We can work on the new songs whenever you're ready."

My eyes land on Mark standing nearby. The hero. I need to thank him, but Vanessa has him cornered. She's wearing a low-cut jog bra, and her ample bosom presses against his arm as she describes some problem in her dressing room with dramatic sweeping gestures. He listens to her, but his eyes keep drifting to mine. Every time they meet, I feel a prickle of warmth under my skin, and even with last night's residual anxiety, it makes me smile.

"What do you have?" Molly's face is annoyed as she watches Mark and Vanessa.

I place the box on the table and open the card. "A gift from Freddie."

Molly sweeps it out of my hand and jumps up. "Dear Lara," she reads with a loud, fake-French accent as she saunters around the table. Everyone, including Mark, looks her way, and I'm trying to figure out what the fuck she's doing with my card. "I wish I could tell you how miserable I am to be so far away while you're in pain."

"Molly," I say through clenched teeth.

"Seeing you fall crushed me, and leaving before I could speak to you was possibly the hardest thing I've ever done."

"Do you mind?" I say louder.

My eyes are fixed on her, so I don't notice Mark walking up behind her until he slips my note out of her hand.

He holds it at his shoulder, which is out of her reach. She squeals, but I can tell her stunt is going better than she expected.

She jumps and tries to grab the paper, throwing her body against his. He towers over her with his broad shoulders, and his blue eyes sparkle. He's more handsome than I remember.

"Is this keep away?" He blocks her with his hand, and comes to where I'm sitting. "This belongs to you."

I can't miss the bandages wrapped around his shredded palms, and gratitude tightens my throat. I place my hand on the back of his. "I need to thank you—"

"Don't." He cuts me off. "There's no way I would've let you fall."

"But your hands—"

"Will be fine in a few days." He takes a knee beside my chair, and my breath stutters.

When he's this close I can't ignore his blue eyes or the memory of how they darkened when he saw me in my costume. His eyes traced every inch of my body, but it wasn't crude or creepy. It was wonder and awe. My skin tingled as if his gaze were the lightest touch. My nipples hardened…

In that quiet space high above the stage, we shared something so intimate, and remembering it now sends smoldering heat between my thighs.

Then he saved my life.

I clear my throat, hoping my face isn't red. "It was pretty brave."

His voice is gentle. "I'm just glad to see you moving around."

"I need to move around. I only have a few days off to recover."

"What will you do?"

With a shrug, I realize I've never really had time off before. I'm always helping Rosa or rehearsing or taking care of Molly or running stupid errands. "I'll probably just go to the library."

"What?" He surprises me with a laugh. "You're in New Orleans, and you want to go to the library?"

"They have computers there." I can look for another job… which sitting here with this gorgeous man smiling at me makes me feel sort of miserable.

"Go out with me. We can walk around the square, go to the French Market, eat fresh beignets…"

"I don't know." Going out with Mark feels like asking for trouble.

"We'll take it slow." His eyes flicker to the letter in my hand. "If you start to feel bad, we can sit and watch the tourists."

He rises and takes a few steps back, studying my face. I blink up at him, and the light in his eyes makes me smile in spite of it all. It's just the encouragement he needs.

"I'll be finished after lunch. Meet me in front of the cathedral."

"Okay," I say softly, and he smiles, straight white teeth and a dimple in his cheek. *Where did you come from, Mark Fitzhugh?*

He disappears in the wings, off to do whatever he does for Darby. I look down at Freddie's letter, finishing his words. *I hope this small token will lift your spirits. Until I see you again. Yours devotedly, Frederick Lovel.*

Standing gingerly, I walk toward the piano. Roland is scribbling on the stack of sheet music, a cigarette dangling from his lips. Dust floats in the sunlight streaming in from above us, and I'm amazed by how quickly things can change...

Small feet scamper up behind me across the rosin-covered stage. Molly is at my side again, and she moves in close as Roland sits and begins playing his newest composition.

"I thought you didn't approve of Mark." Her voice is worried.

"He's in the set crew, which means he's about as bad off as we are." I allow the ache in my waist to sharpen my tone. The reminder is more for me than her.

"You're not being very nice. He saved your life," she scolds, immediately turning swoony. "I think he's gorgeous."

"What?"

"He's so... *big*, and his eyes are so blue."

I don't want to think about Mark's eyes. I don't want to think about his broad shoulders and strong hands reaching out and grabbing a speeding rope to save my life. I can't think of him as my hero, no matter what the girls call him, and I can't swoon about the way he said he wouldn't ever let me fall.

The last thing I need is to think of him as anything more than a stage hand, a drifter. A guy who happened to do the right thing for whatever reason. Nothing more.

"Would you say his eyes are cornflower blue?" Molly continues.

I look down at the box Freddie sent me. "They're like irises."

"Hmm," Molly thinks about it. "You're right. They're so attractive."

"What's so attractive?" Mark is back, right behind my shoulder, and I spin around. *Did he hear me?*

"I'm sorry. I didn't mean to startle you." He goes to where Roland is sitting. "Darby needs the timing for the control box. You said it was off last night."

"Right." Roland stands and walks away, leaving the three of us facing each other.

"You like irises?" A sly grin curls Mark's lips.

"No... I mean, I don't know."

"I think they're beautiful," Molly jumps in, clutching his arm. He only pats her hand.

"I'll keep that in mind. See you in an hour." Those blue eyes hold mine, only now they're more like little blue flames.

"I need to learn the new song." I go around and sit in front of the piano, leaning forward to study the notes on the page, ignoring Mark's smile and how it makes my stomach flutter.

* * *

Mark

Terrence drags the box cutter down the seam of the last of the boxes. We've broken down all of them, and now they only have to be carried out to the dumpsters. We're finished for the day.

"I'm heading to the port after lunch. Fishing boats pull out on Sunday. We can go with them and spend the winter in the Caribbean."

My stomach sinks, and I stop what I'm doing. "What do you mean? You're leaving the show?"

"I'm not leaving the show. The show's finished. At least as far as we're concerned."

Scanning the backstage area, I notice it's clean, the new machinery is installed and tested, and the sets for the revised production wait in the wings.

"Done with us?" I repeat quietly. "For how long?"

"Meh." He shrugs, shoving the cutter in his back pocket. "They run the same production three to six months, depending on how it earns. We'll check in after the new year, see if we want to stay or go out again."

"But what if something breaks in the meantime? Don't they need a crew?"

"Darby can handle anything that comes up. Him or one of the regular guys."

I sit on the side of a set piece. I told Lara I'd be up there every night. I can't leave...

My old idea of joining the police academy crosses my mind. I still haven't given up on it, but I need money to pay for it. Gavin's offer echoes in my ears. *Steady work... not seasonal.*

"What will you do with the house while you're gone?"

Terrence leans forward, gathering the cardboard flats together. "I usually just lock it up."

"Ever considered letting someone stay over? Flush the toilets, keep the rats out?"

"My aunt comes by and checks on the place."

I watch him continue stacking the boxes. "I could do it for you."

"And what else? Work as a bouncer? You'll make more money with me on the boats."

"Gavin offered me a full-time job."

He straightens and frowns at me then. "Doing what?"

I look down at my injured hands. He's right to be suspicious. Hell, I'm suspicious. "I don't know."

He walks over and puts a hand on top of my shoulder. "What happens if you don't like the work?"

"I appreciate your concern." I pat the top of his hand. "But I've been taking care of myself a long time."

He pokes out his lips and thinks about it. "I liked you the first night I saw you. I'll let you stay in the house while I'm gone, and I'll see if my aunt knows anybody looking for a roommate."

"Thanks, man." I grab the stack of boxes and start for the back.

"Hey, Mark?" Stopping at the door, I look up. He's holding out the rubber spiral with the key hanging off it. "Take care of yourself."

One fluid motion, and it arcs through the air in my direction. I reach up and grab it and drop it in my pocket.

CHAPTER 7

"Love is too young to know what conscience is."
-Shakespeare

Lara

"The first hot non-creep, and of course he falls in love with you." Molly is lying on our bed running her finger along the seam of our quilted coverlet.

"I don't know what you're talking about." I lift my shirt and examine the ugly purple bruise. It's as wide as my hands and crosses my stomach like a belt. "No one's falling in love."

She rolls her eyes. "I'm not stupid."

"Neither am I. If I fall in love, it needs to be with someone like Freddie."

"So you're in love with Freddie?" She bounces up, and I glare at her reflection in the mirror. *As if…*

"Give me a chance. I only met him once."

She groans loudly. "I knew it! You're in love with Mark!" She slides off the bed and limps to the other side of our tiny room. She picks up the box from Freddie and holds it up. "Are you even going to open this?"

Then she limps back to where I stand. I frown watching her. "Are you hurt?"

"Because you stole Mark?"

I clear my throat and go to the bed to sit, patting the mattress beside me. "Why are you limping?"

"These shoes." She slips one off and starts rubbing her toes.

"Are they too small?"

"I guess."

I can't believe it. My old shoes have always worked for her. Now I'm afraid *I* might start crying. I drop to my knees and feel her other foot. Her toes are curled in the end of the shoe.

"Shit! How is it possible for you to be smaller than me and have bigger feet?"

"Maybe I'm going to be tall?"

Rubbing my forehead, I groan. "We'll have to get you a new pair of shoes."

Her pouting is completely forgotten. "New shoes!" she squeals, bouncing on the bed. "I've never had anything new!"

"Yeah, well, there's a reason."

I rip open the box from Freddie, and we both gasp. Inside is a large barrette in the shape of a peacock. The card inside says it's covered in Swarovski crystals, and when I tilt it side to side, it glitters like diamonds.

"It's gorgeous!" Molly's hands are clasped under her chin. "You have to wear it in the show!"

"No doubt that's what he wants." I imagine how much I could get if I pawned it.

Returning it to the box, I cross to my dressing table and bend down to the basket hidden behind the curtain. Pulling out pieces of ribbon and a spool of thread, I take out a shiny brass and cloisonné pen. It had been my mother's.

"He's really handsome." Molly is lying on her back now, caressing a small satin pillow.

"Who?" I hold the pen as if I'm writing a letter, turning it side to side so it catches the light.

"Freddie!" she cries as if I'm an idiot.

"Oh, right." With a sigh, I slide the pen into the pocket of my jeans. "I was actually trying to remember what he looked like last night."

She narrows her blue eyes. "He's tall and slim. He has smooth black hair and his teeth are so white and straight. And he has a line in his chin. I love that."

"How did you manage to get such a good look at him?"

"And he's very polite." She nods. "Like Guy."

"Who?" I've never heard that name before.

She's still playing with the small pillow. "Guy. I met him after the show Wednesday. After you fell. He was in the front, and he kept watching me from the audience."

I pull the small pillow down so our eyes met. "Watching you?"

"Mmmhmm. I caught his eye, and he smiled. Then I smiled…"

"Who is he?"

"Friend of Gavin's?"

My mind races. I don't know all of Gavin's friends, but I know they're not all nice.

"He's very sophisticated," she continues. "And he wears a pinky ring."

I don't like the sound of that. "Can I meet him?"

"Not anymore. He went back to Savannah or Charleston… maybe it was Atlanta. But he said he'd be back, and he wants to see me again."

"He wants to see you?"

She nods. "He said I amuse him."

I catch her chin. "He sounds old."

"So?" She jerks her face away. "We were just talking. He likes the way I laugh." She kicks off the other shoe and picks up one of my lipsticks. "Anyway, I was still in love with Mark on

Wednesday, so it didn't matter."

"And now you're not?"

"Mark doesn't look at me the way Guy does." She slides the wine-colored lipstick over her full lips, looking sixteen in the process.

Fear tightens in the center of my chest. "How does he look at you?"

Her eyes drift to the ceiling, searching for the answer. "Like I'm interesting. Like he wants to know more about me."

I silently vow to keep a better eye on her in the future. I haven't lived in New Orleans this long not to know the kind of men who lurk around strip clubs. Pedophiles.

"I told you never to talk to strangers."

"He's Gavin's friend!"

"But you don't know that for sure, do you?" Glancing at the clock, I see an hour has passed. It's not what Mark had in mind, but we don't have a choice. "Come on. If you can limp your way to the Quarter, we'll get you those new shoes."

* * *

Outside, the sky is bright blue, and there isn't a single cloud in sight. The air is crisp and cool, something that rarely happens in New Orleans, but underneath the fresh fall scent is the metallic smell of moldering beer and urine. Odors that only grow stronger as the sun travels higher and the temperature rises.

We make our way up the short alley to the cathedral and across the flagstone courtyard to Jackson Square. My sights are focused on a jewelry store in the northeast corner that I hope will give me a good price for the item in my pocket.

"Wait here, and don't talk to anyone," I say once we're there.

Joyaux Bijoux faces the flagstone-paved square, and Molly can walk among the painters while I haggle. A clerk greets me when I enter.

"I'm looking for Gerard," I say.

She nods and goes to the back. In a few moments, a short man with straight black hair and a monocle strapped to his forehead comes out. When he sees me, he smiles.

"Ah, beautiful Lara, what have you got for me today?" Gerard is going bald right on the top of his head, and it makes him look like a monk.

I take the pen out of my jeans and place it gently on a black velvet pad on the glass counter. "It's genuine cloisonné."

He picks it up and holds it to the light frowning. "Eh," he mutters. Then he rolls it around in his hand. "It's a good piece. But I don't know how I could sell it."

"It's a gorgeous pen. Anyone would kill to have it."

"It's too ornate for a man," he argues. "And a lady would complain it's too heavy."

"Ornate is very popular now. You won't keep it in the store a week."

He holds it in the writing position then twirls it down into his palm. "Forty bucks," he said.

"It's worth three times that amount. One hundred."

He looks at me a split second and twirls the pen in his hand again. "I'll give you fifty, and I'm losing money doing it."

"I'm losing a precious family heirloom. You can give me eighty."

"Your family heirloom, someone else's junk." He rolls it around in his fingers again. The polished brass shines in the light.

"In Europe, this would be worth at least two hundred."

"Ah, but we're in America, aren't we?"

My jaw tightens, and he slants an eye at me. "Seventy-five. Final offer."

He pulls a cash box from under the counter. I sigh and give in. I'll have to hope Molly's feet stop growing. I'm running out of valuables.

He wraps the pen in velvet and places it in a box, and for the last time, I watch the light glint off my mother's precious writing utensil. I fight an unexpected tightness in my throat. I will not cry. Molly has to have shoes, and we both need personal items.

I slip the money in my pocket and pull the tail of my shirt over my jeans. "Pleasure doing business with you." And with a lift of my shoulder, I get on with the show.

Molly is nowhere to be seen in the large square. It's a Friday, so the crowd of weekend tourists is already flooding the popular area. Slowly, I pick my way through the street artists. Someone is always shouting, trying to catch my eye.

"*Enchanté*!" A man corners me. I keep my eyes down and try to move past him, but he blocks my way. "You would make a lovely model. Allow me to capture your beauty to brighten my booth."

"No thanks." I know that scam—he keeps my portrait, and I pay for the honor of his painting it.

Just then I look up and see Molly coming toward me, leading Mark by the hand.

"Look who I found sketching the cathedral!" she cries.

"You're early." He smiles down at me, showing that dimple.

"You're an artist?" I fight the swell of joy in my chest at seeing him.

"I wouldn't say that." He glances at the storefront behind me. "Were you shopping?"

"No, I was—"

"We're shoe shopping for me," Molly interrupts. "Lara had to drop off something with Gerard."

"Who's Gerard?" Mark scans my face, and that look of concern heats my cheeks.

"Gerard's the owner," Molly continues, but I cut her off.

"So if you're not an artist, what were you doing?"

He shrugs. "I was just messing around. Seeing if I might be able to make a few nickels."

"Show her!" Molly takes the sketchpad from him and hands it to me. I lift the heavy brown cover.

"Oh!" I gasp. "Mark, it's beautiful."

"You think?" He steps closer and looks at the drawing.

It's a magnificent sketch of the cathedral, taller and narrower with heavy, dark lines. Rather than a sanctuary, it looks ominous, like a haunted mansion.

"I was experimenting with perspective there," he says.

I look from him to my little friend and I think about extra money. "Would you teach Molly some of this?"

"Oh, would you, Mark?" She grabs his arm, and he looks at me, puzzled.

"I don't know if I'm really qualified to teach..."

My face falls. "And I don't know how I could pay you."

"You wouldn't have to pay me." His voice is gentle, and I look up to meet those blue eyes again.

"It's just that Molly already likes to draw, and I thought it might give her something to do." My gaze meets his then, and I hope he understands. "Something to earn money."

Mark laughs. "Haven't you heard the expression, 'starving artist'?"

"I guess that's true."

A familiar voice calls my name over the bustle of the square. I turn and my eyes land on Evie's. She's walking with two well-dressed men, and the three of them begin weaving their way toward us.

"What a wonderful surprise!" She takes my hand. "Isn't it a beautiful afternoon. Let me introduce Phillip and Armand."

They're very handsome. One has light brown hair, while the other's is darker. They stand close to each other, but Phillip has his hand on Evie's arm. She's wearing a plum-colored mini dress and a black velvet beret, and she looks like a model.

"I love your dress," I say, not really sure how I'm supposed to act. I feel like I know too much about these men to be meeting them for the first time.

"Armand picked it out for me! Isn't it the cutest thing?" She twirls, and Molly's eyes are dazzled.

"You look amazing!" she cries.

"But what are you doing out here?" She studies the three of us.

"I... I was..." I'm drawing a blank. I can't tell Evie and her boyfriends I was pawning my heirlooms to buy Molly shoes.

"I asked Lara to meet me," Mark steps forward, holding out a hand. "Nice to meet you, Armand. Phillip."

"You know Mark... Well, he's actually quite an artist."

Evie's eyes go big. "A hero and an artist? How interesting..."

"And I'm getting new shoes!" Molly announces.

"You are?" Evie studies Mark a moment then looks at me, then Molly. "You know Armand has the best eye for fashion. Why don't we take Molly with us, and I'll bring her home with me."

"Oh yes!" Molly grabs my arm.

"I-I don't know..." Not that I mind her going with Evie. I'm just not sure I can afford Armand's taste.

"Please." Evie smiles, touching my arm. "It'll give me someone to chat with."

I get the feeling Evie is on her own more than she anticipated in this arrangement. "I don't want to intrude on your day. I'm sure Armand doesn't want to shop for Molly's shoes."

"You're wrong." The darker one who isn't holding Evie's arm lifts his eyebrows and winks. "I love to shop for women's shoes."

"That's nice." Leaning forward, I whisper in Evie's ear. "I only have thirty dollars."

"Your money's no good here!" She steps away, waving a hand.

"Evie, I have to pay—"

"Absolutely not," Phillip reaches for Molly's hand. "It's my treat."

My mouth opens and closes, but I'm fresh out of arguments.

"That settles it," Evie says. "We'll see you later tonight. Have fun!"

The four of them take off in the direction of the shops, and I'm left watching them leave. I don't even have a chance to give Molly any final instructions.

"That was lucky," Mark says, turning to face me.

Our eyes meet, and I can't help a smile. The entire transaction with Evie and her boys lifted a huge weight off my shoulders. "I guess it was. I'll have to do something to thank her."

"I think those guys like shopping." He winks and looks after them.

"I won't complain. I hate it."

He nods. "Noted. No shopping for you."

"Unless you need to get something…" I hold out my hand.

He takes it, covering it with his larger one and pulling it into the crook of his arm. "I'm all set for now." We walk along the large square filled with artists, tarot readers, and other street vendors. "Have you had lunch?"

"I didn't have a chance to grab anything before we left the theater."

"That settles it. I'll take you to my favorite place."

"I didn't think you were from New Orleans." His body is warm beside mine, and I can't help noticing the rock-hard bicep I'm holding.

"I'm not, but I get around."

"And you have a favorite place to eat?"

He covers my fingers with his hand. "It doesn't look like much, but I guarantee you'll love it. The best part—no disguises necessary."

I remember my excuse. "I don't think I have to worry about anybody recognizing me yet."

"That won't last long."

I'm not sure how to interpret his tone—is it pride or regret? I decide to let it pass and hold his arm as we walk along the flagstones down a narrow side alley lined with arched brick openings looking into small courtyards. One has a fountain, and the echo of water fills the short space.

"It's so pretty." I lean to look inside.

"Yeah, I didn't really notice last time."

"Are you saying you don't appreciate Creole architecture?"

"I like wrought iron and ivy. Just not when I'm hungry."

A man walks past us carrying a white paper bag emitting a delicious smell, and my hand tightens on his arm. I realize how long it's been since I've eaten.

"I'm beginning to understand."

We continue past several brick-paved streets leading west and away from the square. Mark finally stops at a narrow alley covered by a balcony with black, wrought iron columns and ivy growing up the red bricks. It's shadowy, and he stops me by putting both hands on my shoulders.

"Wait here."

My eyebrows rise. "It's not a restaurant?"

"I'll be right back."

The mischief in his eyes makes me laugh. It's like we're doing something illegal, which I guess we are since you're not supposed to sell food without a permit.

I stand in the narrow alley, watching a stream of water running down the little valley in the center. A few minutes pass, and I slowly walk to the next corner. An Asian guy is sitting in a doorway eating a poboy he holds in a paper wrapper. More delicious scents, and this time my stomach growls.

"Ready?"

"Jesus!" I jump out of my skin, and Mark laughs.

"Why so jumpy? We're not robbing a bank."

He has a white paper bag in his hand. It's just like the one the man from earlier was carrying, and I reach for it. "Give me mine now."

"Hold your horses. I've got another surprise."

Twisting my lips, I frown up at him. "I hope it's not far."

He grabs my hand and pulls me after him. "Come on."

We continue down the same alley for three more blocks until it opens onto a wide street past the French Market. The backs of the kiosks the merchants use to display their wares are facing us. In front of us, the levee goes straight up, tall as the balconies on the facing buildings.

"Sometimes I forget how high the river is here," Mark says.

I remember the flood from when I was a little girl, but the girl's school where I lived was on high ground. We were spared the worst of it.

He tugs my hand forward, and my eyes shoot to his. "I can't climb that."

"Good thing there's stairs."

We walk down a little way then climb a narrow concrete stairway leading to the top of the grassy hill. Damp wind blows cool as we walk down the path to a black metal bench. The currents swirl and crisscross in the center of the wide stretch of river, but I'm not interested in that or the barges slowly passing.

"Let's eat!"

"Now who's not interested in the scenery."

"You're moving slower on purpose."

I reach for the bag, and he laughs, pulling out a foot-long sandwich wrapped in wax paper. The scents emanating from it have my stomach roaring. Mark holds it up.

"I have to warn you. Once you eat this sandwich, you'll be addicted."

"What is it?" I'm practically on my knees waiting.

He unrolls it and I see crisp French bread with lettuce spilling out the sides, pink sauce, and little flakey, golden-brown fried nuggets. He passes me half, and I take a bite. Tangy heat, tomato, the rich copper of oysters, combined with the ocean freshness of shrimp.

"It's the everything sandwich. Fried oysters, shrimp, and fish with Rémoulade and tartar sauce. And a secret ingredient I suspect is crack." He takes a big bite, but I'm already on my second.

"Oh my God," I groan with my mouth full.

He nods, grinning. "Right?"

"Who makes this?"

"Nope." He shakes his head. "Top secret."

"What!" I smack his arm playfully. "You can't keep this a secret now! What will I do?"

"Don't piss me off, I guess."

"Argh!" I squeal before taking another giant bite of heaven.

We sit for a few minutes grinning and scarfing down the sandwich until there's nothing left but paper. I pick up pieces of lettuce with creamy Rémoulade clinging to them and put them in my mouth. My stomach is wonderfully full.

"It's probably good you don't tell me the name of that place," I giggle, rubbing my hands over my stomach. "Bad for business."

"No way. You're too skinny."

"Too skinny?" I arch an eyebrow at him.

He clears his throat and starts collecting our trash. "You're definitely not fat."

Chewing on my bottom lip, I watch his hands moving, remembering the night he saw more of me than any man ever has.

"Why did you come to New Orleans?" I feel certain it wasn't to work at a burlesque show, although I suppose some men would consider it a career goal.

He sits straighter and looks out at the brown water. "I came because my uncle lived here. He was the only relative I knew about."

"Lived here?"

Mark's eyes drop to his hands. "He died."

"Oh! I'm so sorry." I reach out to touch his shoulder. It moves up and down under my hand.

"I never really knew him." He makes a fist. "I'd only been staying with him a few days when it happened."

"I'm so sorry." My voice is softer. I know how it feels to be left alone in a strange city. "Was Terrence a friend of his?"

"Terrence has a house. He rents rooms for cheap. I was only planning to stay one night while I figured out what to do next."

We're quiet watching the currents. A ripple on the water is cut by the prow of a riverboat. "You want to be an artist?"

"What?" His brow furrows, and then he seems to remember. "Oh, that. No, I was just messing around earlier. I want to go to the police academy."

That pulls me up short. "Police academy?"

He grins. "Yeah, I thought I'd be a cop."

"Why?"

"Don't sound so shocked."

"I don't mean... It's not what I expected."

He stands and holds a hand out to me. I take it and we start walking toward the little staircase leading back the way we came.

"I wasn't interested in going to college for four years. I didn't want to join the military... Although, I liked the idea of it, how it works. I like talking to people, and I seem to get along with most of them." We reach the brick paved streets of the Quarter. He looks up at the gray clouds rolling in from the river. "I wanted to be one of the good guys."

* * *

Mark

She's so pretty walking beside me in the fading sunlight. The trees cast speckled shadows over everything and occasionally a breeze freshens our faces. It smells like rain and the promise of fall touches us on every other gust.

Her hand has been in mine or on my arm most of the afternoon, and it's so easy walking and talking with her.

"Will you go to the academy now?" Her pretty blue eyes meet mine, and a touch of worry is in them. I don't want to be stupid and think she cares if I leave... but maybe?

I pull open the theater door, and we enter through the dark lobby. "Going to the academy costs money. More than I have right now."

She stops and faces me in the empty hall. "What will you do? The crew usually leaves once the set work is done."

I rub my forehead, thinking about what Gavin said. His knowledge of my uncle… my limited knowledge of what Rick did, how he died… My creeping sense that working for Gavin would make me one of the bad guys.

Then I see her pretty face.

I saw her beautiful body two nights ago… But she's not like the other girls. When she's with me, it doesn't feel like she has an agenda. She's just sweet and smart and a little shy.

Shoving my concerns aside, I decide to stay. "Gavin wants me to do some work for him. He said he's starting something new."

Her brow lowers, and she touches my arm. "You need to be careful with him." Her face is serious, and I take her hand, holding it in my bandaged ones.

She cares, but I have no reason to believe it's more than friendship. Or gratitude.

"I get that feeling."

Our eyes meet, and she steps closer. When she stands in front of me, she seems so small.

"What did you want to do?" My voice is soft, and I reach up to lightly slide a curl off her cheek. She blinks slowly, thinking.

"Since I was young, I always wanted to be a singer."

"You have a beautiful voice."

"But once you go down this road, it's like you can't seem to get off it."

My chest tightens, and I lift her small hand in mine. "Sounds like we're both making critical decisions."

I won't leave her to take this step alone. The pull in my chest is too strong. I have to keep her safe from things that would hurt her, from the men who come here, from the way the crew talks about the girls. From the way some of the girls see themselves...

"You're so good." Her voice is soft, and she traces her finger along the bandage before lifting her blue eyes to meet mine. "Thank you for buying me lunch. For saving me..."

Without warning, she steps forward and wraps her arms around my waist, pressing her face against my chest, and I don't hold back. She fits perfectly in my arms, and I inhale the sweet scent of her hair just before I press my lips to the top of her head.

Her voice is muffled against my shirt. "It feels so safe here."

"Lara," I whisper in her hair. "I want to keep you safe."

She pulls back, and I loosen my hold. But she doesn't leave. She puts her hand against my cheek, lifting her chin as she rises higher on her toes. Hell if I make her work for it.

Leaning forward, I capture her lips. They part, and our tongues meet, curling together as I hug her closer to me. She exhales a little noise, and her fingers thread in the sides of my hair. I trace a line with my lips to her ear.

"I want you so much," I whisper.

She turns, searching for my mouth, and I kiss her. She fists my shirt in her hands, pulling it up and placing her palm against my bare stomach. I groan deeply, and my hands slide under her ass. I lift her against my chest, and her legs go around my waist. Our kisses are wildfire, fast-moving, lips pulling, hungry for something more. Something just within reach.

She moves subtly against my waist, and the blood rushes downward. I'm hard and she's riding me, stroking my erection with her crotch.

"Lara," I groan.

Her lips still, and she holds my cheeks, looking into my eyes. "That night on the catwalk… The way you looked at me…"

My brow collapses at the memory. "You're the most beautiful thing I've ever seen."

"I only want you to see me."

Her lips are pink and swollen from my kisses. I lean forward and kiss her again, tasting her like she's water in the desert. She exhales a little noise, and it's a charge straight to my cock.

I love her lips. I love her mouth. I want more. I want all of her.

"Does your waist hurt?"

She leans forward, running her nose along my jaw. "Nothing hurts. Everything is amazing."

My mind races through the possibilities. Terrence is at my place. All the people are here. *Fuck,* I don't have anywhere to take her, but I'll be damned if our first time is standing in this lobby.

"Here." I ease her to her feet. We're both breathing hard, and she's still in my arms. "I have to sort some shit out."

Her lip goes between her teeth. "You have to work tonight. Up there… with Vanessa."

She seems to be retreating, misunderstanding my meaning. I catch her waist and pull her to me again. "What?"

She shakes her head and holds my arms, stepping out of them. "I'm sorry, I shouldn't have done that. I shouldn't assume."

Desperation tightens my chest. "Stop." My voice is sharper than I intend, but it works. She stops moving away. "I couldn't be less interested in anyone—"

"Don't. You don't owe me anything."

"Lara." I catch both her cheeks in my hands. Ocean eyes meet mine, and I kiss her with all the heat smoldering in my skin.

A little noise comes from her throat, and she covers my hands with hers, clinging to them a moment before pulling her lips away. Still, I hold her gaze. "Just give me time. I'll work it out." I slide my palm along her velvety, pink cheek. "This is going to happen."

She takes her hands from mine and jogs to the door leading into the theater. I don't chase her. I can't with the raging hard-on in my pants. Leaning my head against the wall, I close my eyes and relive what just happened.

Even if she pulled back, that was real. No way am I letting her get away, and no fucking way am I letting her think anybody else is on my mind.

Pushing my hand down the front of my jeans to adjust myself, I head for the door. I've got to work out these details so when the next opportunity arises, I can take it.

CHAPTER 8

"We can't escape ourselves."

Lara

I have lost my mind.

Jogging to my dressing room my body vibrates with the heat of being in Mark's arms. My brain is drunk on his delicious kisses, and my heart is flying in my chest. It's amazing. I don't have to hide my true self from him, and I don't have to act.

He held my hand and told me to breathe. He kissed me and made me laugh. I've never felt so light and free and happy…

Stopping at the back door, I close my eyes and relinquish the fight. I think of his lips at my ear and the crack in his voice when he said he wanted me. My insides clench, and I remember how we touched.

Riding him, sliding my body against the steel rod in his jeans, I was on fire. Now I ache to finish what we started. I've never felt this way before… not even about Roland. I was a little girl then, dreaming of him writing songs for me and being my boyfriend.

Now I'm a woman, and I'm dreaming of Mark as my lover. I imagine his hands on my breasts, his mouth everywhere.

A loud crash makes me jump. Speak of the devil, Roland bangs through the metal side door and stops when he sees me. He walks to where I'm standing, facing the door to the backstage rooms.

"Hey… I didn't expect to see you here." Dark eyes search my face. "Feel like going over some of the new songs?"

"Not really." My voice cracks, and his gaze fixes on my mouth.

My lips are warm and throbbing from Mark's kisses, and I know he sees it.

"Ahh…" He steps back, turning to face the empty house. "I passed Mark out on the street just now. He seemed different somehow. Happy."

"Really? I wonder why." I'm trying to keep my voice light and failing.

"He's a good-looking guy. Brave… Heroic even." He starts across the stage, headed to the opposite door. "It's too bad he doesn't have any money. Or connections."

Roland continues up the aisle and out the door, leaving me alone. I read his message loud and clear. I need to get my head straight.

Even if all I can think about are Mark's full lips, his broad shoulders, the promise in his jeans… Roland is right. I shouldn't be thinking about men in this place, or if I do, my thoughts should be on Freddie.

Before Molly even opens her eyes the next morning, I'm up and pulling on my jeans and a black sweater. I spent yesterday running around the city with Mark, but I can't afford to be so careless today.

I'm out the side door and jogging up the alley in the direction of the library before the clock even hits ten. Stopping at a coffee truck, I use a few of our dollars to get a café au lait and a scone, then I hurry to catch the streetcar heading uptown to Loyola

University, using another dollar for the short trip.

When I reach Tulane Avenue, I hop off and toss my trash in a green metal bin before jogging up the steps of the public library. The building smells like pine cleaner and old books. The crowd is light for a Saturday—teens wearing braces and glasses, a young guy carrying a backpack—and I consider how there's a whole different world outside the twelve-block radius beside the Mississippi River that defines my life.

People here go to school. They have jobs and families. They worry about gas bills and tuition payments and who's running for President. The math of tickets sold or nights in review or the density of glitter on a thong… the details of my strange existence are light-years from this place. I'm a foreigner trying to belong here.

I find an open computer and sit down, holding my library card under the red scanner until it beeps, giving me access. Minutes pass as the cursor blinks in the white rectangle waiting for me to search for something. Anything…

I consider Mark's question. *What do you want to do?*

If all I want is to be a singer, I can stay on Royal Street for that. Or head one block north and moonlight at a club on Bourbon. I have to think in this world, the world of Loyola and Tulane. I tap the mouse and type in the words *jobs for young women* and hit enter.

A list appears, and I start to read. Most of them start with the word "volunteer." I don't know much, but I know that means working for free, so I keep scrolling. Places seeking interns—again a job where you don't get paid. How do these people eat if they never get paid?

More scrolling.

A foundation seeks a grant writer. I don't even know what that means. I'm attracted to an ad for a videographer and film editor for an independent production company making short films focused on historic sites in the city. Wow. I wouldn't even know where to begin.

A notepad and one of those tiny, half-pencils I've only seen in church sit beside the keyboard. I pick it up and make a few notes. *College degree required* is a common phrase in all the listings.

Several hours pass, and my mind drifts to Mark. He wants to be a policeman, and I can see him keeping the peace. He'd look amazing in that uniform with his broad shoulders and narrow waist. I can see him in those aviator sunglasses, square jaw, and light hair. My stomach flutters and my lip goes between my teeth. I imagine the feel of nylon under my fingertips. His skin tasted salty, and his body was warm... Looking down, my notepad is covered in stars, hearts, and figure eights.

Clearing my throat, I straighten and search a different combination of words, no college degree required. These jobs pay by the hour and take place at times I can't work around my schedule at the theater. I have to find something that will build until I can leave the Pussycat with Molly. I can't support us on any of these starting salaries, and at least we can live in the theater.

Discouragement is heavy in my chest when two-thirty hits. The library closes in a half hour, and I've spent a whole day with nothing to show for it. Standing, I rip the sheet of paper out of the yellow legal pad and fold it several times. I shove the small square in the back of my jeans and head for the door.

The wind is stronger now, and it's starting to rain. I dash across the street and jog up the few blocks to the Walgreens. The metal door swishes open, and I head for the clothes section. Sliding plastic hangers across the metal bar, I choose two shirts for Molly. One is dark green with vertical white pinstripes. The other is autumn orange. They'll look pretty with her complexion, and they won't pull so much across her breasts. The more I can downplay her emerging assets, the better.

Ten dollars spent, and I'm outside again, hopping on the streetcar headed to the river. When I arrive at the theater, it's bustling with the dancers, musicians, set guys, and everyone preparing for tonight's performance.

Gavin is backstage, which makes everyone stress out. Roland snaps at Tanya as she warms up, and Vanessa complains to Rosa about her pasties not staying on her tits. I hunch my shoulders and do my best to disappear in the velvet wings before anyone sees me.

"Lara!" I freeze at Gavin's loud voice. Heavy footsteps cross the stage to where I stand clutching my Walgreen's bag. "You've been shopping?"

"Molly needed shirts," I say quietly, doing my best to hunch to the side, pretending my waist is still in pain. It's not, and he knows it.

"Good. You'll rejoin the production tomorrow night."

My shoulders drop, but I know. Nobody stays here for free. "Yes, sir."

He only studies me a moment before turning on his heel and heading back in the direction he came.

Mark's mention of new business drifts through my mind, and I wonder if that's why Gavin is here.

Vanessa's voice goes loud. "I should be the lead tomorrow. The crowd loves what I'm doing. I bring character to the role."

"Lara can sing," Roland deadpans.

Vanessa glares at him. "I handle it as more of a speaking part."

"It's a singing part." He's not backing down, and as much as I appreciate him fighting for me, I can't deny my anxiety at taking the role.

Being in the spotlight here is like having a bull's eye painted on your forehead—or your crotch. I don't engage. I keep my eyes fixed on the scuffed black floor and pick up the pace, headed to my room. Still, I don't miss Vanessa's final jab.

"Too bad for Mark," she sighs. "Our moments in the dark are so intimate. He knows how to touch a girl just so... Gets the fires burning."

Jealousy tightens my throat, and rage burns my cheeks. My eyes snap up, and daggers shoot from my glare.

"Did I say something wrong?" Her green eyes are round, but the gleam in them says her innocence is an act.

She's baiting me, but I only clutch the bag tighter and push through the curtains. I'm heading to my room, moving fast through the darkness when Mark appears. It's like the force of my possessiveness drew him. I want him to be mine and only mine.

"Lara." His voice is smooth, like a caress to my angry heart. "Where were you today? I was looking for you..."

He's in jeans and a dark gray tee, and he looks like everything good in my bleak little world.

"I was at the library." All the words I don't say drift through my mind. *I couldn't stop thinking about you. I missed you so much. You'll be such a sexy cop. Don't leave me here alone…*

"Oh, right." He looks down and somehow manages to be even sexier in his regret. "I kept you from that yesterday. I'm sorry."

"It's okay." I smile, taking a step closer. "I mean, I wanted to go with you. I wouldn't have missed that poboy for anything."

He steps closer, and his warmth makes my heart beat faster. "The poboy was good, but I thought something else was better."

My back is to the wall, and he leans beside me. The pull is back, the force inside me that craves his touch, his kind words, my dream of escape and safety in his arms.

"What was it?" My words are a hot whisper, and he leans into me.

I don't pull away like I should. I pull closer, reaching for his shoulder, sighing from deep in my soul when his arms tighten around me. I turn my face to gasp for air as he kisses my temple, the side of my hair, my neck. His lips are a match to gasoline. I'm on fire, and logic and reason can kiss my ass—I want him.

We kiss. Our lips unite, move apart, and our tongues collide and curl together. Heat blazes between my thighs with every pass, and I search his waist, slipping my fingers beneath his cotton shirt to his skin. A groan rolls from his throat as I trace the lines on his stomach. I want to go lower. I want to wrap my fingers around the hard muscle I feel straining in his pants.

Our lips part, and he kisses my chin, my neck… He pauses, and his eyes fix on my breasts rising and falling rapidly under my thin shirt. I want to rip it off.

I want him to devour my breasts. My body is melting from the heat, but I hear the footsteps on the stage out front. My reality trickles through the darkness.

"Oh, Mark," I gasp, my legs trembling as I step back. "We can't do this here."

He stands before me panting, his hair tousled, his shirt loose, and God, he's like a dream. I smooth my hair and straighten my sweater. I have to get to my room, but he stops me.

"Wait." I glance up, and his expression, his beautiful, caring face melts my heart. "I hope your search went well."

I nod, turning away so he can't see the mist in my eyes. It didn't go well, and in the smallest part of my heart, I'm glad. I don't want to leave him.

"It's not true…" His voice is quiet. "I want you to find what you're looking for, but I wish we had more time."

My eyes go to his, and I see his struggle. It's my own reflected back at me. "I told Gavin I'd take the job."

"I return to the show tomorrow night."

We're quiet in the face of our shared future.

"It's your last night before you're a star." Slowly lifting a finger, he traces it along the line of my hair, a sad smile curling his lips. "Better rest."

I turn and run into the blackness to my little room as the passage door closes behind me. Two turns and I'm there, but I pause in the narrow hallway before opening the door. I press my fist into my chest and exhale, ordering myself to get control.

But I can't escape him. Images of Mark stubbornly invade my thoughts. His friendly smile, his burning kiss, his gentle touch. He promised to keep me safe.

Is it possible we're stronger than the forces surrounding us? I spent today learning I'm trapped in this machine… Can Mark help us escape? Shaking my head, I know my salvation won't come in time. He's right. I need to make the most of tonight, because tomorrow everything changes.

* * *

Mark

Again I'm in the darkness high above the stage, waiting.

Gavin was pleased when I told him I'd take the job, but he was confused when I insisted I had to keep this task, up here in the dark making sure Lara doesn't fall.

He started to argue. My work for him doesn't involve being on the set crew. Still, I argued I know the requirements of this position, and I've proven I'm willing to do what it takes to keep her safe.

His watery blue eyes slid to my hands, and he agreed to my terms. Whether he knows my real reason, I can't tell, and I don't care. I don't trust anybody up here with my girl, and I won't risk Lara's life as long as I'm here.

I promised her I'd be here every night, and I won't break my promise.

Only this night, it's Vanessa climbing that narrow ladder to the catwalk. With a heavy exhale, I step away, to the farthest point from the swing.

She doesn't wear a robe or any cover over her body. Her costume is more revealing than the one Lara wears, and it's somehow less sexy as a result. Vanessa stands at the top of the platform in a nude thong, a network of glittering strings draping from her neck over her bare breasts, and the smallest pair of wings attached to her shoulders.

Her blonde hair is long down her back to her ass, and her jeweled heels are so tall, our eyes are level. It's clear her outfit is patterned after those runway angels. It's a sexy getup, but for me, it's on the wrong woman.

"Mark?" She trots across the narrow boards to where I'm standing, arching her back so her full breasts lead the way. "I think one of my straps came undone while I was climbing the ladder. Would you check it for me?"

She pauses a moment, standing very straight in front of me. I can see… everything. She's not wearing pasties. She's pretty much fully nude.

"It all looks… fine." Turning my head, I fix my gaze on the show unfolding below. Tanya is doing her contortionist routine, tossing scraps of fabric into the wings with every backbend and twist.

"It's not on the front," Vanessa argues. "It's on my ass."

She spins on her heel and leans forward, thrusting her bare round ass into my crotch and twerking it. *Fuck.* My body responds to her movements because, hell, I'm not dead. Still, I take a step back.

"Yeah, it looks okay to me."

She straightens and looks over her shoulder, eyes narrowed and lips curved in a smile. "I felt that." She turns again and moves closer. "You like what you see?"

I'm at the end of the walk, and she's pressed against my chest, putting pressure on the front of my jeans, and I distinctly feel her hand stroking my cock up and down, running her nails over my growing erection.

"Mmm, it's so big." Her green eyes sparkle. "I'll leave my door open after the show, and you can sink this lead pipe deep in my well."

Reaching down, I catch her wrist and move it off my crotch. "You're going to mess up your costume."

Her hand twists in my grip, and she guides my fingers between her legs. "Feel how wet I am for you."

I pull my hand up and out of hers before she makes it to her cunt. Jesus, how long does it take to get to the musical cue? She's all over me, and I don't want to touch her.

Clearing the thickness from my throat, I move to the side, allowing her to have my place against the metal guardrail. I cross the narrow strip of boards to the bench and pull a pair of leather gloves out of my back pocket.

"You need to get seated and attach the safety harness."

She turns and walks to me like a model on the catwalk, eyes fixed on mine. "You always make me wet, Mark. Do you know that?" Long fingernails trace up my forearm, and I step away, returning to my place beside the rope without answering.

Facing me, she sits, lifting her bare breasts as she holds the sides of the bench. Then she opens her legs wide, flashing me her pussy before crossing them again. The musical cue sounds, and the seat moves out over the open stage, but she looks back over her shoulder and mouths the words, *All for you*.

I almost mouth back, *No thanks*, but it doesn't matter. She's descending. I've made it through my last night in the dark with that naked octopus. I can think of five guys who would give their front teeth for my spot up here with Vanessa, and I'd gladly give it to them. The only catch is I'm not sure I'd get it back when Lara returns, and I have to be here for my girl.

The swing makes it to the bottom without a hitch, and I toss the gloves on the chair, hopping on the ladder and quickly returning to the floor. It's early enough I might catch Lara before she calls it a night.

I know she's tired. I know she's worried about returning to her place tomorrow night. I want to reassure her about all of it. Even better, Terrence leaves for the Caribbean tomorrow. I'll have the house to myself, and I want to ask her to come home with me after the show. I want to keep her safe there, away from this place at night.

My chest is tight, expanding with my dreams of our future, my plans for cheating the system, when Gavin bumps into me in the wings.

"Whoa, there." He steps out from the side door, and seems surprised to see me. "Mark—just the man I was looking for. Come with me."

"I-I was just—" I hesitate, my eyes traveling to the door leading to Lara's room. I'm not supposed to be back here.

"Now." His tone tells me it isn't a request.

I nod and follow him through the side door into a narrow hallway I've never seen before. He walks fast, leading me on a steady slope down. We take a sharp curve, and we're still traveling lower, going underground, beneath the stage to where the trap doors lead. Yellow lights in cages are scattered at distant intervals, casting long shadows through the dusty basement. Still, he doesn't stop.

We arrive at another door at the opposite side of the theater from where we entered.

Gavin pauses, and looks at me over his shoulder. "In this job, you don't talk about what you see." It's a command, given with icy finality.

He waits, and I realize he's waiting for me to acknowledge I understand.

"Yes, sir." My voice seems small in the vast area.

My skin crawls as we pass through the door. It's clearly a secret area, recently renovated with fresh carpet and new wallpaper. My gaze travels up to the ceiling, and I see tiny black domes for surveillance cameras.

I think of what I know about secrets and places hidden underground. Usually when things are secret, what happens in them is illegal. Terrence's warning flickers in my mind, and my muscles tense, bracing for what's to come.

We're in another hallway lined with doors, but it's quiet. I'm pretty sure we're alone. Gavin stops at the first door, pushing it open and reaching inside to flick a switch. It doesn't flood with light. It warms with the illumination of yellow bulbs.

"In here." He stands back as if waiting for me to enter ahead of him. I hesitate and meet his eyes before entering the room.

Immediately, I recoil. My voice escapes on a hiss. "What the fuck?"

A bed is against the back corner, and it's torn apart. Sheets are pulled away and part of the bare mattress is exposed. The smell of sweat and something deeper, musty, hangs in the air, and dark stains are on the sheets, a swipe on the wall, a handprint. On the carpet is a large, black oval. Is it blood? Is this a crime scene?

"Clean it up." He starts to leave, but I go after him, down the short hallway.

"What happened here?"

He doesn't stop, and I reach out to grab his arm.

It's a mistake.

He turns on me faster than I can see, slamming my back to the wall, his forearm at my neck. This guy's as tall as me and twice my weight.

Blue eyes bore into mine, and bourbon stings my nose. "You work for me now," he growls. "You don't ask questions. You don't think. You do as you're told." Tightening his fist on my neck, he pushes me toward the room. "Clean it up. Burn the rest."

"Take it easy, Gavin." The scuff of shoes precedes another man joining us. He's short and beefy, and when he turns, light reflects off a badge. My stomach roils when I realize he's a cop, and he's staring at me, memorizing my face. "Mark Fitzhugh, right?"

I won't confirm or deny.

I don't have to.

"Reese Landry, meet the new guy."

"Kinda young, isn't he?"

"He's young, but he's got guts. He'll do what it takes to stay here."

In that moment, I realize Gavin has my number.

Landry walks closer, taking one glance into the room before smiling at me. "Welcome to our world, Mark Fitzhugh. Enjoy your stay."

Nausea is in my throat, and I watch the two men leave. I'm alone in this strange hidden place facing this dark task.

Two steps, and I consider running. It's not too late to catch up with Terrence and leave in the morning on a fishing boat headed for a tropical paradise. Or simply hop a train and ride it all the way to Chicago. He won't come after me. Why should he? I don't know anything—what happened here or why.

Fuck Landry, the crooked cop. Fuck both of them and their surveillance cameras.

One thing stops me. It's the thing Gavin knew before I did. I won't leave Lara behind in this place. She's the reason I told Terrence no. She's the reason I told Gavin yes…

She's never given me a reason to stay. It's only the barest hope, a few stolen kisses and a dream of something more. We both want more than this life, but now I'm being pulled deeper into it. *Welcome to our world.*

Reaching for the doorjamb, I squeeze the wood in my fist as my stomach churns. I won't leave her here, which means I'm going to do this job. I look side to side in the hallway. He said to clean this up, burn the sheets…

I walk further down the passage, deeper into the belly of this beast, until I come to a narrow door with a brass plate on the outside. No inscription, but I push it open and find what I'm looking for inside. A mop, a bucket, shelves of supplies. Clorox and lighter fluid. It's the start of my work here, cleaning up the mess, burning the evidence, covering their tracks.

I don't know who lost this fight.

I only know I won't be seeing Lara tonight.

CHAPTER 9

"Limits, like fear, are an illusion."

Lara

The bones of the feathered corset cut into my bruised torso as Rosa pulls the laces tighter. The pain almost makes me cry out, but I fight it. Gavin said I'm going on tonight, and that means no more hiding. I don't know if Freddie will be in the audience watching as I make my debut in diamonds. If he is, I don't know how that will change things.

Next comes the glittering top. It's a network of chains, which she attaches with costume glue to the skin under my breasts and up the center of my chest. The collar is snug around my neck, and when I stand straight, it raises my small breasts so they point straight ahead.

"Be still," she says, standing in front of me and taking out the brush and paint.

I stare at the corner where the wall meets the ceiling behind her as she touches me lightly with the brush. Painting my areolas with pink glittered body paint. The strokes of the brush are gentle, and my nipples harden.

"Good," she mutters. "The paint is cooling. It will keep them tight and pointy. Men love that."

My stomach tightens at the thought of Mark seeing me this way, wondering if he loves it. When we kissed, I told him I only wanted him to see me this way. It's still true, but it's a stupid dream. Everyone will see me tonight. My only comfort is in how different I look—almost like my transformed body has become my costume.

"They look bigger… How?" I study my new-and-improved bosom in the mirror. Gavin has often complained about my small breasts, my boyish figure. He'll approve of this development.

"The corset pushes you up," she says. "And perhaps you've grown a bit."

"Not this much." The new corset is blood-red velvet with lines of black sequins running up the bodice. A train of black feathers flows from each of my hips, leaving my ass exposed in only a thong, and the front is the smallest heart-shaped scrap of fabric.

Rosa jerks my corset, straightening it and sending pain shooting through my sides. I wince. "Look straight ahead," she orders.

I look forward and she gathers my hair into a twist of large curls at the top of my head. On my shoulders, thin black feathers flow down and tickle the tops of my arms. With my hair up, the full effect of the ensemble is dazzling. It's the most revealing, decorated costume I've ever seen.

Rosa frowns at me. "I don't like it."

"What?" I barely recognize myself. It's like some beautiful woman with breasts has sneaked in and taken my place. "I think I look amazing."

"You look so old." She drops my hair. "It's too soon."

A knot is in my throat, but there's no changing it. I step forward and pick up the box Freddie sent. I slide the white ribbon from around it and lift the barrette. The crystals send rainbow sparkles through the room when the light hits it, and I hold it up against the side of my head. Rosa looks over my shoulder.

"From Freddie?" she asks.

I nod, and her hands return to my hair, twisting it up and around again. "Hand it to me," she says.

I pass it to her, and she attaches it in the side of my hair. "That'll do. It'll encourage him to see you wearing it during your performance."

She seems happier, and I give her a sad little smile. I never realized Rosa cared about what happened to me, and if I leave this place, I know I'll never see her again. I turn to embrace her in the quiet sadness now filling the room. We're interrupted by a soft knock at the door. Rosa steps back to open it, and my eyes rise to meet… beautiful blue.

"Roland sent me to…" Mark's voice cuts off as he takes in my appearance. Then it drops to a whisper. "You look—"

"I'll check on Molly," Rosa steps to the side and pushes past him out the door.

She's gone, and we're alone in my room. His reaction makes my stomach tighten, tingling heat rises up my thighs, centering in my core. I look away, reaching for the barrette and unfastening it from my hair. One tug and a dark curtain falls across my hot-pink cheeks and exposed breasts.

Mark's breath is audible. "God, you're so beautiful."

My shoulders tremble. I want him to see me—I want only him to see me—but I'm not used to the power of my body. I'm intimidated by its effect on men.

Blinking up, our eyes meet, and his are dark, drinking in my breasts, my legs, my bare pussy hidden behind the dark heart.

"I wish…" His voice trails off.

My voice is barely audible. "What do you wish?"

Navy eyes blink to mine, and the hunger there makes my knees weak. "I wish you were mine. Only mine. I wish I could touch you. I wish I was a rich man, so I could take you far from here."

"Only fools make wishes here."

His head moves side to side, and he smiles. "Oh, beautiful girl, I'd trade being a fool here with you for a lifetime anywhere else."

I don't have a response to that, but he doesn't give me a chance.

"I'd hoped to see you last night," he continues. "I wanted to see you." His expression is different, changed.

"I was tired." It's all I'll say, not that I was defeated and sad and dreaming of him taking the pain away.

"I'll see you tonight." Calm certainty is in his tone as if a decision has been made, a promise.

Our eyes meet, and heat fills me at what's to come, what I've been longing for. I only have time for a nod when the door opens, and Rosa enters my small room.

"They're dimming the lights. It's time to get to your marks." She plants a thick hand on Mark's chest and pushes him out the door, closing it.

"He's a sweet boy," she mutters. "Now face me."

I don't answer. I'm too dazzled by his words, his promise, my beating heart. She dusts my entire body with a large pink brush, and the faintest highlight covers my skin.

"What do you think about him?" she asks.

"Who?" I try to pretend my thoughts are elsewhere.

"I said that Mark seems like a sweet boy," she repeats staring at my face.

"I owe him my life." I step off the platform, aware she isn't convinced, but she pulls open the door and lets me escape without another word.

It's time for me to head to my place and assume the position as star of the finale.

The finale in which I descend from above, the dark angel singing out over the audience.

On that swing.

I race through the sticky rosin, the talc-filled air, past the low murmur of dancers warming up, to the narrow metal ladder against the back wall in the wings. I ignore the hollow stabs of pain hitting my middle whenever I move and once I'm there, I look up.

No robe covers me tonight. My body is bare except for the strategically placed jewels and feathers, and it's time to climb. Rosa stops me before I begin, patting the tiny beads of sweat away from my hairline with a tissue, following quickly with a cone-shaped purple sponge.

"Freddie's sitting stage right," she says, refastening the barrette in the side of my head. "Turn your head so he sees it."

I nod, ready to hurry up the ladder, but as I climb, everything slows down.

I don't understand what's happening.

I'm in perfect shape for climbing a ladder, but the higher I go, the harder it is to breathe. It's like a fist is tightening around my throat.

By the time I reach the top, I'm gasping and shaking all over. My body is covered with a cold sheen of sweat and pain grips my chest. I can't move. Mark is waiting for me, ready to help me into my seat. But all I can do is stand there and grip the rope, paralyzed by fear.

He takes one look at my face and seems to understand immediately what's happening. He quickly comes to where I stand shivering and reaches for me with his still-bandaged hand.

"It's okay," he whispers. "Take my hand."

My wide eyes lock on his, just visible in the dim light so high above the dancers.

"I… I don't understand." I can't explain the panic I feel, why I can't catch my breath. It's more than nerves or stage fright. It's something far more powerful.

"Look at me," he says, holding both my hands. "Breathe."

My chest is tight, but I try to do as he says.

"Vanessa has done it twice. I personally double-checked everything an hour ago. It's not going to break."

I hold his hands, and I can feel the strength that caught me when I fell. I believe him, but my body doesn't want to cooperate.

"I won't let you fall, Lara."

I look into his eyes and focus on taking in air and pushing it out. I study his hands, and I remember him holding me, his wishes, his promise to protect me. Since the accident, since our day on the levee, since every other time he's been with me, I realize we're on the edge of something more, something bigger than this place.

My body calms as my mind filters through these thoughts, as I hold his gaze, and even though my heart beats fast, it's no longer from panic.

It's something very different.

It's waves crashing on the sparkling sand.

It's the kiss of moonlight on a still lake.

It's the most natural thing in the world.

"Don't worry," he soothes. "You're safe with me."

The words enter into my soul, and I know they're true. The music plays below, and the girls perform. The crew mills about, and Rosa carries costumes and makeup from one room to the next.

Bad things happen.

Tragic things happen.

No one knows the things that happen to us here. We don't know the chain of events that have started. I only wait for my introductory notes rising to meet us as he holds my hands so gently.

"I want to touch you." His gaze travels from my eyes to my lips to my hair to my breasts.

"I want you to touch me," I say.

His voice breaks. "If I touch you, I won't be able to stop."

A shiver moves through me. "I won't want you to stop."

"Come." He helps me into position on the swing, fastens the safety harness, and takes leather gloves from his pocket. "I'll meet you on the other side."

"I'll only think of you until I get there."

His hands cover mine on the ropes, leaning closer. I lean closer, tracing my nose against the side of his cheek, inhaling his warm, masculine scent. He groans and turns, capturing my lips, swiping his tongue inside, but quickly easing back. I chase him, pulling his lips with mine, his tongue.

We're careful. My makeup isn't smeared, but it's time. Our eyes hold each other's as I swing out, away from the scaffolding and over the dark house. As I descend, I'm still looking up at him. A lone spotlight hits me, and just when I think I'm too far to hear his last words, they meet me.

"You're beautiful," he says.

My body glitters the bright lights, but I hold his smile, his eyes like two sapphires just visible from here. His hand is on the safety rope, and though my chest is still tight, I inhale a deep breath and sing out over the exclamations of surprise and delight from the audience.

* * *

Mark

Lara is a star.

Her performance is flawless. The audience is in love with her. Tanya might be the queen of the Angels for now, but Lara's the new spirit on the rise.

I think of her before the finale. She blew my mind just a few minutes earlier in her dressing room. Her body was incredible. I could barely speak seeing her for the first time as the dark angel, the seductress. Her silky hair, crystal eyes… not to mention perfect breasts, long legs, delicate ankles.

I was lucky I didn't come in my pants. She obliterated very regret from the night before, every second guess. It's no question I'll do whatever it takes to stay with her.

But when she reached the top of the ladder, she was panicking. I knew immediately it was trauma, and I couldn't believe I didn't anticipate it. We should have rehearsed her descent earlier in the day, helped her get over the residual fear, instead of compounding it with her debut.

I smile to myself remembering the way she pulled it together. She held my hand and found her control. Pride tightens my stomach when I think of how strong she is. She's sweet and strong and beautiful, and I'm doing my best to stay out of sight as I make my way to her dressing room.

Last night, I did as I was ordered. It took me two hours to scrub the blood out of the white carpet. I sprayed the walls, everything with Clorox, then shined the black light on it to be sure nothing was left. No blood, no semen.

Then I gathered all the sheets and everything that wasn't glued or nailed down and carried it across the basement to the enormous fireplace in the back room. A douse of lighter fluid, a match, and the evidence quickly disappeared, taking with it my dreams of heroism. How can I be a good guy now? I was officially welcomed to the dark side by a corrupt cop.

One thing makes my decision worth all I've lost, and I hope she'll agree to sneak out with me tonight. I'm sure she will. I saw it in her eyes tonight in the rafters, high above this place. Our feelings are the same, our needs, our desires, and now we have a place to share them.

I'm in the back rooms, breaking the rules. Only, I'm not sure the old rules apply to me anymore. I've moved into a new realm of lawlessness. I pass the narrow doorways, different girls inside. Some have men with them, and I know enough now to understand the transactions happening there.

Tanya is hunched in the corner of her room, and her voice carries. She isn't trying to hide it. "So I'm a product? A good to be bought and sold? That's all I am now?"

I look inside. Rosa is with her. "Don't kid yourself, it's all you've ever been."

"I have value. I'm a star."

"Why do you think they want you?"

Rosa straps a yellow band around Tanya's upper arm. She's holding something silver, and light reflects off the tray. The door closes, but I know what she's doing. I recognize that glazed, hungry look. Heroin.

My gut twists, and I count the days in my mind. How long before it gets bad, before we find her passed out or worse.

Fuck... I push the dark image aside. I only want to think about my bright angel at the end of this hall, the one I hope will put her hand in mine and take me to heaven tonight.

"*Tres fantastique*!" I pull up short when I see a man in Lara's doorway. "The finale, your descent..." He holds both of her hands in his, and she's dressed in that red robe. "You were a vision coming down from heaven. Pure art."

I step fast into the doorway of an empty dressing room before I'm spotted.

"I'm so glad you were pleased." Lara holds an enormous bouquet of red roses, and while her voice is warm, her words shred my insides. "I thought of you the whole time. Did you notice my hair?"

"It was like waves on the dark ocean." The man smiles. "I mean yes, the barrette. I'm so happy you like my gift."

"I love it." Lara smiles and leans closer.

He lifts his hand to her jaw, and my chest is on fire. He's dressed in a custom suit. On his wrist is a heavy, silver watch. This asshole is clearly rich. He's exactly what she needs to get the fuck out of this place.

I want to kill him.

"I only have one concern." I return to the doorway so I can hear what the fuck he might say. "You're a vision, of course, but ..."

"Yes?"

"Your costume is different." He looks down, and I'm trying to figure out if this shit is serious.

He does realize the Pussycat Angels is a burlesque show, right?

"Does it change our arrangement?" Lara's voice is quiet. "I know you preferred me as the pink angel."

"Not at all," he says quickly. "I'm just sensitive to your feelings."

Shit! I stride across the room, slamming my fist into the back of a velvet chair. It muffles the sound, but it doesn't ease the fury in my chest. If he's so sensitive to her feelings, why doesn't he do something? The cold realization trickles through my veins. It's probably why he's here.

"Thank you," Lara says. "It's hard to find men who understand in my line of work."

The knife twists further in my guts. I have to go, leave her to this rich guy. He's clearly what she needs, and I'm the dreamer who should care enough to let her go.

I step to the door and watch for a chance to leave. For now, I'm trapped. If I go out, she'll see me, and she'll know I heard their conversation. I have to wait and suffer through this.

"Is Gavin making you do it? Because I could speak to him if you'd like."

"Gavin does make the final decisions, but he's controlled by the desires of the audience. I think he'd argue it's part of the act, the artistry."

"I suppose you're right. But if you're uncomfortable in any way—"

"I'll try to manage."

"Excellent. Because your body is amazing…"

His sudden change in tone pulls a feral growl from my throat.

"What was that?" The fucker looks over his shoulder, but I don't move.

He's a fraud. Lara has to know it. He doesn't give a shit about her feelings. It's all an act…

I lean out in time to see him lift her hand to kiss it. Only, I've stepped out too far. Lara's beautiful blue eyes flicker up and collide with mine. Lightning strikes, and her body tenses. Her shoulders rise, and she pulls her hand away.

"I'm sorry?" The man straightens, confused by her sudden withdrawal.

I'm not confused. My eyes hold hers; our connection is undeniable.

"I-I just realized"—her hand flutters to her forehead—"I'm simply exhausted."

"Of course you are, darling. After your fall and your first night back… I hope you'll let me visit you again tomorrow?"

"You'll be back?"

My anger is fading fast. The warmth in her voice is gone. She's flustered and off her game now that she knows I'm here. *Don't be afraid, beautiful…*

"I couldn't stay away. I could listen to you sing until the end of my days."

Hopefully they won't end sooner than he expects.

"Freddie, you're too kind to me."

He goes in for another kiss, and she lifts her hand quickly between them. I don't laugh when I see him pull back.

"Good night, *mon amour*," he says, kissing her hand.

My jaw tightens. I don't like him touching her.

Her smile is tight, and she nods, staying at the doorway as he backs away. I step into the shadows and listen to his crisp steps fading down the passage.

He's gone. We're alone, and she knows I'm here.

What will she do?

"Mark?" she calls softly, and I open the door, emerging from the empty room.

Her face brightens, and it's not an act. It's real.

"I wasn't trying to spy," I say, closing the space between us. "I came to congratulate you."

Her cheeks flush a pretty shade. "For what?"

"You did it. And you were so brave after what happened."

Her eyes are on my mouth. "I couldn't have done it without your help. You kept me from fainting."

"I only distracted you. You're the one who got on that bench. I couldn't have made you do that."

"I couldn't have done it if you hadn't been there." She reaches out and takes my hand. "You saved me once… I knew you'd do it again."

I cover her small hand with mine. "I'll do it every time." Then I remember the pain, the fear, the blood, and I chuckle. "Or let's not let it happen again."

She smiles and steps back, going farther into her room. I glance quickly over my shoulder and follow, closing the door behind me.

Clearing my throat, I can't help it. My feelings are strong, primal. "Who was that guy?"

Her eyes blink quickly away, fingers twisting together. "Freddie Lovel. He's a friend of Roland's… He's—"

"He's rich." I look down at my jeans, my dirty hands, and I hate acknowledging the truth. "He's rich, and I'm… well, I'm just getting started."

"Roland thinks I should encourage him." She turns her back, and my eyes travel the length of her hair, the line of her robe. She's so beautiful. "I know he's right, but... I have this problem."

"What problem?"

She turns and her robe is open. Her body is bare beneath it, and heat rushes to my cock. I swallow the knot in my throat as she steps closer, the sides of the velvet catching on her tight nipples. She takes my hand gently in hers and guides it through the folds to her body. It's the most erotic thing she's ever done.

"I only want you."

My fingers tighten, and both my hands are on her now. I only hesitate a moment when I see the fading mark on her waist. "Does this hurt?"

"Nothing hurts when I'm with you."

I pull her to me, and she grasps my cheeks, guiding her mouth to mine. Lips collide, tongues slide and curl. She whimpers. I groan. Desire flares hot beneath my skin, and the semi I've had for days, every time she's in my presence, rages to full mast, begging for her wet heat.

"This isn't how I'd planned it," I say as the robe slides down her slender arms. "God, you're so beautiful."

My mouth is on her shoulder, biting. Her hands thread in my hair.

"You planned this?" she gasps as I move lower, pulling a tight nipple between my teeth, flicking it with my tongue, smoothing it with my lips. "Oh, Mark!"

I circle the tight bud before pulling back, kissing it and making my way to the other side. "No." I pull that one between my lips, giving it a nibble. "I only dreamed of this."

"Please, please." She's on her toes whimpering, and her eyes follow me. "Stay with me. Show me what you dream of."

A smile curls my lips, and I cross to the door, pushing the brass lock in place. "With pleasure."

CHAPTER 10

"Collect moments..."

Lara

He stands like a god, like an ancient Greek statue in the closed doorway, and he pulls the shirt over his head, leaving his caramel waves a sexy mess. The light from my yellow lamp deepens the lines in his stomach, and I shudder. His body is perfect, tall and slender but strong.

Fire burns in his blue eyes, but it's nothing compared to the inferno raging under my skin. My nipples are cool and tight from his kisses, my knees are weak, and the space between my thighs is slick. I've never been with a man, but my body knows instinctively what to do. My response to him is primal, undeniable.

I cross the space to him, not waiting for him to come to me. He smiles and pulls me close, and I sigh at the feel of the hair on his chest tickling my sensitive nipples.

"You feel so good," I whisper.

"Aren't I supposed to say that?" Large hands move from my waist up the sides of my back, scratching my sensitive skin with his bandages. His lips touch my neck, and the light scruff on his cheek sends thrills radiating to my core.

"I don't know," I whisper, every inch of me burning for his touch.

"I'd planned to invite you to my place," he says against my skin, and I shudder.

"There isn't time." I hold his cheeks so I can find his delicious mouth.

Our kisses are hot and wet. I kiss him slowly, tasting his sweetness, fresh water, a hint of mint. He kisses me deeper, holding the back of my neck as he guides us to my small bed.

Gently, he lays me on my back, spreading the robe apart and running his eyes down the length of my naked body like a caress. I wriggle out of the velvet, an ache spreading in my core, a deep need I never knew existed.

He toes off his boots, first one, then the other, his eyes never leaving me. I slide my palms over my stomach, up to my breasts, circling and holding them as his hands work at the waist of his jeans.

"Shit, Lara," he groans. "What are you doing to me?"

I don't know. I only know my body craves touch, his touch. My hands slide down to cup the need I feel between my thighs. He hisses, watching my fingers slowly circling, and when he shoves his jeans down, my breath catches.

My eyes widen.

He's huge, long and thick.

"Mark…" His name escapes on a sigh, and he fists his cock, sliding the dampness over the tip and down, causing my insides to clench.

His voice is low, like a confession. "It's been a while. I might go fast."

I have no experience to understand what he means, but instead of climbing on top of me, he drops to his knees and wraps his forearms around my thighs.

"What are you… Oh!" My head drops back and my back arches off the bed as his tongue makes a long, slow sweep up the center of my pussy. "Oh, God, yes!"

He stops at the top, focusing tiny licks on that little spot I circled with my fingers, the spot that makes my body shake and my eyes squeeze shut.

"Oh!" I can't stop the noises coming from my throat.

My palms hit the mattress, and I grip the sheets in my fists. His tongue is moving faster, relentless, circling and teasing. His lips close over my clit and he sucks me, making me shudder, pulling me closer when I try to wriggle away.

"I'm coming…" I gasp. "I feel it!"

Heat licks at my inner thighs and they quake with every brush of his scruffy cheek. He's kissing me, licking me, and the wetness is cool on my body. Pleasure expands, ringing through my pelvis, and my forehead burns. I'm shimmering. I've never been so high. I'm not sure I'll ever come down from this…

He's off me so fast, kissing my navel, licking his tongue over my breast, as he travels up the length to ravage my mouth. I barely even register the rip of foil, the hasty roll of the condom. His tongue meets mine and large hands move my thighs apart. His heavy length is on my stomach before he reaches down and positions the tip.

It's pressure, large and hot against my dripping core.

My breath catches…

I can't breathe…

He kisses me again and with a firm thrust, I'm full.

"Mark! Oh…"

"Yes," he groans, sliding in on my orgasm. "Fuck yes, Lara."

He rips through my virginity, and I stretch around him. Rotating my hips, I try to accommodate his size. I never knew I could feel this full…

"God, yes," he groans, thrusting deeper, to the hilt. "You're so tight."

"Oh!" I gasp, unable to hide the pain.

His head pops up, and his brow is lowered. Still, his hips rock again. He's completely inside me, and my knees rise with every thrust deeper. With great effort, it seems, he slows his hips. I clutch his shoulders, doing my best to hold onto him.

"Lara…" Blue eyes hold mine. "Are you a…?"

I don't want this to stop. I want his weight on me pressing me down, skin against skin. I want to find that other side where the sparkling waves of pleasure wait. I feel them there, just out of reach.

"Not anymore." I lean up to kiss his parted lips.

The movement rocks my body forward and my clit slides against his shaft. *There it is…* I do it again, rotating my hips in a dance move, doing my best to grind that spot against his body.

"Why didn't you tell me?" He leans forward and captures my lips again, kissing me long and slow. Kissing me sweet and quick, tracing his mouth along my jaw to my ear.

He moves his mouth into the base of my hair, his heavy breath sending thrills of pleasure down my shoulders and to my clit. His thick shaft is still deep in me, but now his thumb finds that sensitive bud and circles, massaging.

"Yes…" I moan, my body instantly responding to his touch. "Yes, that's it…"

I'm lost in waves of pleasure, and when the thrusting begins, I only want more. I'm crazed and frantic, rocking my pelvis with every stroke.

His tip finds a place inside me, and the effect curls my toes. My stomach shudders, and spasms erupt through my thighs again. I'm moaning and begging, chanting his name and never wanting this to end as my inner muscles ripple around him.

His hand is gone and he's on me, we're stomach to stomach, and I'm meeting him with every thrust, lifting my hips off the mattress to take him deeper until I feel him break.

A low groan and he holds himself, rhythmic pulsing filling me, pushing me higher and higher, yet still holding me down with the weight of his body.

It's so good.

I understand now.

So much makes sense.

I never want it to end, and I'm sure nothing will be the same after this.

* * *

Mark

After months of turmoil, I've found peace.

Soft arms hold me, and Lara's head is tucked into my chest. I'm buried deep in her gorgeous body. Her legs are around mine, and our bodies seem to have melted together.

I'm not sure I can move.

I'm not sure she wants me to.

Lifting my head, I bend my elbow so I can smooth her hair away from her face with my palm. Her eyes are closed, but she's smiling. It does something to my stomach, and I actually laugh. *How long has it been since that's happened?*

"Why didn't you tell me?" I ask her, remembering her pain.

Thin dark brows quirk, and blue eyes blink open. "Would it have made a difference?"

"Hell, yes," I roll to the side still holding her to my chest, still keeping her skin against mine. "I never want to hurt you. I'd have gone slower, been gentler."

"Maybe I didn't want you to go slow." Her eyes trace my face. "I felt like I was burning up inside."

Yeah, I get that.

My mind drifts over our night. I want to remember everything, from her saying she dreams of me to the first time my lips touched her skin.

"I don't think I could've gone slow," I say, threading my fingers in her soft hair. "You're the most beautiful woman I've ever seen. Or touched… or kissed."

She squirms higher in my arms and kisses my neck. "I'll never forget this as long as I live."

Sliding my palm down the length of her back, I follow the curve of her ass, cupping it and pulling her closer. *Her first…*

It changes everything. It plants crazy notions in my head, words like *mine* and *always*. Words I want to say but I can't live up to right now, especially now that I've agreed to work for Gavin, especially when I remember my dark task last night. I could never put her in jeopardy. I could never make her promises I can't keep.

But I don't want this to end yet either. "Go out with me tonight. I want to show you my other favorite part of the city."

Her nose wrinkles with her laugh. "You have a lot of favorites to have only lived here a few weeks."

"I don't have much to do outside of work."

"Sounds like we're in the same boat."

I don't tell her it's a boat I wouldn't abandon for anything. She leans closer and presses her full lips to mine. I roll her onto her back, trapping her beneath my weight and kissing her deeper, drinking her in like water, like air, like the peace I've found. She's a beautiful angel in my arms.

I never want to stop.

She wiggles away. "Where are we going?"

Again, she makes me smile. I can't seem to stop when we're together. "It's a surprise. New Orleans is amazing after dark. You're saying you'll go?"

Blue eyes study my face. "We can't stay out late."

"It's already late." I kiss her again. "But I'll get you home before dawn. Hurry up and change. I'll meet you at the back door in five minutes."

I kiss her lips one last time before grasping the condom and sliding out. I hate losing her warmth, but I kiss her stomach. She makes a little noise, and I laugh, disposing of the evidence and jerking my jeans over my hips, my shirt over my head.

One last look, and I'm out the door. "See you in five."

CHAPTER 11

"Some people feel the rain. Others just get wet."

Lara

The French Quarter glistens in the cool, damp night. The smoky street lamps make rainbow reflections in the puddles, and the sound of music fills the air. As we pass the clubs, I see couples dancing with their arms locked around each other, and I hear loud, boisterous laughter through the tavern doors.

He leads me down several narrow passageways until we're again at the levee, racing up the hill to see the river spread out massive and brown before us. The humid breeze hits us with short, cool gusts, and I know winter is coming, or at least the few weeks of cold weather we call winter this far south.

It's a clear night, and the moonlight dances in silvery sparkles on the mixed-up currents as the sound of a saxophone playing low and a guitar strumming in time drift across the water from Algiers.

I allow my coat to fall open, Mark pulls me to him, and we dance. Only it's not like any dance I've ever done before. It's slow and sensual, and he leans closer to press his lips to mine again and again until I'm drunk with the music and the movements and his tongue touching mine.

Resting my head against his chest, I listen to his heartbeat keeping time with mine. He clasps my hand in his, his other arm tightly encircling my waist, and I try to think of a time when I've ever felt this happy. It's as if for this one night I've been given a holiday—no fear, and nothing bad can happen.

"It's a perfect night," he says into my hair.

I close my eyes and inhale deeply. The dewy grass-scent mixes with Mark's warmth and etches a permanent memory in my mind. The song fades away, and he steps back, still holding my hand, leading us down toward the river. I sit on the grass and he steps to the water's edge.

"It's so huge," he says, looking out at the lights of the riverboat in the distance. Then he spins around to face me, stretching his arms wide. "We could get on a boat and take it anywhere we want."

He takes a step toward me, but his foot slips and he falls, landing with a loud *Oof!* right next to where I sit.

I burst out laughing, loud and clear, and the sound is so strange, I almost don't recognize it. He smiles and slides to a sitting position, dusting his palms together.

"I've never heard you laugh before."

I clear my throat and try to stop, but I'm giddy. Instead, I place my hand over my mouth to hide my grin. "It's always so intense at the theater," I say.

He slides closer to me, and I lean back, nestling into his arms.

"I like your laugh." His face is low to mine, our lips a breath apart.

He slides my hair away from my cheek before gently kissing me. My eyes close as a new song drifts across the water to us. Warm lips part mine and a fresh wave of desire moves through my stomach.

I reach up to touch his cheek and everything melts away, from the damp grass at my back to the clock ticking on this holiday. Reality is only a few hours away, but in this moment, I'm here in Mark's arms. His mouth travels to my cheek and then my jaw, tickling my neck, and I open my eyes to see thousands of stars glittering above us.

"It's so beautiful," I breathe.

Two of us, under the stars...

He lifts his head to smile at me, and I touch his face, his bright eyes, then I run my finger down his nose to his lips, which he pushes out in greeting.

I've never been so light and free, and I can't help laughing again. I wonder if we'll make love here under the stars, but he stands, pulling me to my feet with him.

"There's another place I want to take you first," he says.

"First?"

"On our way to my place."

I pause, and he waits, watching my expression. "Okay," I say, and he relaxes.

"So about this place," he continues. "I'd never seen anything like it before I came here. It's an old hall where musicians gather to play and people stand around and watch. And the music... you won't believe how great it is."

"Is it jazz?"

"It's everything—jazz, Dixieland, blues."

My hand is captured in his, and he leads me over the levee and down the hill again. Short palmettos sprout along the sides of alleys, and twisted wisteria winds up abandoned fence posts and pretty much anything that will stand still. In the spring they drop lightly scented, purple blooms everywhere, but now they're simply ragged green vines that look more like weeds than anything pretty.

We reach the bottom and cross the cobbled street to the square near the statue of Andrew Jackson on horseback. The massive square is empty, and we quickly pass the dark shops. Still, I can't help stopping to look in the front window as we pass Gerard's. A new display is there, and right in the center is a sparkling brass and cloisonné pen.

My breath catches, and the old sadness slips back.

"What?" Mark steps up next to me and looks in the window. "Do you like that?"

"It was my mother's."

The words are out before I can stop them. I've never told anyone how I support Molly and me. Not even Evie.

"Your mother's?" He looks at me. "How do you know?"

I try to laugh again, but I can hear the difference. Instead I shake my head.

"Tell me," he insists.

I gaze into his blue eyes and try not to care. "Remember that day? When I was here running an errand?"

"Yes."

"I was really pawning that for money to buy Molly shoes."

A flash of pain crosses his face and he pulls me to him.

My throat tightens, but I struggle back. "Don't. It had to be done. I can't regret it now."

"Still, it was your mother's."

"No. Not tonight."

His lips press together, and he looks at the window again. My hand hasn't left his, and I pull him into the square again, away from my sad memories, my truth. He takes the lead again, and I follow him past the massive white church with its three skinny, slate-gray spires pointing high into the night sky.

As we walk down the narrow, cobbled streets, I realize except for that one moment, I haven't stopped smiling since we stepped foot outside the theater. We sneak through the city like runaways, and his hand only leaves mine for a moment. It becomes the strongest sense I have of this adventure.

Finally we find the place, and as we enter the dark, smoky hall, there's a room to the side filled with people sitting on chairs or on the floor. Some spill out into the passage where the music echoes off the wood floors and walls. Mark pulls me to the doorway, and his hands find my waist as he holds me in front of him. Smoke fills the air, and men and women of all races crowd together to listen.

Men play trumpets and clarinets. One has a guitar, another an upright bass, and still another a tuba. Mark is right—it's brilliant and captivating, and the crowd sways and nods to the rhythms. The songs stretch on for several minutes as each musician takes a turn improvising.

I study their faces and the silky expertise with which they manipulate their instruments, and something deep within me connects with the sounds. I wish Roland were here to listen.

This is what the city is all about.

This is the brightness.

I study the faces of the audience, black and white, pushed in tight, smiling. Some have their eyes closed; others are laughing and keeping time, starting to dance. Everyone feels it. We're all here smashed together in one hall, and the music erases the pain and darkness that otherwise keeps us apart.

"What do you think?" Mark's lips are close to my ear, and I turn and kiss them before answering.

"I love it. It's my new favorite place."

He kisses me again and smiles, and I return to the show. That's when I see him. Two blue eyes fixed on me from across the room, and my body tenses. Mark's hands tighten at my waist.

"What's wrong?"

Gavin is watching us, and his frown shakes me to the core.

"I've got to go," I say, backing away. Reality rushes back stronger, as if it's angry for being shut out for even a night.

I push through the crowd to the door, Mark right on my heels.

"What happened?" he asks. "Are you okay?"

"I just realized how late it is, and I've got to get back. Someone might see us."

"But... Are you worried about Freddie? Because I don't think—"

"No. I mean, I don't know," I stammer, turning up the collar of my coat. "We could run into anybody out here."

His hand finds mine again, clutching it. The warmth is reassuring, but I'm too shaken to relax. He leads me through the damp streets, and we pause at the Pussycat Angels banner in the front of the theater. It's a black and white shot of all the girls sitting together nude. Nothing is shown, our arms and legs are strategically placed, but sex is in our eyes.

Tanya stands in the center of us with her body dripping in sparkling diamonds. Large, glittering stones are strategically placed over her nipples, and she's wearing a thong. Everything about her is fake, the wig, the makeup, even the jewels, but she's the star.

Soon that will be me.

My stomach is tight as we sneak around to the back entrance. Mark stops me at the door, pulling me to him. "I don't want to leave you here."

"I live here."

"You could live with me." He hugs me close, kissing my cheek, and a pit forms in my stomach.

I shake my head, stepping out of his arms. "I can't leave Molly. She's here because of me. I can't walk away from her—"

"I'll find a different job, a better job. We can leave here, and you can both move in with me."

Leave with Mark...

Leave with Mark...

My eyes squeeze shut as the notion floods tingling warmth through my insides. I want to say yes so much, but like always, my brain forces me to face reality.

"It sounds wonderful." I choose my words carefully, not wanting to hurt him. "But I can't walk away on a dream. The truth is you don't have another job... And I can't take that chance."

As I'm saying the words, a gulf of sadness opens in my chest. Staying in this theater, taking my chances as its star is not the best option by a long shot, but we have a roof over our heads and food to eat. Gavin gave me a promise, and Roland's making him keep it. It's a tenuous layer of protection, but it's real.

Mark's brow furrows, and he nods, thinking. "So it can't happen tonight, I get that, but it can happen." His blue eyes meet mine. "I want you with me."

Stepping forward, I reach for his hand, holding it in both of mine, cherishing the way he comforts me so deeply. He touches the part of me that has stopped believing in happy endings. "Thank you for tonight. For all of it."

"You sound like you're giving up."

I lift his hand to my lips and kiss his fingers. "I'm tired. It's been a busy day."

"You need a phone."

"No." I shake my head and exhale a bitter laugh. "We can't afford it."

"I'll afford it." He pulls me closer and touches my cheek. "Go inside and rest, but believe me. I'm serious about this."

The girls call him a hero. I study his face for the space of a heartbeat, feeling my ability to hope struggling for life. Could he be my hero? It's too early to know.

Instead, I leave him with a kiss, pushing through the metal door and back to my reality.

CHAPTER 12

"An ocean of love flowed over the darkness..."

Mark

Weeks pass, and my world turns into something I don't recognize. Something I've never known.

It's the happiest I've ever been, and when I'm not running errands for Gavin, I do my best to be at the theater. Lara sneaks away to eat, and I meet her with a smile. She didn't say no when I asked her to move in with me. What her body language and actions said was *show me*, and I'm damn well going to show her. I've been working on proving she can trust me ever since.

This morning Gavin sent me to a florist to pick up a box marked *fragile*. I didn't ask questions, but I did buy a five-dollar bouquet. It's not red-velvet roses—the tag says chrysanthemums and lantana—but Lara's eyes light up when she sees it.

I hope it makes her musty theater-home a little brighter, red and gray as opposed to burgundy and black.

"I was thinking I could take a job at the shipyards. Maybe starting at night and working my way up to something full time." She's perched on a large box, and I lean beside her, my arm around her waist.

"No." Her dark head shakes fast. "You'll be exhausted, and the docks are dangerous. What if you were hurt?"

Warmth moves through my stomach. "You'd worry about me?"

"Of course!" She stretches, catlike to kiss my jaw, and I can't resist. I catch her neck and push her lips apart, tasting her sweet mouth. Her cheeks are flushed pink when I straighten, and I smile. She's adorable.

"Okay..." I take out my pocketknife and cut a wedge of apple for her. "I could take a retail job at one of the men's stores... get a clothing discount."

"I'd like that better. You'd look amazing in a suit."

"You like sharp-dressed men."

I laugh and hold the piece of fruit to her. She passes me a bit of cheese. In my errands, I also pick up better food for her and Molly. Better than day-old bread and burnt coffee.

"What would you like to do?" I ask, and beautiful blue eyes meet mine. "Would you want to continue working here?"

She thinks about it. "Only if Gavin paid me a real wage. I'm not sure he'd do it."

Roland calls from the stage, and she swings her legs off the box. I duck down for another quick kiss. Her hands catch my cheeks, and she inhales deeply. I do the same, savoring her delicate flowery scent. She trots to the front, and I follow slowly, leaving our dreams with the rest of the old set pieces.

I watch from where I stand beside a concrete pillar, rubbing the pain in my chest at her departure. I know the pressure she's under. We've only known each other a short time, but still...

Roland plays the introductory chords, and her beautiful voice fills the space. I want her to be happy. I want to make her happy. I want to save her.

Later that night, high above the theater, I'm more forceful. She races into my arms, and I hold her close, nuzzling her hair and kissing her mouth. I want to taste her. I want to show her how I feel, convince her I'm serious. I'm not just another asshole stagehand, hanging around for her body.

"Don't smudge my make up," she whispers. Still, she shudders as my lips trace along her neck and hairline. I know she feels this bond between us.

Her hands smooth the backs of mine as I help her take the seat, fasten the harness. She swings out over the audience, but our eyes remain locked as the words to the song flow from her lips.

You're in my arms, and it feels so right;
But it's simply an illusion…

* * *

Lara

All around us is darkness and night, but I've found a box of matches, and one by one, I strike them, watching the happy flames dancing, allowing the tiny bits of warmth to give me something I've never dared have…

Hope.

Still lurking in the back of my mind are the dark questions. Can I trust Mark? *Yes, I know I can.* What about Gavin? How long will he keep his promise to me? How long can Roland protect me?

What about Molly? Will my promise cover her?

Not yet…

I strike another match and pretend these fears aren't sneaking closer.

I wear skirts to rehearsals hoping for a chance to sneak away with Mark, to meet him in the dark wings. In those lucky times, we're feverish with need. I cover his mouth with mine, and we kiss as the flames consume us.

"This is dangerous," he says against my heated skin.

"We have time," I whisper, my panties on the floor in my dressing room.

He groans as I take his hand, guiding it under my skirt, and I moan as long fingers stroke me, exploring the depths of my desire for him.

He drops to one knee, shoving my skirt away, and my stomach heats, twisting with anticipation as large hands lift me, and spread my thighs apart.

"Oh, God!" I gasp as his tongue slowly circles my clit.

Ever since that first night, all we want is more. It's torture being kept apart. At the same time, it's a potent aphrodisiac.

His mouth touches the crease of my leg, his beard scuffs my sensitive skin, and my body trembles.

"Quiet," he says before touching me again with his tongue.

My eyes squeeze shut as he focuses on that little bud, pulling and tasting, sucking and flickering. My hand threads in his soft hair, and I bite my lip until I taste blood to keep from screaming as the orgasm rips through me. My thighs jerk and my stomach shudders, aching for more.

Heavy velvet surrounds us. The lights of the stage seem far away, and the set crew has disbanded. No one can see us stealing this moment.

He's up, and I hear the clink of his belt, the rip of foil. My insides tighten in anticipation, and I reach for him, needing his kiss, his skin against mine. Large hands are on my ass, and I'm off my feet. The cinder-block wall scrapes my back, but I pull my shirt higher. I pull his shirt higher so I can feel his chest on mine.

My legs are around his waist, he positions the tip then ...

"Mark!" I gasp as I'm filled.

Instinct takes over, and I ride him hard. His legs bend and he thrusts deeper, all the way inside me, and my moans are consumed in his kiss. Our mouths seal, hiding the noises of hunger, satisfaction, and need.

These are kisses I've only read about. Feelings I only dreamed I'd experience. I'm a junkie getting high off the strongest drug I've ever known. He groans and pumps, driving deeper and pushing me higher. His length strokes my inner walls until I'm flying again, pleasure snaking up my legs like vines.

He slaps my ass, and a cascade of glittering ecstasy showers through my core. I whimper, and my inner walls pulse and tingle.

"That's it," he groans, slapping my ass again, making my insides flex.

With a low noise, I feel him break, pulsing and holding deep, filling me so completely I can feel his muscles tremor.

A strong arm is around my waist, and our bodies are flush and slippery. His forehead is against my neck and shoulder, damp with sweat, and I place my hand on his cheek, closing my eyes to treasure this moment.

It's perfect...

Until a small voice cuts through the dim space.

"I knew it!" The sound echoes off the back walls.

We both jump, and I'm on my feet, shoving my skirt down while Mark hastily removes the condom and fastens his jeans.

Molly stands at the edge of the stage with Roland, who looks equally annoyed. I take a hesitant step forward, away from the warmth of Mark, toward the two of them.

"Lara, we need to talk," Roland says. "Mark, you'd better take off."

Mark steps toward me, and catches my hand. I look up and over my shoulder, my chest squeezes when our eyes meet.

"We can talk tonight," he says, lifting my fingers to his lips.

I reach for Molly, but she jerks away.

"Don't touch me," she says. "Traitor."

I don't respond. I've kept her in the dark so long, if she reacts this way, I'm as much to blame.

"Come on," I say, leading her through the door toward our dressing room. "That wasn't what you think."

She follows me, Roland with her. "I'm sorry… You weren't just fucking Mark? Your body wasn't completely entwined with his just now?"

"Language." My voice is low. My inner thighs are scuffed, and my lips still throb from Mark's kisses. I can still feel his face against my inner thighs, and joy like a fountain bubbles inside me. "I didn't think you cared about Mark anymore."

"And I thought you were trying to like Freddie."

"Let's not talk about it."

We reach the room, and I go inside. Roland follows us and closes the door.

"You never want to talk about it," Molly continues. "Except to lie about it."

"Molly, hush," Roland orders in a low voice. "I overheard Gavin talking to Darby. Things are changing, and not for the better."

I frown. "What does that mean—"

"You need to keep an eye on Molly," he interrupts, an angry edge in his voice. "Better than you've been doing."

I look over at her sitting on the bed with her arms crossed, pouting. "What happened?"

He presses his lips together before answering. "Nothing yet, but if what I heard is true…" His hand clenches into a fist, but he quickly releases it and turns to the door. "Let's just hope it isn't."

"I don't understand—" But he's out the door again, striding down the dark passage.

"Get cleaned up and get out here. We need to rehearse."

Frustration lines my brow, and I feel a headache starting. I turn to Molly, who takes one look at me and jerks away, facing the back wall. I cross to my dressing table and dig through the drawers for my makeup remover cloths. I make quick work of cleaning up between my legs, toss them in the trash, then pull on a fresh pair of panties.

Out of nowhere, tears heat my eyes, and my stomach twists at how unfair my life is, how I desperately want to be with Mark doing anything we want anytime we want. He wants to be with me… At least that's what he says, and I want to believe him.

We could build a life together.

We could grow together in happiness.

I'm tired of being responsible for another person all the time, and how can Roland order me to do something, scare me like that, and not even explain?

Life isn't fair.

My mind bitterly responds, *who said life was fair?*

I press my fingers against my eyes until I see white sparks behind my eyelids. Then I take a deep breath and stand up straight, looking at Molly in the mirror. She's still straining as hard as she can to position her entire body away from me, so I go to the bed and take her hands.

"Don't," she says trying to pull them away, but I hold them tightly in mine.

"I'm sorry about what you saw. Me and Mark."

She tries to pull her hands away again, but I hold her.

"I told you I didn't have feelings for him, and I do." I look down and release her as the tears threaten my eyes again.

"I knew it," she says as if it's some great reveal.

I go to my dressing table. Standing beside it, I run a finger down the outline of my brush. How I want to be with Mark. Instead I inhale a deep breath and let it out.

"Roland says you've got to stay close. No more flirting, and that includes Guy." Her description of that mystery man makes me shudder.

"I might as well be living in a convent." She kicks a pillow off the bed and lays down hard on her side.

I go to her. Roland hasn't given me any reason to forbid her to see Guy. I'm only following my gut. "Please just do what I say. I don't like it any more than you do, but we have to trust Roland and be careful."

"You don't want me getting caught?" Her green eyes snap to mine. "Like you?"

"Just work with me, Mol. I'm trying."

"You'd better try harder."

I can't argue. I know Mark and I have been reckless, and we have to stop.

I can't simply do whatever I want.
As much as it's breaking my heart.

* * *

Mark

When I was fifteen, Mrs. Peterson, who lived in our neighborhood hired me to do her lawn.

Dad was gone all the time gambling all our money away, so I took the job. She was a widow, and I told myself we needed the money, ignoring the way she ran her eyes over my body and licked her lips when I said okay.

The first day I was supposed to cut her grass. Instead, she met me in the garage and said she had something special for me. I'd never had sex. I'd only jerked off to porn, so when she dropped to her knees and started sucking me off, I grabbed the side of her car and held on for the ride.

She pulled and tugged, moaning and carrying on as if I were a three-course dinner and she was starving. She took me all the way to the back of her throat until she coughed and gagged, then she did it again. My eyes rolled, my knees buckled, and I shot down her eager throat so hard I saw stars. I cut her lawn that day, and I came back the next day to trim the hedges.

Mrs. Peterson won Yard of the Month in our neighborhood three months straight, and I learned all about what women like. After that summer, she moved away.

I wasn't heartbroken. I was never in love with her. It never hurt me to leave her arms. It was good sex, but I didn't dream of her body when we were apart.

Walking away from Lara each day is like ripping out my insides and leaving them at her feet. Watching her walk away and not being able to kiss her, touch her, tell her I'm serious about making a plan, is like repeated kicks to the stomach. Every night, I lie in my bed and dream of her beautiful body.

Terrence is gone and until January I have this place to myself. With her voice, she could take a job singing at any club in the city. Right now she thinks walking away to be with me is too great a risk. It's a leap of faith because our incomes are tied up in the same place, but I'm going to show her I can take care of her and Molly. I'm shit out of luck on job prospects at the moment, but I'm saving. I'm going to prove we can do it. She can walk away with me, survive, and still accomplish her dream.

"Fitz," Gavin's voice breaks my thoughts. "Report to the basement club immediately after the show tonight. You're my doorman and guard."

He hands me a clip of money. "Get some better clothes. Nice shoes. You work for me now. I want you to look like it."

Turning the clip in my hand, I see several hundreds, and my mind drifts to my plan. "Yes, sir."

I take off into the city, and I barely make it back in time to climb the narrow ladder before the finale begins. It's more of a challenge in leather Gucci loafers as opposed to heavy boots, and I'm amazed Lara does it every night in those stilettoes.

She's already at the top, and when she sees me, her eyes widen. "I thought something had happened to you," she says, running to me.

I hold her at my side, touching her gently, not at all like I want. I want to pull her into my arms and hold her close, tell her I'll always be here. But I can't get her body glitter all over my fucking suit.

"Don't be afraid," I say, tracing the pad of my thumb lightly along the top of her cheek.

"Why are you dressed like this?" She quickly scans my dark suit and pale blue dress shirt.

I adjust my tie with a wink. "It's my new uniform. Like it?"

"You're very handsome." Her chin drops, and she bends an arm to cover her breasts. "I feel underdressed."

That makes me laugh, and I step closer to nuzzle her ear with my nose before kissing it. "You are the sexiest thing in this entire theater."

She responds how I like, a little shiver, a tightening of her fingers. I attach the safety harness and check it to be sure it's secure. She takes her seat in the swing.

"The way you're dressed..." Her beautiful blue eyes are worried. "Are they sending you away?"

I kiss her lips lightly. "I won't even leave the building tonight... But I'm not sure how late I'll be working."

"So I won't see you." Her voice is different, sad, and I don't like it.

"I'll try—"

We're out of time. The music swells, and she moves out over the stage. Our eyes meet, but her smile doesn't reach her eyes.

Still, she sings out the notes, leaning into the act, beautiful as always.

As soon as she's safely to the stage below, I'm down the ladder headed to the dark corridor from my first job. I remember the blood and Gavin's instructions. I'm the guard.

The idea turns my stomach. I'm not sure I can guard if something illegal is happening, if someone's being tortured or killed, but what can I do? Landry fucking welcomed me to the dark side on my first job. He's well acquainted with my face and my name, and I know the point of that meeting was to send me a message. If I decide to turn on them, rat them out, or even not do what I'm told, they've got me right where they want me—with blood all over my hands and all of it on camera.

Gavin meets me at the entrance, quickly surveying my attire. "Good work. The men coming here expect the highest quality—in goods as well as atmosphere. They'll show you their invitations. Check it and let them in."

"What exactly is this?"

He pauses, and I can't tell if he's angry or deciding how to answer. "What happens here is an exclusive exchange for a very high fee."

Again, I survey the hall, the doors leading to smaller rooms. Bedrooms. "What's being exchanged?"

This time he's annoyed. "Private performances. Don't interrupt them no matter what you hear." He starts to leave, then walks back to me. "In fact… it's probably better if you stay outside."

"Outside?" I look around for an exit sign.

He motions for me to follow him, and we go out the heavy metal door to the other side, the side under the stage. The vast, empty room below the trap doors. "I'll have someone bring you a chair. The show's over. They'll be here soon."

Automatically, my mind goes to Lara, and my stomach tightens. Will Freddie go to her room again? Will he protect her? Is he part of this?

My forehead tightens, and I acknowledge the truth. I thought I could take this job, stay close, make money, and be here with her, but I can't. I have to get us out of here.

Buying these clothes obligates me to fulfill my commitment tonight, but I'm done. I'll give them back, return them if I have to, and convince Lara to move in with me... and bring Molly with her. Whatever it takes.

A loud squeak and crash of metal door snaps my attention to the present. The first man appears, and he's not alone.

"What's with the cloak and dagger?" he laughs, and I detect an accent.

It's northern, but not the nasal twang of the Midwest. It's more rounded, Canadian or Pacific Northwest.

"Are you taking us down the rabbit hole, Guy?" Another voice, similar accent.

"Rabbit hole. Name for my next club." The first man sounds intoxicated.

"My brother has a flair for the dramatic." That voice is laced in Deep South.

They stop in front of me, and I stand straight, not smiling. I wait until the one with the copper hair and green eyes, the one wearing a gold pinky ring and carrying a shiny wooden cane holds out a black business card. It's thick and shiny, and one phrase is in the center, embossed in gold lettering.

Under the Lights.

I'd expected something with *VIP* or *Admit One* stamped on it, but when I meet the fellow's cold eyes, I know this is it. He's sinister and challenging, and the good part inside me recoils.

"Something wrong?" His voice is hard, and I know he's not really asking.

I step to the side for him to pass, but just as fast, I block the other two.

"Sorry..." Canada digs in his breast pocket and produces a similar scrap of paper.

"At least security is working." Guy narrows his eyes at the third man, who hastily produces his card.

I stand down, and they pass through the door. Music drifts out from inside along with the faint scent of perfume. I realize there's another entrance. The girls come in a different way...

The click of heels on concrete precedes two more men dressed in expensive suits, both carrying gold cards. I step to the side, and this time when I look through the door, I see Minette, one of the girls from the show.

She's still wearing her costume, a glittering thong, and she's draped over one of the couches allowing the Canadian to stroke her breasts.

I swallow the knot in my throat. Who else is back there? I can't even think her name.

The door slams, and I'm left standing, fear expanding in my chest as vast as the empty space surrounding me. I step to the side, shoving my hands in my hair and trying to decide what to do. My forehead is against the wall when I hear a throat clearing.

Spinning around, I see a fat man in a tux waiting. He holds a card, and I nod for him to enter, which he does without hesitation. This time the noises have started, fake moans and bouncing cries.

It's an orgy.

These men have paid to have sex with the girls in the show, and my job is to let it happen. Tanya's words, Lara's fears, even Terrence's remark about why the crew dwindled so fast filter through my brain like rushing water. The blood I cleaned up—what the fuck was that about?

I drop into the metal chair, my head in my hands. I pull my phone out of my pocket. I want to call her, but she doesn't have a phone. She says it's a wasted expense. She doesn't have anyone to call, and she doesn't want to be monitored.

She's getting one after this night.

The time passes slowly, and I wonder how long I'm expected to stay here. No one else is coming. No one other than the men in there and Gavin knows about this place. I'm pushing off my legs to leave when the door scrapes and opens.

Fake moans set to music filter out along with Guy. He's on his phone, and his face is contorted with anger.

I listen to his words as he stalks past. "She is not what I requested," he growls. "She is not a star. She's a used-up drug addict. Give me what I want or—"

The exit door slams shut, and my throat knots.

I don't like where this is headed.

CHAPTER 13

"Your gut knows what's up. Trust that bitch."

Lara

"Did he kiss you?"

"Sort of," Molly mumbles. "He wanted to talk to me backstage. So I went."

Ice is in my throat. After my performance I raced to my room hoping to get my clothes on before Freddie arrived, and I found Molly sitting on the bed. Her cheeks were flushed, and her arms were wrapped tightly around her waist.

"What did he say?" My heart hammers against my ribs.

She takes a trembling breath. "He asked me to go with him to Atlanta. He said he missed me so much the last time. He wants me with him. Always."

I go to the bed and sit beside her. "Did he say *why* he wants you with him?"

"To keep him company." She picks up a little pillow, and her hands shake. "He says I please him."

I catch her arms and turn her to face me. "But you're afraid."

Her eyes met mine. "I'm not sure I trust him now."

"Why?" She blushes and looks down. I shake her arms. "What happened?"

She moves a strawberry-blonde lock behind her shoulder to reveal a blood-red mark on her neck.

"He did that?" I gasp.

She nods slowly. "And he said he likes the color of my hair."

I bite my lip. "Okay?"

She blinks fast. "Not this hair…" She looks down, wrapping an arm across her waist. "Then he touched me."

My stomach roils. I have to swallow acid in my throat. She's only thirteen. Fear is replaced by a rage I've never felt before. I almost can't breathe for the hatred coursing through me. I stand and begin to pace our small room.

"Don't ever go near him again." She's still looking down, and I can't tell if she's listening. I go to the bed and grip her arms, giving her a little shake. "Listen to me. If you see him, you run away. Run to me or to Evie. Or Mark."

"But how can you—"

A brisk knock at the door interrupts us. "Go behind the screen," I whisper, quickly pulling my dressing gown over my half-naked body.

A giant bouquet of red roses meets me before my devoted fan. "You get better with every performance," he says as I lift the heavy roses from his arms. "And you sing with such emotion."

I put them on the table and return to him, leaning against the doorjamb as my mind swirls with panic, anger, and desperation.

Freddie leans forward to kiss my cheek. "Darling," he starts then pauses. "I suppose you'd expect me to feel this way. I mean, if you knew me at all."

"What is it?"

Fear, my constant companion, prickles at my back. Has he discovered the truth? Has he learned I'm a penniless orphan, many of the dancers are prostitutes, and to make matters even more complicated, I'm responsible for a waif who has become the target of a child predator? *Oh, God, I can't lose Freddie now…*

His voice lowers. "These visits after your shows are nice, and kissing an angel is a little piece of heaven." His dark eyes twinkle. "But I'd like more. I'd like to take you out on a real date. Would you go with me?"

Relief hits me with such force, I almost grab him around the neck in a massive hug. In the time it takes me to recover, Freddie immediately starts backpedaling.

"I'm sorry," he stammers. "I'm sure you have a lot of men in love with you, and you only know me from my visits. You have no idea I only want—"

"Freddie," I say, gazing at his lips. "I would love to go out with you sometime. What did you have in mind?"

His eyes move to mine, and I blink slowly. "Would you have lunch with me tomorrow?"

"Tomorrow would be perfect."

He lets out a laugh before catching me around the waist and pressing his mouth to mine. I'm caught off guard, and while it's not much of a kiss, I notice the front of his pants harden.

He steps back, pulling his coat over his semi and clearing his throat. "Your lips are so soft."

I make my voice breathless, pretending to be overwhelmed. "And yours are so warm!"

"Tell me where you live. I'll pick you up at noon."

"Oh, no… I mean, I have morning rehearsal. You can meet me out front here."

His grin is huge, and he leans forward again. I hesitate, not really wanting to kiss him, but not sure what else to do. Roland said to keep him coming back…

When our mouths meet this time, I allow him to part my lips. He holds me tighter, his tongue timidly touches mine, and I literally feel nothing. I think about tastebuds. His kiss tastes like peppermint candy.

When Mark kisses me, it's like I'm swept up in a wave on the ocean, swirling and spinning, unsure which way is up.

Freddie finally finishes, and he smiles as if we now share a secret. When he speaks, his voice is low. "Kissing you is a dream come true for me. Does this mean you think of me as more than just a devoted fan?"

"Freddie," I touch his arm. "I've always thought of you as more than that."

The expression on his face is utter delight. "Goodnight, my dear. I'm counting the minutes until tomorrow."

Forcing a smile, I lean against the doorjamb, watching him disappear down the passage. Once he's gone, I close my door and roll my back to the wall. Dropping my head in my hands, I rub my forehead with my fingers and try to figure out what the hell I'm supposed to do.

Mark… I need to talk to Mark about all of this. Only, what am I going to say to him? I'm not qualified to do anything except sing. I can't dance for shit. The only reason people come to see me is because my voice is strong, and I look good naked.

"We can't live on that," I groan. "At least not legally."

A soft tap at the door makes me jump, and I hope so much it's Mark. I can tell him what happened, and maybe he can help me figure out this mess. Maybe

Molly and I will run away with him, money be damned. Anything is better than this.

Gripping the doorknob, I sweep it open to the glittering green eyes of a monster.

Before me stands a tall man with ruddy hair and broad shoulders—and a grin that makes me shudder. Remember the cartoon of the fox once wearing a top hat and tails? The very hungry fox, intent on satisfaction? This man reminds me of that drawing, and I try to swing the door closed as quickly as I opened it.

He sticks out a foot and stops it.

"I was led to believe this is Molly's room." His voice is a smooth vibration and his eyes lock on mine. "Instead I've found our star. What are you doing back here?"

I flinch as he lifts his hand, but it passes my cheek and rests on the knot of his tie.

"What are you doing back here, is a better question." All my muscles are tense, ready to fight. "Audience members aren't allowed backstage."

"Oh, little angel," he chuckles. The light from our lamp glints off his large, gold pinky ring. "We both know that isn't true."

Terror has me by the throat. "I'm sorry," I say, my voice tight. "I don't think we've met."

"Perhaps not formally. My name is Guy." His eyes drift down my body and then back to mine. "I've watched you for years, and your... *talent* is beautiful."

I struggle to swallow the scream in my throat. "It's very late. You'd better go."

I try to close the door, but he puts a hand above mine and pushes it open wider, sending me staggering back into the screen. Molly lets out a little yelp as it falls, exposing her sitting on the floor.

"Guy," she cries.

I step in front of her, but he smiles his evil fox-smile. "How lucky. I seem to have hit the jackpot."

I'm going to be sick. "Roland is on his way here, and he... he'll..." My mind is blanking in the middle of my lie.

"Roland is an arrogant little asshole. I'm not concerned with him." Guy's eyes fix on the button holding my robe closed over my naked body. I'm terrified at how vulnerable I am—we both are.

"You have to go." I hate the tremor in my voice. It emphasizes my disadvantage.

Guy moves toward me, lifting a hand. A little yelp comes from my throat, but he lifts a lock of my dark hair, sliding it back and forth between his fingers.

"Such fresh young women. So pure..." I'm sure I'll scream now, but he surprises me by going to the door. "I have to return to Atlanta, but I'll be back in a few days. For now, sleep little angels. You'll need it."

His snarl sends ice through my veins, and he closes the door, leaving the scent of cloves in his wake.

I can't stop shaking. He'll be back.

He's coming for us. He's already marked Molly...

My mind flies through the list of what we need to do. I need a phone. I need to take Molly and run, but how far will we get alone with only my voice? I have nothing to trade, nothing I can pawn to protect us from this. I need to tell Roland. I need to talk to Mark. I'm so afraid.

Desperation claws at my neck, and all I can think of is Freddie and his money and Paris.

CHAPTER 14

"We create our own heartbreaks through expectations."

Mark

"Do you drive?" Gavin corners me on my way to Lara's dressing room. His face is red and sweaty. He looks like he's been fighting.

I'm tired, and all I want is to see my girl, hold her in my arms and forget this shitty job and this shitty night. A quick check in the room confirmed what I felt certain—she wasn't one of the dancers in that fucking orgy.

"Yeah, I drive," I say, not wanting to stand here talking.

He pulls out a set of keys. "You're driving my brother to Atlanta tonight."

Fuck... "Don't you have a car service?"

"Yeah, it's called you." He punches me in the chest, and I feel his anger. I don't understand it, but I know enough not to challenge him.

Grasping his fist, I take the keys. One is black and chunky with the distinctive Lincoln logo on it. "Where you parked?"

"Out the back door. You'll see it. For expenses." He shoves another money clip in my hand and starts in the opposite direction. I slip the bills in the pocket of my blazer and look toward the dressing rooms, wondering if I have enough time to see Lara, tell her what I'm doing.

"Get out there now," Gavin barks. "He's on his way."

That answers my question. Dammit, why didn't I get Lara a phone? She doesn't want one, but this is why she needs it. Atlanta's a seven-hour drive. I won't be back until tomorrow night at the earliest. She'll wonder where I am. She was already so nervous when I was late this evening. I told her I'd always be there.

Exhaling a frustrated growl, I push through the metal door into the back parking lot. Sure enough, a navy Towncar is parked in a nearby spot, impossible to miss. Tapping the key, the doors unlock, and I slide across the leather seat. It's the nicest car I've ever been in.

Staring at the dash, I wait, getting angrier as every minute passes. Where the fuck is this guy? I could've easily seen Lara in the time he's taking to get here. Turning the dial, I find a jazz station and leave it. It reminds me of the night we slipped out and went to Preservation Hall. Looking through the window, I remember everything about that night, her laughter, kissing her under the stars, holding her body against mine as we listened to the band, her mother's pen…

That part sticks in my memory. Her mother's pen…

It was the only time in our night sadness broke through. She tried to dismiss it, to push it away, but I could see how it hurt her.

The door opens, and the red-headed man drops into the back seat. "Let's go."

His door slams shut, and I steer us out of the parking lot. It takes me a few minutes to weave through the narrow streets until I'm on Canal. A few more blocks, and we're on Interstate 10 headed north.

The only sound in the vehicle is classic jazz playing softly. I expect it will be this way until my eyes flicker to the rearview mirror.

Green eyes glare at me, and with a jolt, I fix my gaze on the road. Would it be rude for me to raise the glass partition? This guy gives me the creeps.

"Doorman," he finally says, and even his voice sounds icy. "What's your story?"

Again, I look in the mirror to see his eyes sizing me up.

My hands tighten on the wheel. "No story. Just doing my job"

"What's your *name*?" Impatience drips in his tone.

"Mark." I remember Gavin's response to my name, and hold it there. If anyone is involved in the underworld, it's this guy.

He's not letting it pass. "Just Mark? So you're famous? Like Cher or Madonna? Everybody knows Mark..."

This guy's a total asshole. "No, sir. I am not famous."

"So, Mark what?" he snaps.

Taking a measured breath, I answer him. "Fitzhugh. My name is Mark Fitzhugh."

He doesn't blink, which surprises me. "That's an old one. How did you end up working for my brother?"

"He offered, and I said yes."

Again, his voice heats. "How did you meet my brother?"

"I was on the set crew."

"Idiot." He shifts in his seat. "And you like working as a doorman?"

"Looks like I'm working as a driver now." Our eyes clash this time in the rearview mirror. I'm not taking his shit for eight hours. "Why don't you fly to Atlanta?"

"I don't fly." He looks out the window, and his mind seems to drift. "They're such pretty things, aren't they?"

I'm not sure if he's talking about airplanes or something else. "I've heard flying can be beautiful."

"The dancers." He exhales a long sigh, and his voice changes to longing, sadness... It's chilling. "They break so easily."

My brow lowers, but he leans back against the seat and the glass separating us slowly rises.

I don't care. I have one focus. Getting him to wherever the fuck he's headed and getting back to the theater before tomorrow night's finale.

* * *

Lara

I'm exhausted and moody at morning rehearsal. I spent the night searching for an answer, a way out, and the few times I managed to sleep, a green-eyed fox chased me through my nightmares.

I haven't seen Mark since last night before the show. He looked like he stepped out of a men's fashion magazine. Tall and slim, with his light brown hair falling in perfect waves and a shadow on his cheeks, he made my knees weak. He also frightened me. He looked like he had one foot out the door of this place, and it made me realize how much I've started dreaming he could save us, believing his dream. I can't do that.

Tanya is falling apart. She's late and moody, and her poses are sloppy. Tension hovers over rehearsal like the heavy velvet curtains lining the stage. Gavin lurks in the house silently watching our rehearsals and making Roland impatient and cross.

He's at the piano writing notes on sheet music and as I approach, he glances up at me and smiles before looking down again. "Last week I was worried you were angry with me," he says as he writes. "When in reality, you've simply found someone new."

"It's not like that," I say.

"Certainly looked like that yesterday." He gives me a wink. "Lara's in love."

I push back. "I can't think about that now."

"Come on, Lara. It's your old pal Roland."

Vanessa's loud laugh pierces the air, and I cringe. I decide to put it out there, see how much he knows. How much he'll tell me.

"Who is Guy?"

His body stiffens, eyes narrow. "What?"

His sudden change in demeanor tells me more than his words ever could. "Molly met him after the show a while back, and—"

"Keep her away from him."

"Who is he?"

"Gavin's brother."

I shake my head. "But why have I never seen him? How could I not know Gavin had a brother?"

"He went away a while back. I don't know why he's here now, but it's the reason I told you to be careful. Stay away from him. Keep Molly away from him."

"If he's Gavin's brother, that means—" I try to piece together this new information, understand how it relates to the show, to us.

Roland grips my arm so hard I wince. "Do what I say," he growls.

I bend my elbow and push his hand away. "Don't treat me like that. Tell me *why*."

He exhales and releases me, but the anger is still there. I watch him circle the piano and start to play what he's just written. "I'm not going to repeat stories about Gavin's brother."

"Okay…" Time to push. "We had a visitor last night."

His hands pause over the keys, and his eyes cut to mine. "Guy?"

I nod. "It doesn't seem to matter what we do. The theater isn't that big."

"What did he say?"

"That he knew me, that he's been watching me. That he'll be back and Molly and I should get some sleep in the meantime." I circle the instrument to sit beside him, lowering my voice. "What do I do?"

His lips press together. Five measures pass before he speaks, voice calm. "I'll talk to Gavin. Don't worry about it."

"Don't worry about it? After all you've said?" My voice is a panicked whisper as my grip tightens. "I've seen the look in his eyes before."

He hammers the final three chords and drops his hands to the bench, looking up at me. "Maybe it's time for Molly to go."

Acid rises in my throat, and my fists clench. I've never been so angry with Roland before. "That's all I get? Half-stories and impossible ideas?"

"Calm down." He reaches for my hand, but I jerk

it back and stand. He stands with me. "I said calm down."

"You've got a lot of nerve," I hiss, my chest so tight it hurts to breathe. "I can't send her away. I have nowhere to send her."

He studies me then sits, playing a song I've never heard before. I watch him stringing together notes into a flowing melody like my world isn't crumbling all around me.

"How do you like this?" he asks.

"It sounds like breaking dishes." I spin on my heel to leave.

He stops playing and catches my arm. "I said for you not to worry about it. I'll handle this situation with Guy. Just trust me."

"I can't do that anymore."

I walk away from my old protector and out of the theater. I don't know where Mark is, and I can't wait any longer for a solution.

It's time to take matters into my own hands and do what I can to save us.

* * *

"Here we are," Freddie says, holding a heavy, dark-wood door for me. It's accented with a clear glass panel and a gleaming brass *H* in the center.

Inside is an open, gas-lit space with white plaster walls and dark-wood molding and wainscoting. The floors are tiny white tiles arranged in a circular mosaic pattern with green accents in the center, and the entire place holds about forty small, dark-wood tables. It's classic New Orleans.

A handful of diners are scattered around, and each sit before colorful foods on white place settings atop white linens. A dark-wood bar is situated in the far-right corner with six stools tucked beneath a glossy ledge.

The wall behind it is lined in mirrors and glass shelves that hold bottles of various shapes and colors above clear glassware. A stout man in white shirtsleeves stands beside a bright brass tap station in the center, chatting with a man in a black suit.

The man holds a cigar from which a thin line of smoke curls to the ceiling, and a crystal snifter filled with amber liquid is beside his hand. The low murmur of polite conversation fills the air, and it's all so refined and beautiful. It's completely foreign to me.

We don't wait long at the entrance before another stout fellow with a crisp, white apron tied over a black vest greets us. He recognizes Freddie at once.

"Monsieur Lovel," he says with a bow. "Right this way, sir."

We're led to a small table for two, and when we stop, the host holds my chair for me. Every muscle in my body is tense, but Roland taught me the trick of passing in society—follow one quick step behind everyone and mimic their behavior.

I sit and then jump back as our host places a large, white-linen napkin across my lap. Then he looks at me as if expecting me to say something. I've never been waited on, so I simply smile. A waiter steps up and hands a large cream-colored sheet to Freddie, who peruses it briefly.

"Today's menu looks good," he says. "And bring us whatever your sommelier recommends with each course."

The waiter bows his head, and Freddie looks to me for approval. As if.

I simply smile again.

"Is that acceptable, darling?"

"Of course." I have no idea what I just agreed to eat, but my stomach is in knots anyway.

Within moments a plate of little brown shells arrives. I've heard of *escargot*, but I wait until Freddie picks up the tiny fork to remove a pinch of dark meat from inside. He makes a satisfied noise, and with careful hands, I follow suit. I'm not sure what to expect, but the moment the rich, buttery morsel hits my tongue, I have to resist the urge to groan loudly with delight. No matter what it once was, this is fresh, buttery, and perfectly seasoned—a welcome change from my usual day-old hard bagels.

"*Food & Wine* named this as the premiere bistro in the city," Freddie replaces his small utensil on the white linen. "They are trying to make New Orleans the Paris of the South."

I nod as if I know what the heck he's talking about. Freddie doesn't question my assent as the small plates are removed and replaced with new ones containing a dark green and purple salad.

I watch him pick up the smaller fork and prepare to do the same when he stops moving, sighs, and looks directly at me.

I freeze.

Has he figured out my trick?

"You are so beautiful in this light." He smiles, and I start to breathe again.

"Freddie." I shake my head.

"I've dreamed of being closer to you, and now it's happening." He still holds his fork aloft, gazing at me instead of eating. I try not to appear impatient. My stomach is near growling.

"You have such talent. It must be difficult to only have one part in the show."

I can't tell him it's the furthest thing from my mind. "I try not to let it get me down."

"I love it. Grace in the face of life's challenges. It's great marketing," he says, at last stabbing the bitter green salad he ordered for us both.

I smile demurely and follow suit, hoping to get us off the topic of my occupation and onto his. "Do you go back to Paris often?"

"Not as often as I'd like. My father likes me to stay here and look after our interests."

"Of which you have many?" I smile, hoping I'm not being rude. "I mean, to keep you here so long."

"Hmm." Freddie continues eating, clearly bored with the subject. "Our shipping business is strong and well-established. There's really no need to fuss about it. I'm looking for something new…"

His eyes land on mine as the salad plates are removed. I think about Roland's reasons for pushing me toward Freddie as the servers place a gorgeous arrangement of roast beef with dark gravy and something smooth and white with a little sprig of green in front of us. The luscious scent makes my mouth water, and again I fight back a squeal of delight. I can't remember the last time I had red meat.

"Well, this looks acceptable." Freddie picks up his silver knife and fork and slices into it. I do the same, but he's talking again. I don't want to stuff my face while he's staring at me. Still, I manage to get a piece of roast in my mouth, and I almost swoon at the flavor.

Freddie doesn't seem to notice. "We were doing fine with the usual New Orleans souvenirs, spices and such. Then we added coffee and it simply exploded."

He slices another piece of roast as I study the fluffy white side dish.

"The potatoes are amazing, aren't they?" he says, with a twinkle in his eye. My eyebrows rise. *Potatoes?* I would never have guessed...

"How they get them so smooth is a closely guarded secret," he adds as if reading my mind.

"You enjoy fine dining."

"It's true. I have Epicurean tastes."

Freddie leans back in his seat, placing the white cloth napkin beside his plate. I do the same, although I'm miserable at all the meat left on my plate. I wonder if he'd notice if I slid it into my handbag...

"Do you feel up for a stroll?"

"Of course!"

He stands and takes several bills from his pocket. He places them on the table as he takes my arm, and I feel pretty confident new shoes would not be an issue for Freddie Lovel.

Back on the street, my hand is in the crook of his arm as we walk, surveying the galleries and storefronts along Royal. It's warm in the sun, but with the humidity low, it's bearable. All of the blooms are gone, but dark-green ivy climbs healthy and bright up the sides of buildings and over the wrought iron trim.

A fountain trickles softly in a passing courtyard. It reminds me of my first adventure with Mark to the secret poboy shop, and my stomach cramps. It's only been a day, and I miss him so much. I hate all of this. Where is he?

We pass a shop with a large painting of the Seine in the window, and Freddie stops.

"How I long to be home again," he says.

"Back in Paris?"

"The cuisine here is… well, it's quite good." He covers my hand with his, glancing up at the sky. "It's just so miserably hot all the time."

I smooth my hair off my face. "I'm in the theater most days. I guess I'm use to it."

He nods and looks ahead. "The truth is if it weren't for you, I'd most likely melt into a puddle of *ennui*."

I have no idea what that means, and it never occurred to me that Freddie would be so anxious to go home. "I'd love to see Paris."

"Oh, darling, you would love it." Freddie's eyes take on an expression I usually see after my performances. "It's so beautiful with the flowers and the cafés along the *Rive Gauche*. Our home is in the seventh arrondissement, which is the best place to live."

"It sounds amazing."

"Would you ever consider going?" His eyebrows rise.

I bite my lip and we resume our stroll. "I've never been outside New Orleans, but I've always wanted to travel. With the right person."

Freddie's chest rises. "There are places I could show you that would take your breath away. From Montmartre you can see the entire city spread out below, with its tiny streets. And the shopping on the Champs-Élysées is incomparable."

"I don't know where I'd stay, and I have my little… sister Molly to consider."

"My sister has a large townhouse. I'm sure she would love to have a celebrity guest."

"I'm not a celebrity."

He smiles and pats my hand. "You might not be one yet, but you have the potential."

My brow furrows and I look up at him. "I'm basically one step above a stripper. Wouldn't she find that… problematic?"

"Of course not. Last year's number one song was recorded by a former stripper. One could even argue that Playboy spread made Marilyn Monroe a star."

For a moment my old promise to Molly about what our future might look like feels so close. The limos and the little dog.

"It sounds like a beautiful dream." We walk a moment in silence before I speak again. "Will you return to Paris soon?"

Freddie stops walking and looks deep into my eyes. "Would you care?"

I choose my words carefully. "I've looked forward to your visits. I imagine I would miss them… more than I can know now, standing here, holding your arm. But what could you possibly get out of it?"

I really want to know.

His eyes are warm and he covers my hand with his. "Paris is a much smaller market than America. I'd be honored to be the man who shared your talent with the world. And maybe, one day, you might think of me as more than a friend?"

We're back at the theater, and I think about his words. "I imagine anything is possible."

CHAPTER 15

"The universe loves a stubborn heart."

Mark

I missed the finale.

After dropping that asshole off at a small apartment building on Piedmont, I turned the car around and headed straight back south. But after driving all night, I only made it to Union City before I had to pull into a cheap motel and crash for a few hours. I set my alarm for plenty of time, but a fucking traffic jam in Mississippi cost me two more hours.

I'm tired and aching and worried about Lara when I finally pull into the dark parking lot. Keys in hand, I dash up the back steps headed straight for the dressing rooms, not worrying about who sees me.

I'm pulled up short when I see fucking Freddie again at her door, again with a fucking toddler-sized bunch of red roses, leaning in as if he's ready to kiss my girl. The drop-kick to the chest comes when I hear his words.

"May I kiss you?" He leans closer.

I have to smother the *No!* rising in my throat when Lara's eyes meet mine briefly. They narrow and she closes them as she lifts her chin.

He kisses her.

He fucking… I have to turn into the empty dressing room and go to the opposite wall, planting my fists against the wood paneling.

I'm tired. I'm exhausted from the drive, and I

don't know what the fuck is happening right now. My throat is tight, and it takes all my waning willpower not to charge out there, grab that guy by the neck and throw him out the back door.

The noise of heels clicking up the hall tells me he's gone.

I only see red.

Stepping out of the dark dressing room, Lara stands in her doorway looking directly at me. She's wearing that robe, and her expression is unapologetic.

It takes less than ten steps for me to be directly in front of her. "When did he start kissing you?"

"I don't know." She shakes her head as if trying to remember. It makes me even more furious. "A few days ago? I thought you knew—"

"I didn't," I snap. "I don't want him kissing you."

"I'm sorry," she snaps back, and my stomach clenches painfully. "You don't get to make orders like that."

My jaw tightens, and I turn to walk away. Then I turn back. "What we had… it meant something to me. It means something."

Her eyes move away from mine. "It meant something to me… But my situation has changed. I can't see you anymore."

Three steps and I'm with her again. "What changed?" My hands grip her arms, and I pull her closer. I put my lips in her hair and kiss her temple.

"Stop," she whimpers, but her hands tighten on my arms, holding me. "I can't—"

Releasing her at once, I step back. "That hasn't changed."

Her voice trembles, and tears glisten in her eyes. She fights them. "Where were you last night? Tonight?"

"Gavin sent me away. I had to drive to Atlanta."

"I needed you..." A lone tear falls, but she shoves it away fast, clearing her throat. "I realized I had to take matters into my own hands."

As much as I want to comfort her, I can't. I'm hurt and betrayed. Turning away, I face the wall, but my bleeding insides force me to ask. "Didn't any of it matter to you? That night, the things we said?"

She doesn't answer right away, and when she does, her voice has changed. It's formal, stoic. "What we had is a beautiful memory, but I have to think of Molly and me. Our safety."

My voice rises. "I said I'd take care of you. I just need time."

"How much time?" she shouts back. "You've been saying that for weeks, but still you can barely support yourself!"

A sick misery fills the air around us. She's blinking fast, and we're both breathing hard.

"So you prostitute yourself to a man you don't love?"

"Bastard," she whispers, her voice trembling. "You have no idea what I'm up against."

My anger won't let me take it back. I'm furious and hurting, and I only want her in my arms. "I know more than you think."

"Then you know I have no choice. I have to do whatever it takes to get us out of this place."

We only glare at each other a few seconds longer. Hurt radiates from both of us, but I turn away. I stalk up the hall, pushing through the door before we say another word we can't take back.

The metal door slams against the cinder-block wall as I blast through it. I'm still wearing my clothes from yesterday. Light-blue dress shirt and slacks, but the blazer is slung over a chair. I dig in the pocket for Gavin's keys, ready to give them back and head to the jazz club near Marigny for a car bomb. Or three.

"Hey, Fitz." Eddie, one of the old crew members who never left, stops me. "I get it now."

"What?" I growl.

"Why you kept that job up high."

He nods toward the rafters, and my eyes follow. "What are you talking about?"

"Larissa!" He slaps my shoulder. "Those tits are gorgeous from the stage, but fuck me, up close... I almost—"

Pain flashes through my fist as it slams into his stupid face. I've got him by the throat against the wall, and I'm pounding him with all the fury blazing in my chest.

"Fitz!" His hands are up and he tries to defend himself, but I don't stop.

Another voice shouts louder. "Fitz, stop!"

Two sets of arms grab me from both sides, dragging me off the man. Eddie drops to one knee clutching the blood gushing from his broken nose, his split lips. My hand is throbbing and starting to swell.

"What the fuck!" he shouts, looking up at me.

"Stay the fuck away from Lara!" I shout, and Darby pushes me across the empty backstage area.

"Walk it off!" he yells.

One of the other hands helps him push me to the back door. "Go home and get some rest. Don't come back until you've got it together."

Digging in my pocket, I find Gavin's keys and toss them into Darby's hand. "Give those to Gavin."

Adrenaline surges through my veins, and I can't stop shaking. I'm headed away from Bourbon Street, the bar, my bed, and walking fast toward the river. The alley is wet, and streetlights create rainbows in the gasoline-laced puddles. I splash through them until the alley opens, and I'm facing Jackson Square.

The cathedral looms before me, and it's the same as always, tall, dark, and foreboding. The doors are closed and locked tight. No sanctuary. Crossing the flagstone courtyard, I know I need to ice my hand. The broken bones throb, but the pain is nothing compared to the pain in my chest.

My stomach cramps when I think of what I said to Lara, what she said to me. The image of Freddie kissing her is like a hot iron to my already bleeding heart, and I want to fight more. I want to beat something until I stop feeling this way.

Until I don't care anymore.

Pulling up short, I realize I'm at the jewelry store. I'm standing in front of the plate-glass window, and that display is glittering in the lights. The shiny pen she said belonged to her mother. My hand goes to the glass, followed closely by my forehead.

Standing in the dark, looking at what she had to sacrifice, my fury melts into sadness. Why would I expect her to hold onto me when she's already lost so much?

Eddie's crack about her body clenches my teeth. He was with her there, alone in the darkness. I remember fighting off Vanessa in the darkness, and my rage fans to life again, only this time it's directed at that fucking crewmember I should have finished.

Did he touch her? Did he try to take advantage?

Of course, she's kissing a fucking rich guy. I promised I'd be there and I wasn't. I promised I'd keep her safe, and I didn't. Stepping back, I scan the door looking for the store hours. I see my reflection in the glass, and I see bloodstains on my shirt.

Looks like I have some shopping to do.

* * *

Lara

Fighting the pain twisting my chest, I meet Freddie for lunch again the next day. It's as polite as always, another small café the travel magazines hail as one of the best in the city. We dine, he talks of his business interests, I try to care.

After we're done, he mentions needing to stop by a men's store, and I shrug, not having a reason to say no. It's a lovely fall day. The sky is blue with puffy white clouds drifting by. It seems impossible the weather could be so joyful when my heart is a desolate wasteland.

Freddie holds my hand, and we approach the flagstone courtyard of Jackson Square. The artists are lined up in rows as always, but I resist looking for Mark among them.

"I've been wanting to visit this place," Freddie says, holding the door open to a small boutique. "Don't worry, this won't take long."

I walk inside and step over to a round table holding a rainbow of assorted silk neckties as Freddie goes to the display of topcoats. Everything in the shop is outrageously priced, and I glance up as a man steps up beside Freddie to return a coat to the rack.

My heart stops when I realize who it is.

"I'm sorry," Mark says. "I'm just returning this one."

I stare wide-eyed at him. Again, he looks amazing in a tweed jacket and dark brown pants. At his neck is a yellow tie, and his eyes glow when he turns them on me.

I swirl around, facing the street through the front window, my heart racing. An image of him smiling and catching my neck for a kiss as I trot onto the stage twists an ache of longing in the center of my chest.

"I was considering this one," Freddie says, not even recognizing Mark. My back is still turned when he calls to me, and I fight for control. "Darling, I need your opinion. Is it all wrong for me?"

"Just a moment," I say in an uneven voice as I press my palm into my stomach trying to slow my breathing. I can't let Freddie see me so shaken.

After a few moments, I'm calm. Thankfully Mark has his back to us and appears to be searching through the ties. Freddie smiles, a red tie tossed over his shoulder.

I clear my throat. "It's very nice."

His eyes narrow. "You seem distracted. I'm not sure I believe you."

"I'm sorry," I say, wishing with all my heart Mark wasn't standing here, hearing my words. "You look great. Red is a power tie, yes?"

At that Mark turns, and I can't avoid his gaze. I'm sure the struggle is plain on my face. Freddie is completely unaware as he looks through the shirts. Mark makes his way down the aisle to where I wait.

"See anything you like?" His voice is low, but I shake my head.

"Only what I can't afford."

He runs the back of his finger across my hand. "You can't?"

His touch would've been imperceptible if not for my reaction. My hand quickly turns, and our fingers lace. Familiar warmth floods my chest, but he continues past me, his hand slipping away as quickly as it appeared.

"Do you see anything you like?" Freddie asks, joining me.

"I'm not very good at shopping," I mutter, cheeks flushed.

He pats my shoulder. "We'll take care of that situation."

I might collapse from the tension. I wait as he heads to the register to pay, lingering at the front window as Mark finishes ahead of him and heads for the door. Without a word he leaves, and all the light leaves with him.

Freddie and I leave the shop, walking slowly back to the theater. I'd made up another rehearsal excuse, and I look up at the darkening sky, thinking about the birthday gathering Roland has planned for me. I wonder who might attend, whether Roland will invite Mark, whether Mark will come.

Freddie and I exchange a brief goodbye, and I step into the lobby. My thoughts drift to the rooftop. Has anything changed? Has everything changed? It won't be long until I know.

CHAPTER 16

"She walks like rain…"

Lara

As inexplicably as he'd started, Gavin stopped coming to rehearsals, and the mood in the company relaxed.

After crying myself to sleep last night, I don't see Mark at all the next day. Still, I can't allow myself to care. I can't allow myself to be distracted anymore. My plan has suddenly become urgent.

The pain is almost too much after our weeks of bliss, but I press all those emotions into a tight little pill that I force myself to swallow and be done with.

It's for the best. It was never real, and it could never be real. Mark can't take care of us, and if I keep traveling further down that road, I'll never be able to come back. Not to mention I'll ruin mine and Molly's only hope of a better life, our security with Freddie.

My heart thuds in my chest Thursday night as I go to the ladder for my finale climb. Mark is waiting at the top, and I try to calm my breathing when our eyes meet, when I see the red in his and know his heart is breaking as painfully as mine.

"I'm sorry," he whispers, and tears flood my eyes.

Oh, God, I can't cry. I have to sing.

I go to the bench without answering.

"I wasn't here for you. I said I would always be here and I wasn't. I know that made you feel alone and insecure. I understand that." The tone in his voice is ripping my heart into tiny shreds, but I can't look at him.

He touches my arm when I take my seat. My back is to him, but I don't move away. He fastens the harness, still speaking softly. "I'm sorry I made you afraid, but I meant what I said to you. I'm still working on our plan."

I inhale with a jerk, fighting my sobs as I take in the shape of his mouth, his straight nose, his blue eyes. I shake my head and look down again.

"It's too late. I have to go with Freddie. We have to leave this place now."

He touches my chin and lifts my face. Then he leans forward, lightly kissing my lips and sending aching warmth through my veins. "Talk to me first."

The music rises, and the bench moves. I swing out over the waiting spectators, but when I look back his eyes hold mine, his hands hold the rope, and my heart stays in the heavens with him.

I descend slowly to the stage in a swirl of red and black velvet, singing the words to the "Illusion" finale. The lyrics tell the story of a man so enchanted by a dark angel, he gives up everything, including his life, all for something that will only destroy him.

The words feel prophetic as I sing them, strutting in the lights, sparkling every time I turn until I take my final spin and end with my arms raised over my head in a *V*, my head turned to the side. Breasts high, nipples tight, my eyes close in my nightly expression of rapture, surrounded by a male fantasy of barely clothed, beautiful women.

We remain frozen on our marks until the heavy curtain falls, sending a swirl of musty velvet all around us. It never changes.

Through the darkness in the wings, I take Molly's hand. It's almost like she's still innocent and bad things haven't begun creeping in on us, closer with each passing day. How many days until Guy returns? Until he comes for what he's promised?

"Does Freddie know about your birthday?" she asks once we were in the dressing room.

"No," I sigh, trying to dispel any lingering feelings for Mark as I remove my wings and reach for my dressing gown. I have just enough time to peel off my false eyelashes before the tapping starts. I go to the door, but this time, there are no roses.

"Darling," Freddie catches my waist and pulls me to him. He kisses me without warning, pushing my lips apart and sweeping his tongue into my mouth.

Molly lets out a surprised squeak, and I'm almost speechless. "Freddie!" He's never been so bold.

He winks at Molly and smiles broadly. "I've got the most wonderful news. At least, I hope you'll think it's wonderful."

Molly makes an excuse about finding Rosa and quickly leaves as Freddie reaches into his jacket and pulls out a narrow black-velvet box. I take it and carefully open the lid to find a delicate gold bracelet accented all around by what look like small diamonds.

"It's too much," I say, and he takes it from my hands and fastens it around my wrist.

"I couldn't resist when I saw it. I had to get it for you."

Turning my arm, I watch the rainbow reflection it casts. My eyes go to Freddie's happy gray ones, and I force a smile. "What's your news?"

"I spoke to my sister Annemarie, and she is

thrilled at the idea of having you and your sister stay with her. She has a few preparations to make, but then we could leave here as soon as you like."

A knot closes in my throat. The pain of my fight with Mark is still so fresh, I'm not sure I can be convincing in my answer. Still, I push it all down again and hold it down before my runaway emotions ruin everything.

I slip out of Freddie's arms and turn away, stepping over to my dressing table. "Are you sure that's what you want?"

He closes the distance between us quickly, clutching my upper arms in his hands. I feel the heat of his body at my back. "It's what I've dreamed of for months. Even more in these last few days since we talked."

I squeeze my eyes shut, fighting the pain of what's coming and what it will mean. "It's wonderful news. Like I said, I've always wanted to go to Paris."

"And I can't tell you how happy I am to be the one to take you." He pulls me into his embrace and speaks at my temple. "I know I've said this before, but I still hope one day you might think of me as something more than a friend. Perhaps with time…"

My eyes sting, and my feelings for Mark burn in my chest. I'll shed my tears for him at a later date, when everything is settled and we're safe.

And I'm alone.

Molly's safety is more important than my fairytale ending, which was probably never going to happen anyway.

I inhale a sobering breath and take a step, lifting his hand for the first time in mine. "You've been so good to me. I hope one day I'll be able to repay your kindness."

He traces a line along my cheek. "Those words are enough for now."

Leaning forward, he lightly kisses my lips before turning to go. I watch him disappear through the door and lean my head against the doorjamb, holding back tears.

Molly steps up looking sorrowful. "Oh, Lara."

"What?" I sniff and raise my chin.

"If we leave, you'll never see Mark again."

It's a stab to my battered heart, but I swallow the lump of misery in my throat. "Never is a long time." I go to my table and sit, reaching for my packet of cleansing wipes and scrubbing off my makeup. I grab a tissue to wipe away the dampness that has sneaked out of my eyes. I will not cry.

"But you love Mark."

Our eyes meet in the mirror and for a moment it's only us. The two of us looking into the face of my decision. I turn away again.

"This is about our future and taking care of us. And anyway, I'd expect you to be happy about it."

She rushes over and leans on the dressing table. "So you've started to like Freddie a little? Is that it?"

I think about her question and about my answer. "Yes," I lie.

She frowns, moving away and shaking her head. "I don't believe you. And I don't understand you!"

"Because you're just a kid." My voice is flat.

"You're just a kid!" she shouts back.

"I'm twenty now." And I repeat the words Roland says to me, but with far less confidence. "You have to trust me."

* * *

Evie is the first person I see when I step out onto the roof. A breeze is blowing, and the twilight sky is a mix of pink, amber, light blue, and purple. The fall night is cool and smells of sweet wood fires and approaching rain.

"Happy birthday, darling," she says as she rushes across the space to embrace me. She's wearing an expensive burnt-orange silk dress with a beige open-knit sweater draped across her shoulders. It's tied closed with a black satin bow, and I recognize it from the window of Celeste's Couture when I was out with Freddie. I don't know much about fashion, but I know Celeste's is one of the most expensive boutiques in the city. I suddenly feel very casual in my jeans and long-sleeved black sweater.

"You're beautiful," I say.

Evie has always been so plain, but somehow in the dim light, in the shimmering dress, she's part of the setting sun. She smiles and looks down at her dress. "I'm not sure that's true, but thanks."

We clasp hands as she leads me across the rooftop to where Molly waits with Rosa. Roland is beside them fiddling with a champagne cork.

Molly runs to me and puts her arm around my waist. A popping noise comes from where Roland stands, and everyone cheers and claps as he pours glasses for each of us. He walks over and puts an arm across my shoulders, handing me a glass. Molly walks away with Evie.

"To sweet sixteen," he says with a wink, clinking a cheers with me before draining his glass. "I'm only joking. Twenty is a good age. I remember being up here with you when I turned twenty."

"Don't." My face grows hot.

"Why? You were adorable." He pulls me closer to him. "Your crush was one of the sweetest times of my life. You're the only girl I've ever kissed."

"I don't believe that."

"You'd better." He pours us both another glass of champagne. "And how are things going with the dashing Mr. Lovel?"

I push away and walk to the ledge, clasping my arms over my waist. "You were right. Freddie's nice and rich and he'll take us far away from here. With Freddie we'll never have to be afraid again."

I say the words more for me than in answer to Roland's question.

"You can't say what will never happen." Roland leans against the wall beside me. After a few moments of silence he adds. "I invited Mark. I don't know where he is, but he knew."

It hurts to hear that, but I swallow the pain as I've been doing. "He knows we can't be together."

Roland takes another drink. "Maybe he does. Maybe he doesn't."

I lift my glass of wine and down the entire contents at once.

"Not smart," he says. Then he takes my empty and goes to where Molly and Evie stand with Rosa.

He puts another glass in my hand, but my head feels fuzzy from drinking the first one too fast. Everyone is lifting a toast to me now, so I'm obliged to participate. I take a few sips and listen to the conversations and the laughter. The tears that have been my constant companion lately are a distant memory. In fact, I'm not feeling much of anything at the moment.

I watch Molly try to dance with Roland and smile as everyone laughs. Before I know it, Roland is with me again saying it's time to go to bed.

"Morning comes early, you know." He touches my arm, and I nod.

We're headed to the door when it opens on its own. A low murmur ripples through the group, and I lift my eyes to meet Mark's looking directly into mine. My chest squeezes.

"I'll take Molly down," Rosa says, pulling her through the doorway.

"Time to resume my charade." Evie steps forward to kiss my cheek. "Goodnight, honey."

I kiss her back but Mark's eyes never leave mine. I know because mine never leave his.

"It seems we're no longer needed here." Roland kisses my temple. "Happy birthday, my love, and goodnight."

Within seconds it's just the two of us, standing alone, facing each other. I can't think of a thing to say.

Mark is the first to break the silence. "Happy birthday. I didn't think I was coming."

I nod and look down. The funny thing about champagne is I don't feel a rush of sadness, but I know his words hurt because my eyes are damp.

"I tried to do as you asked and leave you alone," he says.

"You didn't try too hard." My words are a little slurred.

He notices as well and walks over to me. "Are you drunk?" He lifts my chin. I shake my head a bit too vigorously, and he frowns. "Roland shouldn't let you drink."

"It was only two glasses of champagne."

"Baby," he says as his frown relaxes.

I try to walk away, but I stumble over my own feet.

As always, he catches me.

"Take it easy," he says as I fight to disengage myself from his embrace, but it's too late. I know this location too well.

I stop struggling and melt into him. He studies my face a moment before lowering his mouth to mine. With a deep sigh, my lips part, his tongue finds mine, and instantly I'm back in that place of delicious warmth, heat, and desire.

But it's over as soon as it starts.

He pulls back, stepping away, and shoving his hands in his back pockets. "I'm sorry. I didn't come here to do that."

He goes to where Roland left a half-empty bottle of champagne and snatches it up, taking a long drink.

"Why did you come here?" My voice is quiet.

He reaches into his coat. "I got you a present."

It's a long, narrow box, and I take it, wiping my eyes with one hand and turning it over with my other. "You didn't have to."

"Open it."

Tearing the ivory-colored paper away, I find a narrow black box inside. When I lift the top, light hits the gleaming brass, and I realize what it is. A small cry escapes my throat as I collapse to a sitting position, clutching my mother's pen to my chest.

"Oh, Mark," I say through fresh tears. "It's too much. It's more than you can afford."

"I couldn't let you part with it."

Even through the champagne, I feel this pain.

It's the pain of my heart breaking again.

With a hiccupped breath, I reach out for him. He steps forward, dropping to one knee, and I reach for his cheek. He kisses me, and for a moment, all I know is our lips pressed together, our need for each other.

I close my eyes and rest my forehead against his cheek.

I can't fight this.

"What happens now?" I say softly.

"Come home with me tonight. We can sort it out in the morning."

I nod, anticipation heating my skin. My body longs for his, and when our eyes meet, I see the fire burning there. Once more our lips meet, soft and melding together. Our tongues touch, and the heat in my core aches with persistence. A soft moan slips from my mouth to his as his rough hand slides along my neck, his thumb tracing my jaw.

"You're so beautiful," he whispers, holding my gaze in the moonlight. "I really only came here to say that and give you your present."

My forehead tightens. "Would you rather I stay here?"

His beautiful smile appears. "No way. I've been trying to get you in my bed for weeks."

It provokes a tiny laugh from me, but the anxiety in my chest hasn't completely disappeared. I want Mark so desperately, but that threat, that fear is still nudging at the back of my mind. *Don't think about it for one night…*

Leaning closer, I kiss his lips once more. "I want to be in your bed."

His hands are on my waist, sliding under my sweater to tease my bare skin. My lower stomach tightens. Our lips unite again, and I'm growing desperate for more.

"It'll take me a second to pack a bag," I whisper.

"Meet me at the back door."

I hurry down the narrow stairs, wondering how long it will take for me to learn to relax, to stop looking over my shoulder. The room is empty, and on my dressing table is a note that reads, *Molly is with me. Enjoy the night. Happy Birthday, Rosa*

My worried mind says to go to Rosa's room and carry Molly back, stick to the plan. I run my finger down the side of the sparkling barrette Freddie gave me and think of my old promise. I think of Mark in the shop, our fingers entwined.

A tapping on my door startles me. Mark must've grown tired of waiting.

"Come in," I say softly.

My eyes go to my small bed, and I remember our first time, the intensity, the heat, the pleasure. I remember his mouth on my pussy making me come so hard I screamed. I can still remember his lined body and how my breath caught at the sight of his cock. Heat fills my panties at the memory, and I hurry to the door wanting him now. We'll get to his bed eventually...

"I'm sorry to disturb you so late," Gavin says, stepping into the light.

"No!" I jump back, ice in my veins.

Gavin never visits me, and all I can think of is Roland's warning.

"Happy birthday," he says, placing a small box on my dressing table. "I got you just a little something."

I silently watch his every move, waiting to hear why he's really here. He looks around the empty room.

"Where's..."

"Molly is spending the night with Rosa."

He nods, and looks down. "I wanted to talk to you about her."

A shuffling in the hall interrupts us. We both look at the doorway where Mark is now standing. My breath disappears, my throat is tight. We're not forbidden from having boyfriends, but I know when it comes to sex, Gavin expects a cut.

"What are you doing here?" His sharp voice echoes in my small room.

"Sorry," Mark answers fast. "I was returning this."

He hands me my mother's pen, and Gavin watches our exchange with a stern expression.

"Let yourself out," Gavin says. "I'll deal with you tomorrow."

Mark hesitates, but we don't have a choice.

"Goodnight," he says softly and disappears into the passage.

Gavin steps out behind him, watching until I hear the click of the back door and my heart sinks along with my dreams. Gavin returns and goes to my table.

"I saw you out with him the other night. And I've seen him watching you."

"Is that so wrong?" Losing my chance at happiness, even if it was only for one night, has me bitter.

Gavin's mouth tightens. "It's not very smart. It can cause… conflicts."

I glare up at him, knowing what he means but unable to argue. Getting involved with a woman whose sexuality is a commodity is a recipe for disaster.

"Just don't get pregnant. And take better care with your valuables." He exhales and turns to the door. "I came to speak to you about the little one. My brother finds her interesting."

In that moment, I feel distinctly as if the hand of my worst nightmare has reached out from the darkness and grabbed me by the neck.

"He's asking for her—" Gavin continues.

"No." I forget all my fear. My eyes are clouded as I rush to the door and grab his arm. "What does he want?"

"It appears you know what he wants." He looks down at my hand clutching his sleeve. "He wants her for himself."

"He can't have her!"

"She has no family, no talent, no education. It's probably the only way she'll ever make money."

"She has me. I'm her family. And she doesn't need to make money. She's never cost you a dime."

"That's not the point." He covers my hand, loosening my fingers. "Guy holds the deed to this place. He gets what he wants."

My head is spinning, and for a moment I think I might collapse. Then I remember his words, what he said about watching me grow.

"He can have me. I'll take her place." It's out so fast, I don't have time to reconsider. I look down at my clenched fists.

"No," Gavin says. "You're too important to the show."

"I won't let him hurt her."

Gavin presses his lips together in a tight line. We stand in a silent impasse, him in the doorway, me facing him down, fighting to pull air into my lungs.

"I'll hold him off a little longer," he finally says. "Perhaps he'll lose interest."

I don't speak as he turns to go. I can't stop trembling. He stops before closing the door again. "I hope you like your gift. It was your mother's favorite."

Then he shuts the door, and I'm alone in the lamplight. After a few moments, I turn and slowly go to the table, my whole body tense. I lift the box he put there. Inside is a tiny bottle of what looks like perfume, and when I pull the stopper, my room fills with the scent of tea-roses and ocean air, the scent of my mother. I remember her dark hair, the soft folds of her cotton gown, being a tiny girl and pulling these things around me for comfort, for protection.

I close my eyes and sit in my chair, pulling my knees to my chest. My body shakes harder, and I hug my legs tighter as I rock back and forth, afraid of what's coming.

CHAPTER 17

"I broke my own heart loving you."

Mark

The back lot is dark.

It's chilly and drops of rain hit my face. I look up at the sky, but I can't leave. My fists tighten and release, and I pace the dirty asphalt. I don't like Gavin in Lara's room. I don't like what he might be saying to her, ordering her to do... and *fuck*, I'm pissed at losing our night together.

I look at the chunky stainless steel watch I got at the shop when I bought back her mother's pen. Ten minutes. I reach for the handle, ready to face the consequences and storm back in there, when it pushes into my fist.

Gavin steps out into the darkness. "Figured I'd find you here." His voice is a growl, and he shoves a square slip of paper in my hand. "Take that to the Walgreens on Magazine Street. Tell the doc it's a standing order."

"But..." I look down at the paper. Narcan is written on it, and some physician signed it. I can't tell if it's real or a forgery. "There's no name on this."

He steps closer, speaking through clenched teeth. "That's why you go to the fucking Walgreens on fucking Magazine Street. What the fuck have I said about you questioning me?"

My jaw tightens. This asshole has given me close to five thousand dollars in the past week alone. Half of it went to clothes. A little bit went to gas and the hotel in Union City, but enough is left over to keep me on the line. If I have a few thousand coming in every week, it'll be enough for me to keep my promise to Lara and even include Molly in the process.

I back down. "When do you need it?"

His shoulders relax along with his voice. "I want it in my hands first thing in the morning. We have the situation under control for tonight."

I know he's talking about Tanya. I know what I saw, and if she was already shooting up, her situation is progressing fast.

"It's late, but I'll go there before I go home."

"You have a car?"

"I'll catch the streetcar."

"Better get going."

He stands in front of the door with his arms crossed, and I'm pretty sure this errand is as much about getting me out of here as it is getting what he needs to revive Tanya when she overdoses.

Shoving the paper in my pocket, I start walking south toward Canal. I'm two steps away when he stops me.

"If you're smart, you'll keep your hands off Lara."

I look up over my shoulder. His expression isn't cruel or menacing, and I'm sure he's trying to give me good advice like Terrence did my first day.

"I've never been very smart."

The rain is picking up, and I keep moving.

* * *

Lara

Like a giant wheel, our week begins again with stale breakfast, never enough, rehearsals until we dance in our dreams, costume adjustments, set repairs, and then back to bed to sleep until it all begins again.

Mark finds me in the wings, where I watch as Fiona works with the dancers. One look, and I'm in his arms. It hurts so much, I can't push him away. We're behind the heavy, dark curtains, and our times here making love are like muscle memory. His tongue finds mine, and he kisses me long and hungrily, warm breath whispering across my cheek, strong hands lifting me against the hardness in his jeans. I slide my fingers into his soft hair, but this time I'm wearing yoga pants not a skirt, my panties firmly in place.

"I miss you so much," he says beside my ear, and despite my panic and fear, I cling to him, battling tears as he kisses my cheek then my lips again. "Maybe we can try tonight?" Then he sees my expression. "What's wrong? What happened?"

It rips at my heart to let him go, but I steel myself. "I can't. I have to stick to my plans with Freddie."

"Why are you saying this now? What happened?"

"It doesn't matter. I made a promise, and I have to keep it."

"No, you don't."

I nod, swallowing the pain in my throat. "It's my fault Molly's here. She's in danger because of me—"

"She's not a puppy, Lara."

"I never said she was."

"Yet you dedicate yourself to her as if..." he pauses, looking for the right word.

"As if I were her mother?"

"Yes."

"I knew you wouldn't understand." I turn and go to the door leading to the backstage passage. My hand is on the handle just as his finds my waist and arm. He pulls my back against his warm body, and my insides melt.

"Wait," he says. "Don't go yet."

"It's better if I do."

"But what about us?" He presses his face into my hair. "Don't we matter?"

"I could never forgive myself..." My voice fades, but the truth remains.

I could walk away and leave her behind to face whatever fate awaits her... And I'd never be happy as long as I lived.

His grip relaxes, and he steps back, releasing me. "So you're determined to end it."

Pain wrenches my insides. "I'm sorry."

He starts to say something, but I'm through the door before I can hear it, running to my shared room as fast as my legs will take me.

I've given up on dreaming about a future with Mark, but each afternoon a small token appears on my dressing table.

First it was a single blue iris. Then it was a tiny chocolate, next a little sketch of two hands, the fingers entwined.

By Thursday, I have a collection in the small basket beneath my dressing table, along with the box that holds my mother's perfume.

Tonight he behaves as if nothing has changed. He watches me climb from the top of the ladder with a calm expression on his face, and while we wait, he holds my hand and caresses the top of it with his thumb.

It's excruciating, but I'm too overwhelmed to argue. I don't understand why he's behaving this way, deluding himself and killing me.

"Nothing's changed," I whisper in the moments as I get in position, belt around my waist.

"I'm not letting you go."

Pain. "I'm leaving with Freddie."

"Not yet."

I shake my head and turn away as my seat moves out, and I present the same song of disillusionment to a new set of dazzled faces.

Freddie is preoccupied in my dressing room, but I do my best to keep my demeanor light. "I hope you're not growing tired of me," I say, tracing my finger up his hand and slipping it under his cuff. "It always makes me happy to know you're out there watching."

He laces our fingers and kisses my cheek. "I'm afraid I've got some bad news," he says, releasing my hand.

Panic tightens my neck. "Bad news?"

"I've got to go to Paris tonight... in just a few hours, actually. Not enough time to take you with me, I'm afraid."

My heart slams to the floor, and I don't have to pretend to be horrified. "*What?*"

He pulls me against his chest. "I know, and normally I'd be thrilled to return home. This time all I can think of is not seeing you."

I'm afraid I might lose it. "For how long?"

"A month, three weeks at the most. Apparently some urgent business matter requires my immediate, personal attention." Then he smiles. "But the good news is there's a divine little jewelry store just off the Champs-Élysées. I have the perfect gift in mind—"

"A month." My voice is quiet as fear trickles into my veins.

"Will you forget me?"

"Of course not."

He kisses my lips then reaches for his breast pocket.

"To be sure, my adorable little Luddite, I bought you something useful and something to help you remember me."

I'm numb as I take the box and open it to find a golden locket. He opens it to reveal a tiny picture of himself inside.

I stare at it, unable to smile.

He chuckles and turns me around to fasten it at my neck. It's too long and slips between my breasts. When he turns me back around, I don't lift it for him. I hold my breath as he silently observes its position.

Maybe if I sleep with him…

The air is charged as I wait for his response, ready to welcome anything that might take us away from here to Paris, but he only pulls the delicate chain, lifting the locket into his hand.

Our eyes met, and my almost-tears are real this time. "How can you leave me?"

"I know, it's excruciating, but now for the something useful." I watch as he again reaches into his breast pocket and removes a slim, white device. "I took the liberty of buying you this, active and ready to go."

My eyes flicker down to the phone in his hand.

"And your number…" He takes my mother's pen off my dressing table and writes on a tissue. When he finishes, he rolls the pen around in his fingers.

"This is a nice piece. Where did you get it?"

"It was my mother's."

His eyebrows quirk up, before he continues. "Roland programmed his number, and of course my number is saved. We can video chat every night. It'll almost be like we're together."

I only nod. "Goodbye," I say, causing Freddie to clutch me again in a long embrace.

"I confess, your fatalism warms my heart, but I'll be back before you know it. Sooner if at all possible. And in the meantime, I'll just be working around the clock so as not to be constantly thinking of how miserable I am without you."

I can't reply or even make eye contact.

"One last kiss, and I have to get to the airport." He squeezes my hands before pressing his lips to mine and giving me another long embrace. "I adore you, *ma petite chou*."

My eyes are fixed on the floor as he disappears from my life, and a cold certainty trickles down my spine.

It's over.

I go to my dressing table as if in a trance. I place the phone there and put my hand around the golden locket, staring at it a few moments. Then by force of habit, I let it go and reach for the packet of face wipes to clean off the makeup. My hand falters, and my glance flickers to the mirror. My eyes are the same blue they've always been, and my hair is swept away and up in a style that sends my large, dark curls cascading down my back.

But I've changed.

I'm haunted.

Desperate.

Again I imagine taking Molly and running away.

But where would we go? I could pawn these new gifts Freddie has given me—the diamond bracelet, the barrette, this locket—but for how much? And how long would it last? Would it be enough for us to get away?

Just then Molly enters the room, her eyes as round as mine. "I heard Freddie say he's leaving without us."

My own anxiety rushes back, and I go to the door, shutting it and double-checking the bolt before answering. In the face of her fear, a determination I didn't know I possessed rises. We are *not* trapped, and I *will* find a way to save us.

I slide my hand under my pillow to retrieve the white tank I sleep in. "Get ready for bed," I say.

She robotically obeys, and as we've done since her first night here, I pull her back into my chest and smooth her hair away from her face, trying to calm the tremors that keep passing through her body into mine.

The moonlight streams through our tiny window when I begin to speak. "Your mother was a gorgeous dancer..."

Her body shakes hard, but I take a deep breath and continue. "And when she met your dad, she couldn't help but love him. He played such beautiful music on the guitar."

My arm is tight around her waist, and I feel as her trembling begins to subside, her fear dissipating because she trusts me. It's all she knows to do.

My eyes grow damp, but I clear my throat and keep going. "He had no money to marry her, so he went away to find his fortune. But before he could return, she was married to another man. He came back anyway, and she went to him. And nine months later, you were born. But your beautiful mother had to return to her husband, so she left you with me until she could come back to get you—"

"It's all a lie," she cries out. "She's never coming back, and something terrible's going to happen to us."

"I won't let anything terrible happen to you." My voice is low and firm. "I told you that, and you have to believe me."

She doesn't answer, so I continue to my next story. "In a month, Freddie'll be back, and I'll quit the show. We'll move to Paris, where we'll live in a house on the Avenue Montaigne and I'll have a limo and diamonds—"

"And a little dog," she says, the smallest glint of hope returning.

"And a little dog." I repeat, swallowing my fear. "And we'll never think about this place. Ever again."

CHAPTER 18

"Being scared means you're about to do something brave."

Lara

Hours pass as I lie in the darkness listening to Molly breathe. Desperation has me by the throat, making it impossible to sleep. I can't stop thinking of how we might escape until finally I give up and slip out of the bed.

I creep to the door, sliding the bolt and stepping out into the dark passage, and I make my way down the hall to Rosa's room. Her light is still on, but I'm frozen in place by what I hear inside. It's Tanya's voice, whining and fighting.

"No," she mumbles. "Let me go!"

"Stop doing this. You're going to kill yourself."

"Then let me die," Tanya shouts, her voice breaking.

The noise of something banging to the floor has me leaning forward to look. Tanya is on her back, eyes closed, and in her hand is a crumpled piece of aluminum foil and a lighter. The room smells like vinegar, but I don't understand any of it.

I lose my balance, and my shoulder hits the door. It creaks open, and Rosa's face snaps to mine. Her brow collapses.

"Lara," she sighs. "Get out of here. You shouldn't see this."

"What's wrong with her?"

"Heroin. Fentanyl." Rosa pushes off her knees and sits in the chair, leaning forward with her face in her hands over what looks like a sleeping Tanya.

"Why would she do that?"

"She's an addict. It's getting worse. Fast. If we don't get her clean, she'll die."

The words are terrible, horrifying, but instead of fear, something different blooms in my chest. I scan the place, mentally logging the items surrounding the skinny girl on the floor. The wheels are turning, and I can't stop the idea growing bigger by the second...

"It's powder?"

Rosa frowns. "Yes.

"How does she get it?"

"I've heard some of the voodoo shops have it, but you can probably buy it on Bourbon Street if you know who to ask."

I'm out the door, headed to my room while she's still speaking. Molly is asleep, but it's still pretty early. I pull on my jeans and grab the black sweater, jerking it over my head and down to cover the white tank. Calm fills my mind. The calm of knowing exactly how I'm going to handle this. My path is plain, and I know I won't falter.

But first I have an errand to run.

Tapping on my new phone, I text Roland to meet me at the corner of Royal and Orleans in five minutes. I grab a coat and small hat on my way out the door. It's brown tweed with a black band and a little feather on the side.

Roland grins when he sees me, and we set off down the narrow street toward Bourbon. I pull the collar tight at my neck. The sky is overcast again.

We stop at the corner, and Roland lights a cigarette. "Care to tell me where we're headed, old boy? I have to admit this drag you're wearing is working for me."

I cut my eyes at him and start walking again, slipping my hand in the pocket to clutch the money I grabbed from pawning my mother's pen. I've never made a drug deal, and I can only hope it's enough to get what I need.

We reach the small shack on St. Anne's just as Roland finishes his cigarette and tosses it to the ground. "Voodoo?" he chuckles as he grinds out the butt. "Now will you tell me what the hell we're doing?"

"I need to buy something. I didn't want to come here alone."

"At least you're smart."

"Come on."

The house seems deserted, but Roland dashes up the steps and holds the door for me. It's as cold inside the narrow cottage as it is outside, and the pungent scent of pipe smoke mixed with spicy patchouli oil surrounds us.

We pass counters adorned with dolls and alligator claws, crude noise-makers, and other assorted *gris-gris*.

An olive-skinned woman in a white turban with frizzy hair sticking out the bottom passes through a beaded curtain that divides the front of the house from the back. She comes to where we're standing and looks us up and down, frowning.

"Children," she mutters in a thick, New Orleans accent, shaking her head. "What do you want?"

Roland points at me.

"I need something." I hesitate, then I lean toward her. "Fentanyl."

"You don't come here for that," she snaps. "You need a prescription."

"I just need an ounce."

The woman doesn't react, but Roland catches my arm and turns me to look at him. His eyes narrow, and he drags me back to the entrance. I struggle against him, but he's stronger than me and has me outside in two steps. Then he fixes those brown eyes on mine.

"What's going on?" he demands.

I glance down and a huge gust of damp wind whips my hair up and around my face. "I have to do this."

"Do what?" His arms are crossed, and I simply look at him until he lowers them again. "Who?"

"Guy."

At that, he grips my arm and pulls me back to the street, the way we came. I struggle to break free of his hold until he finally stops walking and turns to look at me again.

"First, there's no way you'd ever get him to take it. And second, what makes you think you could hide something like this by yourself?"

"He's coming for Molly." My throat grows tight, and I can't finish. I can't tell him what I said to Gavin, my dark bargain.

Roland spins on his heel and throws out his arms. "So let him have her!"

My hand clenches into a fist, and I hit him so fast, it surprises both of us. He staggers back, covering his mouth, and I rub my fingers. The pain brings tears to my eyes.

Then he grabs my arm and jerks me to him with a force that makes me cry out. "Don't *ever* hit me again," he growls through clenched teeth.

Two tears hit my cheeks.

He shoves me back, still holding his lip. A trickle of blood appears, and I dig in the pocket of my borrowed coat to find a tissue.

I hand it to him. "I said I'd take her place."

Anger flashes in his eyes, and his teeth clench. "Who did you tell that?"

"Gavin."

He explodes a loud exhale. "He'll never let that happen."

"I won't let Guy have her!" My voice is desperate and tears blur my vision. "This is the only way to stop him. For good."

I start back for the cottage, but Roland catches my arm, gentler this time, and pulls me to him. "Calm down," he says, stroking my hair. Then he wraps his arms around me and presses my head into his chest. I shiver as the tears fall.

"Why have you stopped caring about her?" I whisper through the thickness in my throat.

"I haven't. It's just… you have to learn when to fight, and when to let go. There are those you can save, and those you can't."

"And into which category do I fall?" Anger rises in me again, and I don't want to be in his arms.

For a moment he simply looks at me. Then he steps forward and catches my face. I'm about to speak when he bends down and kisses me, pushing my lips apart with his.

My stomach clenches, and the metallic taste of his blood is in my mouth as I fumble with the scratchy wool of his coat, trying to get away. He holds our lips together a second longer before letting go and pulling back.

Then he looks directly into my eyes. "Which do you think?"

"Why did you do that?"

"Because there's a bond between us. You know it."

I seize that sentiment. "Because you looked out for me when I came here. Don't you see? That's how it is with Molly and me."

"It's not the same."

"It is!" My throat is tight again.

"Molly has none of the history we share. None of the debt I owe your mother." His voice softens at the words, at some memory I don't know. He steps to me, and smooths the tear off my cheek with his thumb. "That I owe you."

"You have no debt to me."

But he smiles and waves a hand, and just like that I watch his own invisible curtain rise. "I'll help you. But I won't let you put yourself in danger."

I'm still trying to understand what just happened, but his words give me hope. "You'll help me?"

"Of course. But not like this." He motions to the cottage. Then he crooks his arm and nods in the direction of the theater. "Come on."

With hesitation, I take his arm. I believe him, but still… He doesn't have to know if I return to the cottage, and there is only one way I know to stop Guy permanently.

I'll be back, if only for insurance.

* * *

Mark

The men are back.

All of them.

Since the night of Lara's birthday, I've been to Algiers to basically stand with my arms crossed while men unloaded crates from a barge, I've made two more trips to the Walgreen's on Magazine for Narcan, which turns my stomach, and I drove to the airport to pick up the Canadian and the other guy, Esterhaus.

Tanya is fading fast, and I'm pretty sure her decline started the night I stood outside the door, guarding the gangbang happening under the stage. I didn't see her there, but a few of the girls said they were given pills to "help them relax."

I'm not doing that job again.

I've made five thousand dollars in five days, and every cent I don't spend on food, gas, clothes, or prescriptions, I put in the Bank of the French Quarter. It's small, but it's cheap. I'm lucky to be living rent-free, but when Terrence returns, I'll have to start coughing up rent money. My hope is by then, I'll have found a better job and a place for the three of us—Lara, Molly, and me—to live.

The last time I held her, she tried to push me away, but when I kiss her, I feel where her heart is. She's mine. I just have to show her I can and I will take care of her. And Molly. I lost points that night I went to Atlanta, but Lara has a phone now. I don't even care if that rich guy bought it. I have her number, and I always tell her where I am, whether she wants to know or not.

For instance, tonight I had to go all the way to Holly Grove, almost to Metairie to collect payment from some asshole who runs a laundry service.

It turned my stomach because it felt like the kind of shit Rick was into before they blew him away. As far as I've been able to learn, Guy is the puppet master in all their seedier affiliations, but I'm puzzled that Gavin knew my uncle and he didn't.

Gavin only appears to run the Pussycat Angels club, and, to my knowledge, Rick didn't have any dealings with strippers or prostitutes. That I know of…

I'm still working that one out.

The rain hasn't let up for a week, but it's not storming. Mist hangs in the air, almost as if it's too saturated for precipitation. I hop off the streetcar at Dauphine and continue walking toward the theater. I've got less than an hour to get there before intermission.

Pulling my topcoat closer at my neck, I lean into the wind, keeping my eyes on my feet as I cross, block after block, headed to Orleans Street. I stay east of Bourbon, trying to avoid that mob as long as possible.

I pull out my phone, scrolling to Lara's number in my recent calls, grinning at the nickname *Wifey* I've given her. I study the photos I've taken of her. Her smiling, her looking tolerant, her in my arms, her face buried in my chest.

She still says we have to break it off, but that Freddie bastard is back in Paris, and I plan to tell her my money situation and make another pitch for staying with me when I get back tonight.

A dark figure in a long black topcoat jogs fast south. The wind whips around me, fanning my coattails and shooting the runner's hat off his… her head?

"Lara?"

She's panting and leans against a brick wall, looking at the sky. We're surrounded by buildings in the middle of a block, and I can tell she's disoriented. My stomach tightens, and my fists clench, preparing for a fight. I don't know why she's running, but I'll kick some ass if someone's bothering her.

A quick look left, and I cross the one-way street to where she's collapsed against the side of a building. "Lara," I say louder, and she lets out a little yelp.

Her eyes are huge, and I reach for her arm, pulling her to me. "I thought that was you. What are you doing out here?"

She takes a step as if she'll bury herself in my topcoat against my chest—a welcome place for her always—but she stops herself.

"I... I..." She looks away and then down at her hand in mine. "I lost my way."

"Well, lucky for you Gavin sent me uptown this afternoon. I'll take you back."

We walk beside each other in silence for a while. The strong gusts hit us in the face, and I want to pull her to me, put my coat around her, and shelter her from the damp. She glances sideways and our eyes catch.

"How are you?"

She shakes her head. "The same."

"Something's changed. Freddie's gone."

"Just for a month."

Catching her arm, I stop our progress and turn her to face me. "It gives us more time. There's still a chance for us."

She looks down, and her eyes blink faster. "You're so good." She places her narrow hand on the sleeve covering my forearm. Her slim fingers widen and narrow as she pulls it back. "I would give anything for that to be true."

We're at the corner of Royal and St. Anne Streets, and before I can pull her to me and reassure her it can be true she turns. Her pace quickens, and she's jogging ahead of me to the theater.

She hurries through the back doors, and I let her go for now. She has to get ready for the show, and I'll be able to kiss her cheek and hold her to me in a few minutes. We will be together. She'll believe it once she knows what I've done.

CHAPTER 19

"In the end she became the journey."

Lara

My moment with Mark before the finale is brief, but he holds my hand and promises to meet me after the show as I'm swept away. I descend to the floor to perform, and following the rush of musty velvet curtains, I race to my room.

Molly has been with Evie since I left this afternoon, and I consider running to that luxurious apartment myself.

But it's too late.

My stomach fills with icy fear when I burst through my dressing room door to see Guy standing before my mirror, holding my mother's pen. At the sound of the door opening, he turns.

With a hiss he leers at my exposed breasts then takes a step closer, placing a hot palm on my shoulder. "What you're wearing pleases me, but I want this body paint off."

A bustling in the passage causes us to look up. Roland leads Gavin toward my room with Darby close behind, and none of them are smiling.

"What's going on?" Gavin says as his brother steps back to cross his arms.

"This one made a deal with me. I'm here to collect." Guy steps forward to take my arm, and a knot of panic twists tighter in my throat. I have to get my hand in the pocket of that topcoat before we go.

"Just let me slip into something more comfortable," I say, trying to smile, to act calm. Everything about me says I'm lying. My voice breaks and my body trembles.

"We aren't leaving the building," he says with a glittering smile.

My heart beats so fast, it's painful. "But you want me to wash off the body paint, yes?"

Gavin frowns at me before turning to his brother. "Tomorrow," he says, patting Guy's arm as if to calm an attack dog. "Let's us men do something tonight, and we can trouble Lara tomorrow."

"I've waited long enough." Guy flings his brother's arm away, and another bustling in the hall causes us to look up.

It's Mark, and his fists are clenched, nostrils flaring as he strides toward us.

"Lara? What's going on?" he snaps, but Roland steps out and blocks his path.

"Best head on home now, Mark," Roland says. "Lara will see you tomorrow."

"The fuck she will!" Mark tries to push past him, but the two struggle until Darby steps up and takes Mark's arm. "Come on, son," he says, smiling apologetically.

"I'm not your fucking son." Mark shoves his arm back. "And I'm not fucking leaving."

He pushes forward again, but Roland holds him.

My eyes grow damp and for a moment, I imagine running to him. Pushing through Roland and Darby and taking Mark's hand, letting him sweep me far away from this terror.

Instead, I go into my dressing room, and with trembling hands, I begin removing my false eyelashes and taking down my hair. Mark can't stop what I said I would do.

"Give me five minutes," I say.

Gavin backs up and turns to walk away, back down the dark passage without another word.

"Fine. Get that shit off your tits," Guy says, his blue eyes gleaming. "I'll wait."

"Let me go!" I hear shuffling of feet and grunts as Darby and Roland wrestle with Mark.

"Lara!" he shouts, and my eyes squeeze shut.

"Lara!" A tear stripes my cheek black as his shout comes from farther down the hall.

He calls my name once more before the metal door slams shut, and my stomach twists. Then the banging starts. I can hear Mark's voice shouting from outside, but the metal door muffles it.

A sob jerks my body, and I wipe the makeup away with my tears. I rub the cloths over my shoulders, over my breasts again and again until the paint is gone. Stepping across the room, I pick up my dressing gown and a plastic knife I took from the breakfast table earlier this week.

It has a sharp point, and if worse comes to worse, if the drugs don't work, maybe I'll be strong enough to do some damage with it. Going to the coat hanging on the back of my chair, I slide my hand to the pocket and remove the small glass vial of bright white powder.

Guy waits in the passage, and when I emerge, his eyes travel the length of my body under his furrowed brow.

"Open it," he orders.

With trembling fingers, I unfasten the button in the center of my chest and open it to reveal my mostly nude body still wrapped in the network of glittering chains from the show.

"*Enchanté*," he says, taking my hand. "This way, Dark Angel."

I follow him down the hall, away from the noise of backstage. We don't go where I expected—down the narrow stairway that leads to the small rooms in the back. Instead we turn right and descend a different stairway to the trap room beneath the stage.

Our heels click on the concrete floor as we cross the large, open area and then go through another door and then another into a small sitting room lined in black wallpaper, embossed with a black velvet floral design.

Two chairs stand before a table, which has an ornate Tiffany lamp in the center, but we don't stop. He hastens me into another, larger room and closes the door behind us. All the walls are lined in the same embossed fabric, this time in deep red, and in one corner is a red velvet chaise lounge.

In the center of the room, a smaller table stands between two red velvet armchairs. Enormous mirrors hang on every wall, and the fireplace mantle is decorated with stained-glass lamps and small candles.

More fear. I've never seen this place before, and it feels very far from the theater and any help that might be back there for me.

"Hungry?" He lifts a plate of tiny cakes from the table.

The light glints off his pinky ring, and I take one. Eating is the furthest thing from my mind, but I need to stall and watch for any chance to slip the powder into whatever he drinks.

"Where are we?" I ask.

"My private suite."

He walks around behind me, sliding my hair back and sniffing my neck. Chills fly down my arms, and with one rough move, he turns me to face him and rips my robe open, sending the button flying.

A little cry comes from my throat as he pulls it off one shoulder. I've got to get that vial out of my pocket... but where will I put it? I'm doing my best to stay on my feet. Only my costume is beneath this robe, which means I'm all but nude.

I'll be weaponless. He'll be able to do what he wants, but a light tap at the door interrupts us.

"What?" Guy shouts, and Roland enters, carrying a crystal decanter on a tray with two tumblers.

"Ah, my first little conquest." Guy steps back and his voice makes my skin crawl. "Such a pretty little ass."

Roland's smile is tight, and a wave of nausea passes through my stomach as I understand the meaning of his words.

Roland's face is a mask of casual indifference. "Sazerac," he says, placing the tray on the smaller table.

"You know I prefer Chartreuse," Guy snaps.

"Chartreuse isn't as popular, I'm afraid, and it's hard to keep fresh when so few drink it. This should work." Roland's eyes meet mine briefly as he turns and walks back to the door.

"Sure you won't stay?" Guy calls after him. "I always enjoy a *ménage*."

I'm going to be sick, but Roland only pauses and glances at him. "I'm far too old for you now." Then he disappears through the door.

"Arrogant little faggot," Guy mutters, walking to the table.

My eyes fill with tears, and I'm fighting to keep it together. Roland brought me what I need. He's helping me again the only way he can. I'll deal with the onslaught of understanding when I'm out of danger.

Fucking get it together, Lara…

Guy removes his red velvet blazer and drapes it on one of the chairs. His trousers are black, as is his shirt. His skin is pale and he lifts the decanter, pouring the amber liquid into two short glasses holding thin lemon rinds. He hands one to me and lifts his to the light.

"He knows I hate this shit," he says. "But we'll sample it anyway."

"I don't drink—"

"You will tonight," he cuts me off.

He clinks our glasses, and I'm sure my chance is gone. My heart sinks, but a little bell sounds in the small room.

"God dammit," he shouts, slamming his small glass on the table without taking a sip.

He digs in his coat pocket and pulls out a slim black phone.

"What the fuck?" He turns his back, and I've got seconds, less than seconds to do what I need to do.

My hands shake, but I step in front of the small table and turn the vial of powder upside down, emptying it into his glass. *Please let it dissolve fast,* I silently pray as a hand clamps on my shoulder, spinning me around.

"What are you doing?" He looks me up and down, but I've dropped the vial and covered it with my foot.

"I-I thought you'd want privacy," I manage to answer.

"Take your glass."

I lift the small crystal and he clinks his against mine. I watch as he takes a sip. I follow suit and my nose wrinkles as the sharp, burning flavor of whiskey covers my tongue.

I go to the fireplace repeating my silent prayer over and over in my mind. "What do I do?"

He follows me, taking another sip. "We've got all night to find out."

I cringe and take another, longer drink, draining my glass. Then I gaze at the crackling fire, thinking of another room somewhere far away from here, where a man I love lives.

"I don't know much."

He looks me up and down. "That's the point."

Then he turns and takes one of the little cakes from the tray. "Open your mouth."

A cold chill passes over me. He's in front of me, glaring down with sinister green eyes. My lips part, and I open my mouth. Without ceremony, he shoves the petit four inside, smearing icing on my lips.

I whimper, and light hits his eyes as he watches his hand, his fingers moving down my jaw, smearing the bits on my neck.

"Not quite enough," he muses.

He moves away for another cake, and I try to distract him. "How long have you been back?"

"Long enough to find the little morsel you've been hiding in your room. She's very beautiful."

My chest tightens at that backfire, and I steel myself. "She's not for you."

He quickly crosses to where I stand. "Everything is for me if I want it."

I know I should be afraid, but my muscles feel weak. My feelings are drifting like the night on the roof when I shot my champagne. He pours us both more Sazerac, and I lift my glass draining it quickly. Maybe I can drown the memories of this night before they happen. The less I remember, the better.

"It's the only thing that keeps this place open." He stares at his glass a little too long, and my hope is restored. *Is it working?* "I should've shut this place down years ago."

"Why close something that's making money?"

"I'm not interested in owning a theater. Or playing pimp to a gaggle of used-up dancer-whores. If it weren't for you and that little girl, they could die in the streets."

I wince, but my numbness intensifies until my lids feel heavy. I step away from him and go to one of the velvet armchairs, wondering if I'll even make it to sit before I collapse. My fingers fumble for the chair, but I drop to my hands and knees on the floor.

"Yes." Guy comes closer. "That's a position I like."

A thud on the carpet behind me makes me look over my shoulder. He's at my ass, and his hands fumble clumsily at his waist. "This will be painful at first, but don't fight me. If you fight me, I'll be sure it hurts."

He's saying the words as if to reassure me, but I can tell. He wants me to fight. He wants to hurt me.

I no longer seem to care. My emotions are gone as his hands rip the thong aside. His nails scratch the skin of my thighs as he moves my legs apart. I'm exposed, and I feel him touching my body. I know what's coming, but I close my eyes and slip away…

CHAPTER 20

"Someday you won't remember this pain…"

Mark

"Lara!" My fists slam against the metal door again and again until I'm sure my bones will break.

My voice is hoarse.

My knuckles are bleeding, but I feel no pain.

Adrenaline is driving me now.

I'm on my knees at the back door, and this place is like a fucking vault for how sealed tight it is. I shoved my fists through the glass windows, but I couldn't remove the bars covering them.

She's in there.

That fucker has her.

I'm locked out here in the cold rain, yelling and beating against this door as my insides crumble to dust.

All my promises.

All the times I told her I'd protect her.

When she needs me the most, I fail her.

I can't take it. I push off my knees and look to the lot. The Towncar is parked in its usual spot, and I check my pockets for the keys. Nothing.

I go to the gleaming navy car and hit the glass window with my fists. It doesn't budge.

Stepping back, I look for anything to break the glass. I'll hotwire it and drive it through the brick wall then I'll find her. I know all the hiding places in this fucking hellhole.

My eyes light on a broken red brick at the chain link fence, and I hustle to where it lies and snatch it up. I'm running back to the car as fast as I can, the brick raised, ready to smash into it with all my strength when a voice grabs my attention.

"Mark! Come in! Come now!" Roland stands at the door, holding it open.

"What the fuck?" The brick slips from my fingers, and I pivot, running to the steps and pushing him out of the way as I fly up the hallway.

"Stop," he yells. "She's in her room. This way!"

"What?" I freeze and turn, heading back to the small room I passed in my haste to get to that fucking basement.

We meet at the door, and I burst in to see her lying curled in the fetal position, unconscious.

"What did you do to her?" My voice is a hoarse growl from twenty minutes of screaming in the rain.

I grab that fucking pianist by the lapels of his black coat and jerk him to me.

"Let me go!" His black eyes flash, and his expression is as enraged as mine. "I fucking saved her!"

"You let him take her!" I shake him hard. "You shoved me outside and let him take her!"

"I needed time." His eyes squeeze shut, and he grips my fists. "I was there almost immediately."

Releasing him, I drop to my knees at her bedside. Her face is placid, and I run my eyes over her body wrapped in that red robe. I don't see any signs of injury, but I can't see her skin. Roland braces a hand on her dressing table as he catches his breath.

Anguish squeezes my chest, breaking my voice. "Did he hurt her?"

He stands over me a moment, then assesses my hand on Lara's head. "I didn't see any signs of that. They were both out cold in ten minutes."

He leaves the room, and I continue smoothing her hair away from her face. "You'll be okay," I whisper. "I won't let them hurt you."

Roland returns and places a bowl and ace bandages on the bed beside me. I keep one hand on her head as he doctors my wounds. "What made them pass out?"

"Rohypnol." He places a gauze pad over the worst of my cuts. "Hold this."

My hand leaves Lara's head long enough for him to wrap it. "The date rape drug," I muse.

"Works fast, and they're out for six hours." His lips are pressed into a thin line as he washes the blood off my knuckles. It stings, but I don't care.

"Where did you get it?"

"Not important. I slipped it into the Sazerac and hoped Lara would understand to drink it."

He finishes wrapping me up. "Thanks," I say, standing. "I'm taking her to my place. It's only a few blocks away. I'm not leaving her here."

I lift her into my arms, and he digs a set of keys out of his pants pocket.

"I'll drive."

* * *

Lara

Comfort, clean fresh air, bright whiteness. Strong arms wrapped tightly around my waist, and a deep sense of safety. Surfacing through the mist, I'm greeted by so many pleasant sensations, I think I must've died and am waking up in heaven.

But as I continue to regain consciousness, I realize actual arms are around me.

I open my eyes, and I'm in a bright room with large windows. I'm lying in a bed with another person behind me, holding me close against him. One breath and I know who it is. If this is a dream, I don't want to wake up. Still, I know I must.

I pull forward and into a sitting position as his blue eyes blink open. He smiles and warmth tightens my stomach.

"What happened?" I look around the huge space. "How did I get here?"

He sits up beside me and kisses the top of my shoulder. "Roland helped me bring you here. To keep you safe."

I struggle to remember last night, but nothing comes. It's like a blank space in my timeline. No fear, no pain. Nothing.

I'm not sure if I should be afraid or relieved.

I look down at Mark's bandaged hands. "You're injured again?" I take one in mine.

He shrugs. "It's nothing. Just some broken glass."

Shaking my head, I look at him for a second and then slide out of the bed, walking toward the large windows opposite us. I'm wearing a thin white tee I assume is his. It's thin enough that my dark nipples are visible through the fabric, and while it's ridiculous, considering how many times he's seen me naked, I want to be covered.

One of Mark's dress shirts hangs on a chair nearby. I grab it and slip it over me.

"I don't remember anything." My head is groggy, and I'm tired. Then a chill grips me.

"Did he... did I—"

"Roland said it didn't look like anything had happened."

I hug my body in relief. "I think he's right." I don't feel like I was assaulted.

When I turn, Mark is lying on his side, gazing at me. He smiles, and I feel self-conscious. I push my hair behind my ear and look down.

"How long have I been here?"

"Eight hours."

I glance around the sparsely furnished apartment. "Where are my clothes?"

"You only had the robe. It's there."

I follow his point and see my velvet dressing gown draped over another wooden chair.

"Is there a bathroom?" We're in one large room with a nice wall of windows overlooking the river, but there's nothing else. No closet, no kitchen. Just the single space.

"It's downstairs. When Terrence left, I brought a bed up here and started sleeping in the loft. It's got a better view." He slides to the edge of the double bed and swings his legs off to stand. "I'll escort you down."

He's only wearing boxer briefs, and my stomach tightens. I'm certain I shouldn't respond to him the way I do. Not after last night. But it's hard not to remember the feel of his muscular body against mine.

"I can wait. I need to check on Molly anyway."

I step toward my robe, but Mark catches me and pulls me to him. "Roland said to tell you she's safe, not to worry. And he said for you to stay here with me until he comes to get you."

I watch his lips, thinking how nice it is not to remember anything. How nice it would be to pretend the danger is behind us. I breathe deeply, fighting the urges humming under my skin. The desire to give in and embrace him back, to stay here and act like the only thing in the world is us in this room.

"It's probably not the best idea," I say.

"You were just fine with it a few minutes ago."

"I was unconscious."

"I won't tell anyone you woke up."

His hands gently slide to my waist, and I rest my palms against his warm skin.

"Has it started for you? Are they trying to... make you do things for money?"

"No. Last night was something different."

"Why are you so afraid, then? Why did Roland want me to tell you nothing had happened if he wasn't trying to—"

"I can't explain it all now. It's something I said I would do. But no one's forcing me."

"What did you say you'd do?" His face is so full of concern, so ready to understand, but I don't want to talk about it.

"It seems I didn't do anything." I step out of his embrace, toward the chair that holds my dressing gown, but he catches me by the waist.

"Don't keep me out, Lara. Let me help you."

I can't answer, and after a moment of silence, he exhales and gives my hand a little pull.

"As long as you're here, you should come back to bed. Roland could be a while, and it's chilly this morning."

I allow the dress shirt to slip off my shoulders, leaving me in only his white tee. "I suppose we ought to keep warm."

We crawl into the blankets, and I snuggle close to him. His arms go around me, and I rest my head on his bare chest, listening to his heartbeat, his breath swirling in and out. It's the most soothing thing I've ever felt, pulses of comfort with every soft beat.

He rolls me onto my back and studies my face. "You had a bad night. I'd like to comfort you, but if you'd rather sleep, I'll understand."

I watch his full lips as he speaks. "My head is fuzzy, but I'm not afraid... or hurt."

"May I kiss you?"

I slip my hand up to his cheek and guide our lips together. They barely touch when that familiar heat races from my stomach to the arches of my feet. His tongue finds mine, and my hands begin exploring everything under the blankets.

I trace the lines across his back and shoulders, and he quickly slides the thin tee up my sides and over my head. We both sigh as our bare chests press together, and his mouth covers mine.

His tongue dips once into my mouth before his lips move to my jaw, my neck. I close my eyes as waves of pleasure ripple through my stomach. His mouth is on my tight nipple, pulling, licking. He gives it a suck before kissing his way to the other side.

"Mark," I whisper as he repeats the process, sending little sparks to my core, clenching my inner muscles.

His teeth graze my nipple, and a moan slips from my throat. A groan rumbles from his as he kisses my ribs, my waist, making his way lower.

"I've missed you so much," he says against my stomach, and my toes curl.

He hooks a finger in my panties and pulls them away with one swift tug.

"Oh, God!" My back arches off the bed as his expert tongue finds my clit and begins to circle.

Circles, kisses, sucks and strokes. He's eager,

hungry, and I'm gripping the sheets, gripping his hair, writhing and crying out in ecstasy. Sparkles of pleasure shudder through my legs, and he gives my pussy one more kiss before he slides up quickly and covers my mouth with his.

My taste is on his tongue as it curls with mine. He spreads my thighs, and I feel that delicious pressure, the sizzling anticipation just before he pushes in with one deep thrust.

"Yes," we both groan together.

He's inside me so deep, filling and stretching me all the way to my core. Once seated, he stills, both arms beside me, the weight of his body holding me down. Our eyes meet, and his burn with so much emotion. I'm certain mine reflect the same passion, the same deep need, the same burning hunger.

Then he starts to move.

My back arches. I lift my knees, and my eyes close. My mouth opens as his thickness moves me, hitting my clit and igniting my second orgasm.

My face is buried in his neck, and I clutch his shoulders, holding on as the sparks of pleasure tingle through my limbs.

"Mark," I cry. "Don't stop."

His mouth covers mine, and we kiss, long and savoring. Our mouths move again and again in time with our hips. We're grasping and holding, hungry and consuming. He pulls back, and I follow. I move to the side, and he chases me.

Instinct takes over as my orgasm crests. My legs are tight around him, and I break, arching and moaning, feeling the spasms rippling through my insides.

"Oh, fuck," he gasps, and he's suddenly out of me.

I feel his heavy erection on my waist, and hot liquid shoots over my stomach again and again with every groan.

His forehead is against my shoulder, and he reaches down to tug his cock. My hand follows, and I mimic his movements, wanting to give him pleasure like he's given me.

"Fuck." It's a shuddered whisper as I take over, wrapping my fingers around his thick shaft and gently pulling rhythmically, over and over.

I feel another pulse in my hand, another touch of heat on my stomach, and he groans so deeply.

"Lara," he whispers, and I feel a shiver move through his body. "That's so good."

My pumping slows, and I kiss his sweaty cheek. I run my tongue along his jaw, wanting his salt in my mouth. I want all of him, even his come on my body.

A guilty smile is in his eyes when he lifts his head. "I didn't have a condom."

"You pulled out," I say, grinning back. "Now I'm a mess."

He leans away and glances down. "A beautiful mess."

And in a flash he's off me, out of the bed and grabbing the tee I was wearing. "Mark!" I shriek. "It's freezing."

The shirt is on my stomach, and he cleans me up fast, bundling the cotton material and dropping it on the floor before scooting in behind me again, his strong arms around my waist.

"I'll warm you up." His mouth is at my ear, and his beard scuffs my neck.

"Tickles!" I cry and lean forward, but he chases me, kissing the top of my shoulder blade and doing a little growly laugh.

I laugh, too, and his warmth soothes my insides. I straighten until my back is firm against his chest. His arms are solid, holding me close. My eyes start to close, and I allow my body to relax in his embrace.

He kisses my head, and the last thing I hear before I sleep is his deep voice saying, "Sleep, Angel."

* * *

Mark

Lara is in my arms.

She's in my bed, safe beside me.

Her eyes are closed, and I listen to the sweet whisper of her breath gently gliding in and out. I feel the movement of her chest under my arm.

I never want to let her go.

My face is buried in her silky hair, and her scent of little flowers surrounds me. It's fresh and hopeful. I want to tell her about my plans, the money I've earned, and my goals for January.

Only I'm not waiting for January anymore. She'll stay with me here from now on, and I'll escort her to and from that fucking theater if she even wants to continue with the show.

I expect I'm fired. Can you attack your boss's brother and still have a job?

It changes my plan slightly, but I still have money in the bank.

And I still love her.

I love her.

The words enter my mind unbidden, and for a moment I let them stay there, take root. Lowering my chin, I place my lips against her skin and think of all the ways I love this woman. I love her laughter and her strength. I love her beauty and her talent. I love how she loves the same things as me, and even her devotion to Molly, as much as it complicates her life, I love that she won't break her promise.

Kissing her higher, I slip my tongue out and taste her skin. It's soft and clean, and she exhales a little sigh. She starts to wake, moving her ass right against my cock, which brings that member to life.

From my position, I see her eyes blink open, and I grin. Her gaze lowers to my fist at her breast, and she pulls my hand to her lips, placing small kisses on my fingers just above my bandage.

I kiss her neck, moving into the back of her hair, and she makes a little noise.

Add those little noises to the list of things I love.

She opens my palm and kisses it before placing it on her breast. Rocking her hips, she massages my erection with her ass, and it's enough of an invitation for me.

I reach down to open her thighs, positioning my tip at her tight little core before sliding in to the hilt.

"Oh, fuck," I hiss at finding her so wet and ready.

"Mark," she whispers, arching her back as my pace quickens.

Her hands cover mine on her soft breasts, and I'm not slowing down.

My head is feverish, and a deep and primal need in me drives my thirst for more. One hand leaves mine, and she's circling her clit. Her inner muscles contract rhythmically, and it's more than I can take. My eyes squeeze tightly shut.

Just a little bit more.

"Mark!" she gasps, and fuck me.

I pull out quick as streams of come trail down her ass. A slim hand moves around and grips my pulsing cock, massaging and milking as I rest my head on her shoulder, riding out the blinding orgasm radiating through my ass and legs.

We gradually slow, and I pull her back against my chest again. For the space of several heartbeats, I only hold her, feeling her small body mold into mine. She's everything. We're everything together.

"I've got to get more condoms," I whisper.

She's giggling, and I move back, allowing her to face me. The light in her blue eyes is irresistible. I lean down to cover her mouth with mine, kissing her long and slow, curling my tongue with hers.

Slim arms wrap around my neck, and our chests press together. Warmth flows from me to her, healing the wounds, binding us together.

Leaning back, I gaze deep into her blue eyes. "I'm glad you can smile. I only want you to be happy."

Her brow pulls, and she drops her gaze to my lips. "It's hard to be sad when I'm here in your arms. We can almost pretend—"

"No more pretending. I've saved almost ten thousand dollars. We can live here for free."

Her eyes go wide. "Ten thousand! But… but how?"

Clearing my throat, I don't want to tell her. I don't want her to know how deeply involved I am with Gavin's illegal activities. Even more, I don't want it to seem like I blame her for anything, from my work to my doing without.

"I've been saving. Since I'm watching the place for Terrence, he stopped charging me rent."

"For how long?"

"Until he comes back in January… but by then, I hope we'll have a place—"

"We..." She's thinking, processing everything I've said. "Molly too..." It's barely a whisper.

"Molly too."

She moves into my arms again, resting her cheek against my chest and holding it there, tightening her arms around my waist and holding her body to mine.

"Can we really be free of that place?"

"Do you want to go back?"

"I have to go back. I have to get Molly and our things... we don't have much, but even replacing what little we have would add up."

My hand is in her hair, smoothing it down, holding her neck, her shoulders.

"I don't want you to be alone there. I'll go with you."

"Didn't you say Roland was coming to get me?" She leans back to study my face.

"He is, but I don't trust him."

Her face relaxes. "I do. Don't worry."

"I'm always going to worry. Until the day you're with me for good."

Blinking quickly she nods. She stretches up to kiss me lightly before rising to a sitting position. She leaves the bed, taking the tee from last night and using it to clean her backside. She takes the dressing gown off the chair and slowly pulls it over her body, fastening it at her waist.

"It's time."

* * *

Lara

My head is still thick despite having slept most of the day, but I have to get back to collect Molly and our few belongings. Mark kisses me as I pull the dark topcoat Roland brought for me over my shoulders.

"Don't be afraid," Mark says. "I'll shower and change and be with you in fifteen minutes or less. Roland promises he'll look out for you until I come."

The sky is growing dark, and I guess it's getting close to the start of the show. I'm not planning to perform tonight, if ever again.

After a few moments of silent walking, I notice Roland's watching me.

"What?"

"I've been waiting for you to ask how I did it," he says.

"Mark said you roofied us."

He nods. "Gavin gave it to me, along with the Sazerac. You both passed out—it looked like at about the same time. Guy was in the process of undressing, so that was a fun sight."

I shake my head, not wanting to hear this. "Thank you," I say quietly, thinking of the mixture I poured in his glass.

"I told you to trust me."

"Did anything else happen to him? Is he sick?"

"I don't think so." Roland looks straight ahead, but his hand goes to his pocket. "Worried about this?"

He holds up the small glass vial, and my lip goes between my teeth. "Did it work?"

"What was it?"

We're less than a block from the theater, and I decide to confess. "I went back and bought heroin laced with fentanyl. I poured it in his drink. I hoped it would kill him."

His jaw clenches, and I watch his face, waiting for what he's going to say. He only exhales deeply. "It was a valiant effort, if life-threatening and completely stupid."

I jerk his arm. "I had to do something!"

"Heroin doesn't dissolve in liquid. And even if it did, by the time it finally got through his stomach, it might make him lightheaded. Today."

My shoulders fall. "It was all for nothing."

"I'm afraid he'd have done all he wanted with you while you were waiting for him to keel over."

The theater yawns before us, and I shrink back, fear tightening my throat. "I can't go in there," I whisper.

Forget our shit. They can have it. Not my mother's pen, not even my need to protect Molly is stronger than this fear. Standing in front of the looming edifice all the memories I didn't know I had come flooding back. I remember his eyes, the way he ripped at my clothes, the things he said.

Roland steps in front of me and grips my arms. "Gavin has him under control. He's been slipping him a sedative all day, telling him he has a cold."

"And it's working?"

"It's working for now." His voice is grim, and my body trembles violently. "Come on." His arm goes around my shoulder, and he leads me to the back entrance where I see large dents in the door, and the small windows at the ground are smashed.

"What happened?"

"Mark was determined to get in last night."

My stomach drops, and I can't walk anymore. My emotions overwhelm me, and of all the things I've forgotten, the sound of his beating on the door, his shouts, him calling my name—all of what happened before floods my mind.

"I love him," I whisper as a hot tear falls on my cheek.

Roland pulls me into a hug, his hand on the back of my head. I feel his lips press to my temple. "I know."

My insides are raw as we enter the back door. I follow my old friend down the corridor, and when we turn the corner, I let out a little cry. Gavin is standing in my dressing room. His face is red. Perspiration coats his upper lip.

"Can you perform tonight?" he asks, running his eyes over my body. "Tanya can't do it."

Roland releases me at once. "What's happening?"

"See for yourself."

Roland takes off down the hall, leaving me alone, facing the man behind this. The one who callously gave away Molly then saved me when I tried to take her place. My tattered emotions don't know where to start.

"Can you do it?" Gavin repeats, watching me. I can tell he's doing his best to maintain an air of control.

"Where's Molly?"

"I haven't seen her since yesterday."

"Evie was supposed to bring her back here today." Roland didn't tell me if she knew what happened. I look around for my phone, but I have no idea where I left it. Perhaps it's in the topcoat I wore to the voodoo shop.

"I still don't see why she's so important." He steps to the door.

"Thank you," I cut him off, anger flaring at his words. "For the drugs."

"I don't know what you mean." He's pretending not to know, but I don't care to question why. "I need you to take Tanya's place. Will you do it?"

"Why should I?"

"You'll be the star." His eyes flicker to the dressing table. "It's what you always wanted."

I no longer care about being the star in hell, but walking slowly to the small table, I lift the brass pen still sitting on top. He told me to be careful with my valuables. He recognized this piece as belonging to my mother. How much loyalty do I owe to him?

He did stop what was happening last night...

The noise of footsteps jogging up the passage interrupts us, and when I look up, Mark stands in the doorway. My fears diminish, and my eyes heat. The mere presence of him in this room gives me the strength I need.

"Where the fuck have you been?" Gavin shouts at him. "I'm out of Narcan. I need you to get more fast." He holds out a brass clip of cash.

My eyes are still on Mark's, and he pushes past Gavin's hand.

"Are you okay?" Mark's voice is warm, and he puts both hands on my waist. "Have you found her?"

"I think she's still with Evie," my voice is soft. "I need to find my phone."

He pulls it out of his pocket and hands it to me. I step forward and wrap my arm around his waist, my head against his chest.

"Well?" Gavin's voice is insistent. "What's it going to be?"

Roland's back in the room. "Where's the—"

"Mark's just leaving to get more." He extends his hand again, the brass clip tucked inside.

"You'll have to take my car." He gives Mark the keys.

"Lara?" Mark is waiting, and I nod.

"Go. Help her if you can. I'll do this one last time."

"I'll be back before the climb." With one last hand squeeze, he's gone.

"I don't know any of her dances." My eyes go to Roland's.

"We can do the new songs," he says. "You can do it like a concert. Wear her costumes."

"She lost so much weight, I don't know if they'll fit me."

"Work out the details," Gavin snaps. "I'll take care of the front."

CHAPTER 21

"I broke my own heart loving you."

Mark

Anxiety twists in my gut as I race through the wet streets.

Tanya was on the floor of her dressing room when I left. Rosa had given her one dose, but it wasn't working. She told me to get two more. My chest is heavy with the idea Tanya's life is in my hands, but truthfully, my main focus is Lara's safety.

Roland says Guy is sedated, and Lara will be onstage performing. She should be safe while I make this short trip, but fuck it. I don't like her there alone.

Every muscle in my body is tense, and pain radiates through my fists when I tighten them on the wheel of Roland's Fiat. I should probably have my wrists wrapped as well as my hands. I beat on that metal door a good fifteen minutes last night before breaking the glass.

The light turns, and I punch the accelerator. The rain has stopped, but the streets are still wet, and the tires skid on the slippery asphalt. A quick glance at the clock tells me eight minutes have passed.

I throw it in park when I reach the store and push my way to the pharmacy counter. A man with gray streaks in his dark hair sees me and moves quickly, bagging the syringes and handing them over as I pass him three hundred dollars. We don't even bother with receipts. He knows the look in my eyes.

I'm in the car racing back to the theater in less than two minutes. Skidding into the parking lot, I throw the door shut and sprint up the back steps and down the narrow hallway to the dressing rooms.

"Give it to me," Rosa says, and I pass her the bag.

She pulls out the first box and assembles the syringe. Her hands tremble, but she moves slowly, calmly inserting the glass tube into the plastic syringe.

"Stay with me," she murmurs as she works, and I see red handprints on Tanya's face from where it appears Rosa slapped her, trying to keep her conscious.

Tanya's red hair is frizzled around her face, and her skin is sallow. Her cheeks are sunken, and she looks like she weighs ninety pounds. She's so small, she's like an abandoned doll, left out in the rain.

It appears Rosa has what she needs, and I leave them in the dressing room hustling to the backstage area so I can be ready for the finale. I've missed most of the show, but from the sounds of the audience, Lara's killing. In my heart, I hope she can enjoy it, but in my head I know she's as anxious as I am about being here.

Making my way through the bodies, I accidentally bump into a woman standing in the wings. "Oh, I'm sorry," I say, catching her by the waist.

She's fully clothed, which means she isn't performing, and when she turns, I recognize her face. "You're Mark?" Her eyes are bright and she smiles. "I'm Evie. We met in the square a while back."

"Evie," I repeat. "You have Molly."

That makes her laugh. "I had Molly. I left her in their room."

As she speaks, I scan the backstage area frantically. Molly usually waits in the wings with the dancers, watching as Lara performs. I don't see her, and I jog back toward the dressing room. I'm just at the door when the music changes. It's time for the finale. I promised Lara, but I hesitate. She'd want to know Molly is safe.

I see one of the new guys leaning against a set piece watching the show. He's smaller than I am, and his eyes are fixed on the topless dancers.

I grab him by the throat and push him up against the wall. "What's your name?"

"Hey!" His eyes bug out, and he grabs at my fist while his feet dangle around my shins. "J-Jeffrey. My name's Jeff."

My fists throb, and I release him. He falls back, gasping and holding his neck. "Look at me," His eyes snap up. They're filled with fear, which is a good thing. "I need you to get to the top of that ladder, to the catwalk. You hold the safety rope as she descends."

His eyes follow where I'm pointing and down, and he nods quickly. "I've seen her do it."

My hand is on his throat again, and I back him against the wall. "If she falls, you die. If you look at her body, you die. If you touch her body, you die. Understand?"

Sounds like my new motto. His hands are on my wrist.

"I'll be back. Now get up there." I shove him toward the ladder and head through the door to the backstage area.

Running up the passage, I reach Lara's dressing room. Sliding to a stop, I go inside, looking all around. I see the dressing gown, the pen, a small bag, Lara's phone with a text on the face…

We're here, the text from Evie reads.

No signs of Molly.

My pulse ticks higher, and I'm out the door again, headed for the stage with a bad feeling in my stomach. Pushing through the door, I make the entire run through the wings on both sides, catching dancers and asking if they've seen Molly.

Nothing.

All the members of that sick sex club are back, and Lara's bargain is in my head. She offered herself in exchange for what? Gavin sent me to buy Narcan, so who does he have guarding the basement?

Slamming into the passage, I sprint to the basement stairs. Taking the steps two at a time, I reach the bottom and race across the large empty trap room with only my phone for a light. Skidding to a stop at the door leading to the hidden rooms, I grab the handle only to find it locked.

I press my ear to it, but my thudding pulse and rapid breathing are louder than what's happening inside. When I was here the last time, I could hear music. I could hear the occasional fake orgasm. Now all I hear is silence.

Nobody's here.

Rolling my back to the door, I look up at the stage floor above. The show is over. I have to get to Lara.

* * *

Lara

My dream is coming true, and I'm terrified.

Gavin renamed the show "Bright Angel," and Roland decided my performance should be me walking around the stage singing all the new songs while my wardrobe changes leave me wearing less and less.

I start with my former innocent angel outfit of pink feathers covering my breasts and large wings on my shoulders. From there it progresses until the finale, where I sashay around the stage, breasts fully exposed and wearing only a thong. A triangle of silk keeps me from being totally nude.

It's a mixture of my dream come true combined with terror of being in the spotlight and not being able to find Molly. The curtain falls, and I don't even care about the applause. The fear is back full force, and I hurry to my dressing room.

Pushing through the door, a little cry escapes my lips. Tears blur my vision, but I slam the door, pulling my robe over my body before going to the bed where she lies, curled in a ball and shaking.

"Molly?" My voice wavers. Her lips are cracked and bleeding. "What happened? Are you hurt?"

Her eyes are glazed, but looking down, I see blood on her dress. She's wearing a white sweater dress with leggings, but the leggings are ripped. Large holes are in the front of her thighs and around the back.

The hem of the sweater is dirty with what looks like rust stains, but the closer I look, I realize it's blood on her skin. Flaky, dry white patches are on her thighs.

"Oh, God, no!" I shriek, covering her with my body.

She shakes harder, but she doesn't speak to me. I'm not sure if it's because she's been drugged or if she has mentally retreated.

Please let her have been drugged. I don't want her to remember this.

Suddenly she starts to cough. She coughs so much, her face turns red, and she begins to gag. I'm off her at once, running for the small trash bin for her to puke in. She vomits, but only bile comes up. I hold her hair, rubbing circles on her back.

"It's okay," I whisper. "I'm going to fix this."

Tears are on my cheeks, but rage twists in my belly.

I jump to my feet, throwing my robe on a chair and grabbing jeans and a long-sleeved shirt. I take a blanket and wrap Molly in a tight cocoon on the bed. Snatching up my phone, I send Evie a text.

Come to my dressing room now.

"Stay here. I'll be back," I whisper, smoothing her russet hair.

Fury drives me down the hallway to that basement room I remember from last night. At the top of the stairs is a narrow red box I've never given much thought. Grabbing the metal rod, I break the glass and yank out the small axe inside.

I charge down the steps and cross the trap room, determination driving me. Roland said they'd been sedating that bastard all day. I plan to find him and cut his dick off.

What I don't expect is to be met at the door by an enormous bouncer. "The girls come in from the other side," he growls, crossing his massive arms.

"Who are you?" I ask, holding my weapon behind my leg.

"Who are you?" he growls back.

This guy is huge. He's at least six-four, and his arms are like concrete pillars.

"I'm here to see Guy," I say, forcing authority into my voice.

"Nobody gets in this way without a card."

My grip tightens on the handle of the axe, and I realize I haven't thought this through. Taking a step back, I slam into another body, and just as I spin around, my wrist is caught in an iron-like grip.

"Let go!" I scream when I recognize Guy smiling down at me.

"This is a pleasant surprise. Come to finish what we started?"

"I came to finish you," I shout, jerking my arm, trying to get it out of his grip.

"Devin, take this."

The massive bouncer easily rips the axe out of my hand and tosses it into the darkness where it clatters against the concrete floor far away from us.

"We're not to be disturbed," he tells the man as he holds up a gold business card.

Devin steps to the side, opening the door for us to pass through.

"No!" I shout, falling back. "This is a mistake!"

We're through the door, and I see the larger room has been set up for a party. Finger foods sit on small plates with several champagne glasses scattered about. Guy doesn't stop, he continues down the shorter passage to the room we were in last night.

Throwing me ahead of him, he closes the door behind him and locks it.

"Let me go," I shout. "I said I'd do this to protect her, and you violated that agreement. You hurt her, and you're—"

He crosses the room to speak directly in my face. "I told you everything is mine. I took what was mine, and now I'll take you."

My voice gurgles as his hand clamps around my throat. Heat floods my face, and my eyes burn.

"That's right," he says in a soothing tone.

I gag and claw at his hand, but his grip doesn't loosen. I twist and beat his forearm, but he's too strong. I'm losing consciousness. My hands fall weakly at my sides.

"That's better," he continues, loosening his grip just as I'm about to pass out.

I gasp and roll to my side on the small sofa, coughing and covering my neck. I can't speak. My eyes are blurry and my knees weak. It takes several minutes for me to gather my strength, and he stands over me watching the entire time.

"Poor thing. Now look what you made me do," he says, holding what looks like a glass of water. "Have some water."

My eyes are on his, but I take it with trembling hands. He watches as I sniff it, but I don't smell anything.

"Are you afraid to drink it? You think I don't want you to fight me?"

I take a tiny sip, holding it in my mouth. It tastes like water, so I drink a little more. It's salty, and it helps my throat.

He walks to the mantle and looks at his phone. "Take a few minutes to catch your breath."

The longer I sit, the heavier my eyes grow. My jaw feels slack, and my muscles are like jelly. "Liar." My words are slurred like I'm drunk. "Fucking liar. What was in that?"

My head is spinning, and I hold the arm of the couch to keep me steady.

"Take off your clothes," Guy orders, then he tosses a black sleep mask at me. "Put that on and get on your knees. I expect you to be ready when I get back."

"No." My head falls forward.

He grabs the top of my hair and jerks my head up, snarling. "Do what I say." He shoves my head back and roughly ties the mask over my eyes. Then he's gone.

I'm too weak to remove it, and slipping off the couch to my knees is actually a relief. My hands are on the tops of my thighs, and I feel buzzy. *Did Guy want me on my knees? I can't remember.*

A long time seems to pass before the door opens again. This time, the voice I hear is one I absolutely love.

"Lara?"

"Mark?" I turn my head in the direction of his voice, and he's on his knees beside me.

He pulls the mask off my face, and it takes me several blinks before his face comes into focus. When it does, I lean forward, holding his neck. "You're here."

His face contorts, and I don't understand why he's not happy to see me. "Why are you doing this?" he asks. "What's happening?"

Noises break out on the other side of the door. I hear men shouting and what sounds like muffled banging. Mark stands up quick as the door opens.

"Who the fuck are you?" A voice that makes me think of a wild animal snarls from the doorway.

"I'm taking her out of here." Mark's hands grip my arms, pulling me to my feet, but all at once, he's gone.

I look around and see he's on his hands and knees on the floor.

"Mark?" I drop down beside him, the good

feelings dissolving, but still just within reach.

"He's going to be a problem." Another man is in the room, and I look up just as the first voice answers.

"No, he's not. I'll take care of this fucker."

His leg flies back, and I scream as he kicks Mark in the chest. A sick *Oof!* comes from his throat, and he falls on his side.

"No!" I scream, terror cracking my drug-induced haze.

Mark staggers, trying to get to his feet, but the man kicks him again in the stomach. I can't stop screaming. The men keep kicking him. Blood is on his mouth.

"You want to be a hero?" the man shouts, kicking him again. "Heroes don't last long around here."

Blood drools from his mouth, and his head flops to the side.

"No..." My voice breaks, and I cover my eyes as the thuds of the men beating my love continue. "Stop, please!" I cry.

Mark's swollen eyes meet mine, and I feel the hot tears slick on my face. He tries to reach for me. I reach for him.

"Lara?" His voice breaks.

The big man kicks him in the head, and his body goes limp.

"Oh, God, no!" Snot covers my upper lip, and my cheeks are hot and wet.

With swollen eyes I watch them drag Mark out of the room. His face is black with bruises already forming and blood flows from his mouth, but he's not fighting. Sick fills my stomach as fear creeps in. *He's dead.*

"What is this?" Guy is back.

"Got ourselves a hero," Wolf-man taunts.

"Take that body away. You know what to do."

The men leave, dragging Mark away, and Guy comes to me. "My little angel, did that frighten you?"

His voice is strange, but the haze floods my brain again. The calm feelings are back. "Why did they do that?"

He wipes my face with something soft and pulls my sweater over my head. "Let's do this."

The mask is back, and I'm in darkness. He takes a handful of hair from my shoulder and jerks my head to the side as his lips press against my neck, hands fumbling with my jeans.

A startled cry flies from my throat, but my feelings are flat. He clutches my breast, squeezing it repeatedly. He's sucking my neck, and as he presses himself against me, I feel his erection hard on my leg.

I don't want this...

The thought passes through my mind completely detached from my body. It's like a strange beast is at my side groaning, pulling, and licking my skin. I try to slide away from him, but he grabs my waist, pushing me forward onto my hands and knees.

"Yes," he hisses, and he's at my backside again.

I feel him ripping the thong, pulling it away until I'm completely bare except for the mask. I want to curl into a ball, but his hand fists my hair, holding me up. I try to pull against his hold, and he only laughs, shoving me face-first into the carpet and gripping my arms behind me.

"Hurts!" I yell, but my voice is muffled in the pile.

He's holding me in position, and I feel the slip of fabric down my thighs. Fleshy hardness is against the skin of my ass. I brace myself, tensing every muscle as he forces his way into my body, like a knife cutting through paper.

Pain…

My eyes close behind the mask. The haze is right there, and I take its hand. I allow it to guide me deeper into the darkness, until I'm somewhere far away…

CHAPTER 22

"Tears travel to God when we can't speak."

Lara

When I open my eyes again, everything is pain.

I'm alone in my small bed. I try to move, but my body shakes as if my muscles are too weak to support me.

So I don't move.

I lie motionless, facing the wall.

My throat hurts from screaming and my stomach cramps. Light from the window above says it's afternoon.

The passage is unusually quiet, but I don't care.

Nothing matters now.

I don't remember much of last night, but two things flicker like slivers of a dream. Mark on the floor, blood covering his face, his lifeless body dragged from the room. A shudder of grief cramps in my chest. I open my mouth to say *No*, but nothing comes out as tears flood my eyes.

The second memory is a cruel green gaze that shoots terror through my veins. My entire body seizes, and I slam the door shut on that memory.

I never want to go back there.

Not ever.

Someone enters the room. It's a woman from the scent of her perfume, but I don't move as she walks to the bed and leans over me.

I hear her breathe and recognize her sigh.

Evie.

"Will you eat?" she whispers. She waits, but I don't move. "I told Roland you wouldn't sing tonight."

I'll never sing again.

"He begged to see you, but I told him to wait." The side of the bed dips as she sits beside me. Her hand goes to my arm and begins to rub. "He was a wreck when we finally got to you. Guy was gone or I swear Roland would've killed him with his bare hands."

She waits, but I don't speak.

"I've never seen Roland cry." Her voice is quiet.

"Molly," I manage to whisper. A sharp inhale twists the fear in my stomach. "Where's Molly?"

Evie's voice wavers when she answers. "She's going to be okay… She'll heal."

I turn my head into the pillow as the tears flow and my nose grows warm.

I failed.

Evie pats me and stands. "Just rest. Tomorrow you'll feel better."

I will never feel better.

Sleep must've come because when I open my eyes again, it's dark. No moon lights the night, and the only slice of bright in the darkness comes from the crack beneath the door. I have no idea where Molly is, but it's too hard to care about anything anymore.

My only feeling is pain.

And emptiness.

I haven't moved from my position facing the wall when I hear the door open slowly. Footsteps cross the space, and I feel the bed depress. A warm body snuggles in next to me.

Soft sobs shiver through her, and I allow myself to wonder how she feels. I don't move, waiting for her to sleep. A long time ago, I might have told her a story.

It all seems childish and foolish now.

Her small hand touches me in the darkness, and I stare at the wall.

Somewhere, something mattered. I just can't remember what it was.

* * *

The smell of coffee wakes me. I'm alone in the bed, and I slowly turn to face the door for the first time. Roland sits in the chair across from me, and when our eyes meet, he drops to his knees at my bedside.

"Will you eat?" he asks softly.

I struggle to sit up enough to take the mug from him. I cup it in both hands and sip, allowing the soothing warmth to travel through my body as my eyes close.

He watches me silently for a few moments before running his index finger down my arm. "I'm sorry I was too late," he whispers, his voice thick. "I'm so sorry, Lara."

His head drops onto the bed, and tears sting my eyes.

I don't want to cry.

I don't want him to think I blame him. He looks up, his eyes wet, and a knot forms in my throat. I blink and two salty drops fall.

He rises to slide his arms around me and presses his lips to my head. "I'm so sorry you were hurt. I'm so sorry I didn't save you."

My body shudders fighting tears, fighting ribbons of memory.

Heroes don't last long around here…

The voice echoes in my ears, and I know he would have failed if he'd tried.

Just like Mark.

My insides crumble, and I start to lose control. With all the failing strength left inside me, I push that door closed again. I can't face that memory. Not yet.

I won't come back from that pain.

We're quiet as he holds me. He's faint cigarette smoke mixed with warm coffee. After a few moments, he stands and takes a tissue from my dressing table. He touches his eyes and crumples it in his fist then he turns away from me.

"I was much younger than you when it happened to me."

My eyes fly to him, but he doesn't look at me. He looks past the mirror to some distant memory.

"I didn't dream of killing him. I dreamed of permanently disfiguring him."

I don't know how to answer.

"I thought that punishment would fit the crime," he continues. "But it was never possible, and eventually he moved on to another one."

He returns and touches my face. "I never thought it would happen to you. And I'll do whatever it takes to keep it from happening again."

My coffee is on the verge of coming back up.

It could happen again?

Fear grips my throat. For all I know, he could still be here, waiting. It doesn't matter what he's taken. He can come back for more…

I know he will.

"This came for you." Roland holds out a letter, and I recognize Freddie's handwriting.

I'd all but forgotten my old plan, my old safety net, and I watch as Roland places it on the bed beside me.

"It feels impossible, but you'll get through this," he says. "Now I'll get breakfast. Be right back."

The door shuts, and I place my cup on the small table, grimacing as I move. My entire body feels covered in bruises. The place between my thighs feels torn and damaged. Even my ass…

A shudder moves through me.

Push the darkness away.

I reposition myself and lift the letter to tear it open.

My Dearest Angel,

I know how you eschew modern technology, so I decided to write you a letter. I hope it pleases you, although my handwriting leaves much to be desired and I have no idea if this will make it to you before I do.

Please forgive my poor communications. I'm afraid this business has kept me far busier than I anticipated.

Let me reassure you, you are <u>constantly</u> in my thoughts, and I count the hours until I see you again, which will actually be sooner than you think.

Sadly, as a result of my business concerns, my return from Paris can't be permanent. In fact, I will have to fly back within a day of my arrival in New Orleans.

However, Annemarie says her preparations are complete, and we are both eager for you to join us here, especially in view of what I read on the web of your debut.

I can't begin to tell you how crushed I am to have missed it, but I hope I'll be able to see it at least once before you and your sister join us here in Paris.

Please consider what I've written as I must have your answer when I see you again. I should be back at the theater the second week of November, and I hope you'll say the prospect of joining me in my beautiful city fills you with as much joy as it does me.

Your devoted friend,
Freddie

I stare at the letter a long time before lowering it to the bed.

It's still here.

Our way out.

Yet all I feel is hopelessness and misery.

I look up as Roland returns to the room and watch him place the stale bread and a few pieces of fruit on my table—and a surprise.

"You managed a piece of ham." My voice is hoarse, and it sounds different to me.

He glances up and smiles, then carries it to the bed. "Had to move fast. I hope it warms your insides."

He slices it and hands me a piece. The savory meat gives my mind something to settle on apart from my wretched state of affairs.

"Back soon?" He nods to the letter, and I pass it to him with my free hand.

His eyes quickly scan the thick ivory paper, and as he reads, his expression changes. He stands and goes to my dressing table, sets down the dish he's holding and turns to me.

"You've got to get up. If his date's an estimate, he could be here as soon as tonight."

I blink. "I don't understand."

"Get up," he orders, jerking back my blankets and pulling my legs around. "You have to clean up and start moving."

My feet touch the cold floor and tears jump into my eyes. I try to lift them back into the bed, but he catches me and pulls me to my feet. I start to cry.

"Come on, Lara," he urges, giving me a little shake. "This is the best news you could get. It's a way out, and tomorrow's the tenth!"

I close my eyes and drop my shaking head. "I can't do it anymore. I don't feel anything. I only want to die."

Roland catches my chin and lifts my face to look at his. His lips are drawn tight and his dark brow furrows. "You have to find it. Grab what's inside you and force it to stand up."

Tears flood my eyes as I look at him, but he doesn't soften. He clenches his jaw and gives me a harder shake. "Do it!"

I suck in a halting breath and grasp his arms. His hands are still clenched on my shoulders, but I take a step back and turn toward my dressing table. The reflection in the glass gives me a start. My eyes are red and my skin is pale. Even my hair seems dull.

He steps behind me to look at my reflection over my shoulder. "Clean yourself up and be the star you are."

"But…" My voice falters. I can't say his name. "I lost him."

My whisper breaks as my shoulders collapse and the tears run from my eyes. He pulls me against his chest, holding me tight as I break, as the waves of pain I can no longer hold back radiate through my chest.

Mark…

I lost him.

"I know," he whispers, stroking the back of my hair. "You have to lock that away. You have to hold it down until you've escaped."

"I can't."

"You *can*. You're an actress, Lara."

"I was never an actress. All I can do is sing. I'm not even sure I can do that now."

He wraps an arm across my shoulders. "You're a terrific actress, and you *can* sing. You must. It's a chance none of us ever had. He would want you to take it."

I look into his eyes once more, and for a second he allows me to see the pain he keeps at bay. It's not enough to give me hope. Still, something in my chest shifts. I don't know what it is or why.

Perhaps I still want to live, to survive this. Perhaps I believe it's what Mark would want me to do…

Only, how can I live without him?

Roland gives me another hug, and I close my eyes as a tear slides down my nose. Then I nod.

"That's my girl," he whispers, and with a quick kiss to my ear, he releases me and goes to the door. "Come as soon as you're ready, and we'll practice the songs. Exercise your voice."

The door closes and I turn to the mirror. I stare deeply into my own eyes, clear blue sky. They're still beautiful, but they're broken now. The eyes I want to see are gone, lost to memories, but Roland says I have to box that up. Put it away and run through the door that's open.

* * *

My pace slows as I approach the stage. The scrubbing and brushing has done little to change the hollow in my chest, but a quick survey in the mirror shows my appearance has improved.

My soles crackle as I tread on the rosin left over from last night's performance, and as always, I inhale the faint smell of cigar smoke mixed with earthy mildew as I approach the lighted stage.

I'm still in the wings when I see a familiar figure.

"You're up," Molly says, her arms around her waist.

She doesn't come to me or reach out for a hug. She seems completely closed and distant. She's changed. I'm not sure how much she knows about what happened to me, so I go to her and touch her hair, trying to calm my racing heart. The thought of walking into view onstage almost causes me to run back to my dressing room, but Roland is right. I have to get back out here for her as well as me.

"Do you feel like singing today?" She frowns as she studies my face.

I force a smile. "Doesn't matter. The show must go on, right?"

"I wouldn't if I were you."

"Working helps me feel better," I lie. "And Freddie's coming back."

Her brow furrows. "We're still doing that?"

"I promised you—"

"A lot of things." Her voice is flat.

"I need to find Roland."

I walk toward the lighted stage as the piano music starts a fast tune. I hear the tapping feet of dancers out front and wait a moment before stepping forward. Molly's presence, watching me, is the only thing that keeps me moving.

Everyone stops when I step into the light. Bea crosses to embrace me, and I stiffen.

"How are you feeling?" The soft concern in her voice is fake, but I follow Roland's instruction and force a smile.

"Better."

She squeezes my hands and then walks back toward Vanessa, who watches me from afar. Bea says something quietly to her, but I don't try to understand what it is. I focus my gaze on the piano and continue walking.

Roland looks up and smiles. "You look very good." I reach across the top of the piano and grasp his hand for a moment. "Feel like singing?"

"Not really." My insides are numb, and as I dressed, a major roadblock to our escape had entered my mind. "We don't have passports."

"Shit! Passports…" He stands in front of the piano, brow furrowed as he thinks. The cigarette goes between his lips, and he blinks away the tendril of smoke. "I have an idea… I'll take care of it."

I'm about to argue it's impossible when Gavin's voice stops me. "Better today?"

His tone is gentle but I'm unable to fight my response. *Pure rage.*

Roland reads my face and jumps in. "We're just about to go over the songs for tonight. Do you need us?"

Gavin shakes his head. "Just wanted to check on Lara."

I look away as he tries to catch my eye. I can't forgive him for letting this happen. To anyone. I don't know which is worse, the monster or the monster who hides him, who allows him to prey on the innocent.

"Well, on with the show," he says and turns to leave.

Roland stands and comes around to me. "I know how you're feeling. Like you want to scream at everyone. But you can get through it."

I look up at him.

"Remember tonight and Freddie and leaving this place."

CHAPTER 23

"One day I will have a body you have never touched."

Lara

By the finale climb, I'm weak and exhausted from acting.

I don't feel happy or sad.

I don't feel anything.

But in the show I have to be ecstatic, so I raise my arms and smile as hard as I can while the spotlight flashes off the crystals in my costume, in my hair, and the glitter on my skin.

At the top of the ladder, Jeffrey is back, and it's like a spear down the inside of my body. For the first time, I understand Tanya's motivation for taking the drugs. It's going to take something very strong to kill this pain, if that's even possible.

I walk to the bench and sit.

My eyes are fixed on the dark crowd far below, and as I descend I glance back out of habit.

No one is there.

My grip loosens on the ropes and I consider letting go, falling and letting my body be smashed on the stage floor below.

The end.

But I hold on and open my mouth as the smile and the song pour out with no soul attached to them.

Onstage, I'm the dark angel. I prance and swirl as my voice rings out. The final *V*, the swirl of musty velvet curtains, and the crowd roars—a standing ovation.

I walk slowly back to my dressing room, and when I open the door, a bouquet of roses greets me. Instantly I'm onstage again.

"Darling!" Freddie's voice is euphoric, and I almost don't have time to recover before he grasps my hand and drags my entire body to his chest. His mouth covers mine, and it takes all my strength not to pull away.

"Freddie." I fight to seem happy. "Careful, your shirt." I step back and pretend to dust makeup off his shirtfront.

"I couldn't care less." He smiles, running his eyes down my bare breasts. I quickly step over and pull my dressing gown around me. He clears his throat and seems to wake from a spell. "You were incredible tonight. I've never seen you so stunning. I take it you're well? Did you get my letter?"

"I did. It made me so happy."

Relief passes over his face, and again he catches me by the shoulders. His gray eyes are warm as he pulls me to his chest, kissing me longer this time. I inhale his rich, spicy scent and try not to think of fresh air and citrus.

"I couldn't be apart from you another day," he says. "But I only came to get you. Our flight out is tomorrow afternoon. I hope that gives you enough time?"

My eyebrows rise, but I nod with forced anticipation. "The sooner the better."

He breathes a laugh and steps past me into my small room, squeezing my hand as he does.

"And… it's not a problem to bring my sister?"

"Of course not! I could never ask you to leave her behind."

A flicker of relief moves through my heart. Gratitude is an emotion I can use to fight the pain. I focus on that and take his arm. "I've never traveled—"

"And you need a suitcase."

"How did you know?"

He grins and touches my nose. "I guessed."

He pulls out a thick leather wallet and hands me several hundred-dollar bills. My breath catches at the sight of them.

"Buy whatever you need. And don't come back with anything left, so if you see a dress or two or a little treat, anything else you like…"

I step forward into his arms and hug him tightly. He chuckles and hugs me back. "You make me very happy, *mon chou*. I hope I do the same?"

His eyebrows arch as I look up at his face. "Thank you, Freddie."

He leans forward and touches my lips with his, then pulls me into another hug. "God, I'm so happy to see you again. It felt like I was gone an eternity."

He releases me. "Get some rest now, and I'll pick you up around lunchtime, yes? What's your address?"

"Here. I'll be here saying goodbye."

"Of course," he smiles. "And I'll be counting the minutes."

Then with one last kiss, he bids me *adieu*.

The door closes, and I collapse into my chair. I lean forward on my dressing table as tears fill my eyes.

"Oh, Mark," I whisper, eyes closed. "Mark…"

I ache for him, but I have to follow Roland's instructions. I have to hold that pain away for a little while longer, until we're safe. I lift my head slowly and stand, but in that moment I hear a voice in the passage.

"Just a quick visit." It's Guy, and panic grips me.

I break out in a cold sweat and quickly search for anything I can use as a weapon. My lamp? No. A shoe? No.

My door is still unlocked. I dash across the small room, but it's too late. He shoves it open and knocks me back with it, standing tall in the doorway.

"There you are." His gleaming eyes scan my body. "None the worse for wear, it seems, and I trust you've been dreaming of me?"

I'm screaming, scrambling to crawl away, but he lunges forward and grabs my arm, jerking me to my feet.

"Come now, let's have a little kiss. We can catch up right here."

He slides his hand inside my dressing gown, down below my waist, and presses the pad of his finger against places that haven't healed.

My knees buckle, and I scream.

But just then I hear a hollow *thump*. Guy's grip goes slack, and his expression changes. His eyes roll, and as I step aside, he drops like a stone onto my dressing room floor.

Roland steps over his body and tosses a wooden stage pin onto my bed.

"I saw him in the hall and got here as quick as I could." He closes the door. "Change. Fast."

My dressing gown slides to the floor, and Roland goes to my closet. I hear him quickly sliding hangers aside as he pulls my clothes out of the closet.

"You shouldn't stay here tonight."

I step into my jeans, my entire body shaking as I stare at my attacker lying powerless on the floor. The pressure of his fingers still echoes on my skin, on my hips. I look at the hand nearest me, at the golden pinky ring.

He strangled me with that hand. Images of the panic I felt flash through my brain. Images of the men beating Mark. I remember the noises of pain, the way Mark's body slumped, but they never stopped beating him even after he was...

Tears flood my eyes, and I step over his leg and pick up the wooden stage pin from my bed. It's the size of a baseball bat. I hold it a moment, testing its weight as I stare at Guy's unconscious body.

It isn't enough just to knock him out.

"You can leave this." Roland's back is to me. "Grab a bag. We haven't a moment to lose."

Just then Guy's head moves. He makes a sound, and faster than I can think, I raise the pin over my head and slam it down as hard as I can on his skull. A dent appears in the side of his temple. It's strangely satisfying, so I raise it again and slam it down, then I do it again harder.

My eyes are hot and damp, and a strange roaring fills my ears. I can barely breathe, but I keep slamming the pin into his skull. The dents turn into holes, and the holes turn into sticky red-brown mush. Particles fly up and stick to my face, and I keep slamming.

I hit him for raping Molly.

I hit him for raping me.

I hit him for hurting Roland.

I hit him for the men who viciously beat Mark.

I hit him for destroying my love.

I hit him for all the used-up dancer-whores he wanted to see die in the streets.

His head bounces slightly off the floor, so I hit him again for that.

It's then I realize something is slipping, fumbling to catch my forearms. I hear myself screaming and close my mouth. Bright-red blood covers my arms and hands. It's rushing out onto my dressing room floor like someone dropped a gallon of milk.

I've reduced Guy's skull to a glittering black hole, and a sick satisfaction fills my stomach. I almost smile.

That's enough.

He'll never hurt anyone again.

"Oh, God." Roland holds the bloody pin. "Oh, God, Lara."

He steps across the body, drops the weapon, and rips the sheet from my bed, doubling it then folding it again before wrapping it fast around Guy's head. He wraps it several times, covering the bleeding pulp like a turban then he stands back and stares at it.

"He's dead." His hands shake as he wipes them on a towel. "Clean yourself. You've got to get out of here."

For a moment I don't move. I wait for the fear to come, the guilt.

All I feel is glad.

"Don't stand there staring, clean up! Get your clothes!"

I pull out a makeup remover wipe and clean my arms. Then I take my black sweater and pull it over my head.

Once I'm dressed, Roland takes my hand and leads me over Guy's dead body to the doorway.

"The sheet will hold him for now, but you can't stay here. I'll make sure Molly stays with Evie then come back and dispose of the body. You've got to stay at Mark's."

I freeze. "I can't do that. I can't go there without him."

"I don't have anyone else I trust to keep you, and if I get caught... you can't be here."

"I won't let you take the blame. I'll stay and help you."

"If someone calls the police, murder won't be the only charge brought against us. You've got to hide until you leave with Freddie, whether it's at Mark's or somewhere else. Now come on."

We creep into the passage, and Roland pulls out a key, locking my room. A door slams a little further down, and we both jump, setting off in a run. Around two corners and down another narrow passage, and we're at the opposite door. I stop as he helps me into his overcoat and hat.

"Just go out and stay close," he says. "I'll come looking for you as soon as I've made sure everyone's settled."

I slip out into the cold night and walk west a block, then north. I'm not sure what to do, so I wait, leaning against a wall. My hair is tucked inside the coat, making it difficult to tell if I'm a man or a woman.

In the darkness, my whole body shakes. I'm not sure what I feel, other than numb. I think of Guy lying dead on the floor, and I'm not sorry.

A car passes slowly, and I duck my head. Then a couple walks past, but they're too involved in their conversation to notice me. I'm beginning to worry when I hear my name being shouted in a whisper and I run toward a dark figure in an overcoat.

"It worked," Roland says when I reach him. "He's secure in your room for now, and everyone thinks you're in there asleep. They won't disturb him."

The horror of it all has me strangely giddy, but Roland takes my hand and pulls it into the crook of his arm. "Don't be afraid now," he says. "I'll take care of it. Come on."

We set off at a brisk pace away from the theater. We take the few blocks north to Bourbon and then over to the Marigny.

My heart clenches.

Unbearable pain twists in my stomach the closer we get to his door.

"I can't do this," I whisper. "I can't be there without him."

Roland stops and faces me, studying my face. He turns on his heel and we start off in a different direction. We go two more blocks north and then another block east. We walk up to a narrow house, and I realize he's taking out a key. One half of this small place is his.

We step inside, and I'm in a living room. Just past it is another room, I assume the bedroom. Finally, in the back is the kitchen with a small bathroom off to the side.

"I've always wondered where you live," I whisper, stepping slowly on the wide plank floors.

It's clearly an ancient structure, but the inside is restored and well-decorated with traditional New Orleans trappings. Fleur de Lises and slate tiles, vintage wood and leather. He drops onto the couch shaking his head. Then he almost laughs.

"You did it. That bastard thought he could get away with it, but you did what I could never do. I actually feel like celebrating."

I sit on the floor in front of his large coffee table. "It's wicked to feel that way… isn't it?" My stomach is so tight.

He shakes his head. "Perhaps. But you can't say you wish he was still alive."

I'm quiet several minutes, thinking. I remember my arms acting on their own, almost instinctively. I killed him the same way I'd slam my shoe against a palmetto bug. Repeatedly.

"I'm glad he's dead," I whisper. "But what now?"

Roland exhales and takes my hand in his. I study his face, which has become serious.

The muscle in his jaw twitches, and at last he speaks. "Now we continue like nothing happened. You leave with Freddie and stay in France. It's the only place you'll be safe until we're sure no one knows what happened."

I pull my hand back. "I'm afraid."

"Of what? Staying in France or being caught?"

"All of it. That I did it. That it makes me happy, and that I have to run. That I'm a murderer, and I don't care."

"You're a survivor. You did what you had to do to protect yourself and the ones you love from a monster. A predator."

Tears fill my eyes. "I want it all to go away. I want none of this to have ever happened to me."

"But it did happen. You have to face it, accept it for what it is, and then put it behind you. It's a part of you now."

My insides recoil at the thought. "I don't want this to be a part of me."

"Too late. It happened and there it is. If you pretend it didn't, it wins."

I don't answer. I cross my arms over my middle, and turn away. "It's too much."

He slides off the couch to sit beside me on the floor and pull me to him. "It's safe to admit that. But you will get past this."

I shake my head. "I won't. I'm not as strong as you."

Instantly he releases me and laughs. "What? You're strong enough to kill a man. You're dangerously strong." He slides a curl off my cheek. "Stop being afraid. Own your bravery."

"I'm afraid of it," I whisper.

"Oh, Lara," he breathes. "Look at all the things you've survived. And you're alive."

"And this is what I have to live with."

He slides his hand down the back of my head, holding the side of my cheek. "It's going to work out. It simply has to. We won't let the bad guys win."

I lean into him, and he holds me for a bit in silence as I think about him and what I know of his past. He was abused like me, but unlike me, he isn't trapped. With his talent, he could go anywhere, do anything.

"Why did you stay in New Orleans?"

He doesn't answer, instead he glances at me with warmth in his eyes, sadness, too. My stomach tightens as I realize what he'd never said, the things he'd never spoken, but he'd demonstrated in so many other ways.

"You stayed for me."

He shrugs and tries to swagger. "Well, not *entirely* for you. I also had this fabulous offer to be the musical director at a… somewhat decent burlesque show in town."

"Somewhat decent," I repeat.

"You have to admit, darling, between your voice and my songs we really took the old girl over the top. Take tonight, for example. You were phenomenal."

"You didn't trust Gavin. You stayed to make sure I was safe."

Roland sighs and pats my hand. "Your mother got me out of more trouble." His voice becomes tender. "She saved me."

I study his handsome face. I don't remember my mother. "I can't leave you like this. I can't put you at such risk."

"I have always been at risk. At least now it'll be easier. I won't have to be constantly watching your back, too."

He tries to act cavalier, but I'm not convinced.

"There's nowhere else for you to go," I whisper, and for a moment he doesn't answer.

But with a wave of his hand, it's gone. "Now that sounds very dire indeed." His smile returns along with his playful arrogance. "I prefer to look at it as 'limited mobility.'"

I shake my head and look down. He puts an arm around my shoulders. "It's hard for you to see things clearly right now, but it'll pass."

"I don't know what you want me to see."

"That I love this city. I love to make music. And dance." He waves his hands and rotates his slim hips. "I'll handle this, and I'll be fine. Don't you trust me?"

I close my eyes, leaning my forehead against his cheek. "I do."

"I'm more worried about the show now," he says. "You're my muse, you know."

The thought of saying goodbye to him overwhelms me. My first love who has always made me smile. My gallant music man who taught me to survive.

"Oh, Roland, I wish I could be more like you."

"Darling, I wouldn't change a thing about you." He leans forward and kisses my nose. "Now come. Time for you to sleep."

CHAPTER 24

"Hope is like a bird that senses the dawn and carefully starts to sing in the darkness..."

Lara

Dancers and crew members are stirring and arriving as we sneak in through the back door the next morning.

Roland leads me down the dark passage to my room, looking around before pulling me inside. We dash into the narrow space, and I'm amazed. It looks exactly the same as it did before. No signs of blood, no signs of any disturbance.

"What did you do?" I ask.

He lets out an exasperated sigh. "There's no place to bury a body around here, and it was too far to drag him to the river by myself."

"So?"

"I did the next best thing. I scrubbed everything clean and put him in his bed. Once you're away, I'll tell Gavin, and we'll have someone come and dispose of the body."

I swallow the knot in my throat. "Will Gavin go along with that? It's his brother. I can't believe he'd just... do nothing."

"What can he do? For all we know, someone sneaked in and attacked him. Plenty of people hated Guy, and Gavin won't risk a police investigation here. Too much is at stake."

Then he gives me a reassuring smile. "Try not to worry. It's almost over. You're almost free."

I hug myself. "I wish I could believe that."

"Freddie will be here soon to take you away. Then you'll be safe."

"But what about passports?"

"I've already told you. I'm on it. Now pack."

I follow him to the door. He slips through it, and I slide the bolt behind him. That ache is back between my shoulder blades as I walk to my bed stacked with the clothes we pulled from the closet. I look down at the floor that was once covered in blood. Now it's spotless. No trace of my crime here.

Dropping into the chair before my mirror, I lay my head on my hands. I changed everything last night when I raised that pin. I inhale a shaky breath and look at myself. The haunted look is back, but Roland is right. I have to prepare us to leave.

Freddie gave me money to buy a suitcase. I tucked it in an envelope and left it for Roland. Now I go to my closet and run my hand down the jeans and old shirts I've worn for years. His sister will see right away that we have nothing, but I hope she'll chalk it up to my commitment to fame, my limited time.

A tap on the door causes me to jump. I step to it and listen, although I have no reason to be afraid. Am I expecting ghosts?

"It's me," a small voice says.

I quickly pull Molly inside and hug her to me. "Were you okay last night?"

She nods stepping out of my arms. "Evie gave me this suitcase for our things. Armand picked it out."

"That's lucky." I take the large case. "It's plenty for our shabby wardrobe."

Molly frowns. "When do we leave?"

I glance at the clock and see it's after ten. "Not long now. Freddie said he'd be here at noon."

She nods, but her movements are as robotic as I imagine mine are. It's going to take a while for us to heal. Hopefully we can find a way to pick up the pieces in Paris.

I put my arm around her shoulders. "We're almost there," I say, giving her a squeeze. "Just a few more hours."

* * *

Our suitcase is packed and everything collected. I take one last look around my small room, and then drop to my knees. Spreading the drapes on my dressing table, I pull out the basket hidden there. From under the discarded stockings, scrap material, and ribbons, I take Freddie's barrette, the remaining money from the purchase of Molly's shoes, and the diamond bracelet.

The golden locket is in a silk pouch, and the last two items are my mother's pen and the tiny perfume bottle. I hold them in my hand a moment before turning to tuck them into my suitcase.

"Here," I say, holding the diamond bracelet together around my wrist. "Help me."

Molly's eyebrows rise. "It's beautiful."

"It was a gift. From Freddie."

She nods. "It's going to be a different experience having money."

I stand and take her hand.

"Let's go," I say, leading her from the room.

Together we walk up the passage, through the maze of boxes and discarded scenery, through the wings, and onto the stage. The dancers, who, for all these years have been our strange family wait to embrace us both. Tears spill over as I hug Rosa then Evie.

"It's your happily ever after, yes?" She smiles through her misty eyes.

I nod back. "If only there was one for you."

But she shakes her head. "You're the star. In the end, you're the one to ride off in the carriage with the handsome prince."

I choke back another surge of emotions and try to smile.

"Take care of you," I say. "Thanks for the suitcase."

"Armand has ten of those cases." She kisses my cheek, and with a brief hug, Molly and I continue to the front of the stage and then down the short flight of stairs and into the house.

We walk up the aisle to the bright lobby where Freddie waits in a pale gray overcoat. A stocky man wearing a wrinkled suit stands near him. I don't recognize him, and he regards me with curiosity. I look away, at Freddie's smiling face.

He steps forward to take my hand. "I trust you had a relaxing evening?"

I answer quickly. "I couldn't stop thinking of you and our exciting trip."

He kisses my cheek. "Roland gave me these." He holds up navy blue booklets with PASSPORT stamped on them in gold. "He said they were in the safe."

My jaw drops, but Gavin joins us in the lobby. "Best of luck in your new life."

Rage simmers just below the surface of my skin, but I hide it for Freddie's sake. "I'll never forget how you took me in and gave me my start."

He bows slightly, then turns to the small man watching us. I hope never to see his face again, and I can't help wondering what will happen when he learns of the body in the salon under the theater.

"We're almost finished here, Detective Landry."

"I'm supposed to question everyone who was in the theater the night of the disappearance," the strange man growls. "Otherwise—"

"I can assure you, Lara and Molly know nothing of your business."

My pulse beats faster as I wonder what the stocky detective is investigating, but Freddie is back, taking my arm.

"As soon as you're ready, dear." He carries my suitcase out to the waiting Towncar.

I follow him quickly, anxious to get out of here.

Molly is right beside me, and despite her hollow eyes, her pale skin is bright. Her smooth curls glow with auburn highlights in the sun.

"A limo," she muses. "You're wearing diamonds. All we need is a little dog."

I give her a tight smile and take her hand.

Freddie touches my lower back. "Ready?"

"Oh—wait." I leave them and jog to where Roland stands near the back doors of the house.

He's watching from afar, and I know, like me, his tears are waiting to be shed in solitude.

"You did it," I say.

"I told you I would."

Our eyes hold each other's for the last time. I blink back the tears. "I have a phone. You promise to keep in touch?"

"I'll be waiting for your first text."

"Thank you," I whisper.

"It was always my pleasure."

I step forward into his embrace and hold him a few heartbeats longer before letting him go and walking slowly to the waiting car.

"Now," I say, and Freddie helps me inside.

My eyes drink in the buttery leather interior of the small limo taking us to the New Orleans International Airport. My stomach is fluttery to be leaving here, not knowing what awaits us in a new country where we don't speak the language and our only friend is this man who thinks we're something we're not.

The car rumbles quietly forward, and Molly spins in her seat to look out the back window. My eyes are fixed on the man sitting in front of me as the soft strains of classic jazz surround us.

Freddie reaches for my hand. "It won't hurt my feelings if you shed a few tears. I know it's hard to say goodbye to the people you know and love."

"You're always so kind to me."

"Only because I adore you." Freddie gives my hand a squeeze. "And I really do think you're going to adore Paris as well. Perhaps I can make you happy there the way you've made me happy here."

"Perhaps."

"Annemarie's already planning to take you shopping," he continues. "Make a list of everything you want to do and see."

Molly finally turns around, and for the first time in two days, she slips her small hand into mine. Her head is on my shoulder, and she speaks quietly.

"Lara loves diamonds. And she wants a little dog."

Freddie laughs. "I can't wait to get to know you better," he says, tapping the end of her nose lightly.

His gesture fills me with an emotion I've almost forgotten.

Hope.

The car hastens our departure, and I look down at the small hand holding mine. She's safe now, and perhaps one day we'll learn to forget the things that happened here. Maybe one day we'll learn to never think about this place, ever again.

There's no reason for ghosts to follow us across the Atlantic.

EPILOGUE

Mark

It's black as pitch when my eyes open again.

Time has passed, but I don't know how much. My entire body is wracked with intense pain, and the coppery flavor of blood is in my mouth.

I try to move, but my wrists are tied to my ankles. I try to roll, but my shoulder collides with hard wood. I'm in some kind of box or a crate. Getting still, I listen.

The rhythmic noise of clattering wheels on metal rails is unmistakable. I rock side to side, and I realize I'm tied up in the dark in a box on a train.

I didn't save Lara.

She's still back there.

She's still in danger.

I can't let myself think about how those men might have hurt her. I've got to get out of here and get back to her.

This isn't the end of my story…

* * *

The story continues in UNDER THE STARS, live Jan. 22!

"Sundown" is a special bonus novella that occurs between *Under the Lights* and *Under the Stars*... Get it today on Amazon!

Keep turning for an Exclusive Sneak Peek...

(A slightly different version of "Sundown" appeared in THE VAULT anthology.)

See the inspiration board for *Under the Lights* on Pinterest: http://smarturl.it/WWTpin

Check out the Book Trailer on YouTube:

* * *

Never miss a new release!

Sign up for my New Release newsletter, and get a **FREE Subscriber-only story bundle!** (http://smarturl.it/TLMnews)

Join **"Tia's Books, Babes & Mermaids"** on Facebook and chat about the books, post images of your favorite characters, get EARLY exclusive sneak peeks, and MORE! (***www.Facebook.com/groups/TiasBooksandBabes***)

* * *

Get Exclusive Text Alerts and never miss a SALE or NEW RELEASE by Tia Louise! Text "TiaLouise" to 64600 Now!*

(U.S. only.)

Your Opinion Counts!

If you enjoyed *Under the Lights,* please leave a short, sweet review where you purchased your copy.

Reviews help your favorite authors more than you know.

Thank you so much!

* * *

Books by Tia Louise

KINDLE UNLIMITED

Stand-Alone Romances:
When We Touch, 2017
The Last Guy, 2017*
(*co-written with Ilsa Madden-Mills)

The Bright Lights Duet:
Under the Lights, 2018
Under the Stars, 2018

"Sundown" (*A Bright Lights novella*), 2017
Hit Girl (*A Bright Lights VAULT novel*), **coming March, 2018!**

Paranormal Romances:
One Immortal, 2015
One Insatiable, 2015

BOOKS ON ALL RETAILERS

The Dirty Players Series:
The Prince & The Player, 2016
A Player for A Princess, 2016
Dirty Dealers, 2017
Dirty Thief, 2017

The One to Hold Series:
One to Hold (Derek & Melissa), 2013
One to Keep (Patrick & Elaine), 2014

One to Protect (Derek & Melissa), 2014
One to Love (Kenny & Slayde), 2014
One to Leave (Stuart & Mariska), 2014
One to Save (Derek & Melissa), 2015
One to Chase (Amy & Marcus), 2015
One to Take (Stuart & Mariska), 2016

Most available in audiobook format!

EXCLUSIVE SNEAK PEEK

"Sundown"
(A Bright Lights Novella)

Part I: Confidence

"I was quiet but I was not blind."

Mark

This time it's different.

I've made the annual journey from British Columbia to Juneau and back on the White Pass-Yukon Route for as long as I've been a detective. It's a treacherous route in the winter, one with no direct connection to any other railway.

Tourists will ride it in the summer to see the glaciers, gorges, waterfalls, and steep grades. Now, only a very few individuals with proven business in the remote stops are allowed to travel this line.

Perhaps that's why I do it each year at this time, for the adventure.

Perhaps it's nostalgia, missing the dusty clutch of regulars riding these rails for their line of work.

I'd say I'm doing due diligence, keeping tabs on the outer reaches of my territory. This part of the country is so remote and isolated, anyone could get away with anything, and it would take months if not years for the authorities to notice. If it were even reported.

The truth is I'm here for a very specific reason.

I'm here waiting for him to slip up, to give me the reason I need to nail him.

"Confidence." The slender man's pronouncement breaks through my musings.

He leans forward on the bar, grasping his chunky shot glass in three fingers. Emerald-green absinthe swirls around inside the cup.

"Confidence is the key to everything," he slurs. "The best criminals know this."

Dropping back onto his stool, he slides two fingers along the corners of his thin mustache, pushing down his shifty grin. Aleister is a hustler, and he seems to be feeling the effects of his liquor.

Or it could be a lie… a grift. He could be stone cold sober and trying to get my guard down. He knows I'm searching. He wants to know why, what for.

His brown tweed three-piece suit has the finishing details only a tailor would know, tabs on the lapels, specialty labels. It's old, but it's expensive.

"Is that so?" I take a small hit of my scotch, poker face in place.

Unlike this fellow, my suit is off the rack, and I wear a beard, although I do keep it neatly trimmed. He's a relic from another way of life. I'm the younger generation he feels compelled to educate.

"Yes," he continues, "no matter what happens, the authorities will walk right past a perpetrator if he acts like he's supposed to be there. No one questions him."

I smile at that. "You don't have much respect for my profession."

The dining car sways, and I clutch my tumbler to keep it from sliding across the glossy wooden bar.

Everything about this line is vintage. It's filled with highly polished antiques, and the smell of cigar smoke, wax, and days gone by.

"*Au contraire*!" Aleister places a palm flat against his vest. "I have great respect for law enforcement. I am merely a lifelong student of human behavior."

"I see." I take another sip. The alcohol warms my chest on this frigid night. "You're a profiler. I'm afraid your line of work has fallen out of fashion, my friend."

"Pah! I'm a profiler of the profilers," Aleister argues. "Profilers make judgments. I merely watch for patterns. Men see what they're looking for, and they're looking for suspicious behavior, fear, defensiveness. The most cunning serial killers—the Unabomber, the Boston strangler, Jeffrey Dahmer—they all walk around in plain sight because they're confident. They're calm."

My lips tense, and I'm ready to argue when the double doors slide apart, and my insides go completely still.

A woman enters the dining car.

I don't believe my eyes.

It's her.

She's more beautiful than ever. Her long, brown hair is perfectly straight, and her skin is as gold as the California sand. I meet her bright blue eyes, a spark flickers, and it's gone.

Still, she recognized me. My stomach is tight, and I can only imagine she feels the same. It's the first time we've seen each other in five years.

She continues, poker face in place, and behind her is the girl. Stike that, behind her is the young woman. She's grown and changed, and while I know she's eighteen, she seems more mature. Her hair is now bleached pale blonde, but her skin is still peachy.

Her body is much curvier, and she moves like she's become accustomed to attracting the male gaze.

They're both stylishly dressed for dinner. Lara wears tight black pants and a flowing burgundy blouse that reveals her slim neck and elegant collarbones. She still has the body of a dancer, long and willowy, and her skin is as smooth as I remember her voice. My fingers curl at the memory.

Molly is in a short skirt and thick sweater. She's completely new to me—almost like a different person.

I watch Aleister studying her ass as they go to a table near the window, and I can't help thinking she's the wild card in this game of cat and mouse.

Outside, winter white blurs our view of the scenery. It's all mountains and treacherous canyons, but as they sit, Lara turns to us.

"Our route is appropriately named." She smiles, and her voice is smoky silk and longing. "White as far as the eye can see."

My drinking companion is quick to answer. "The White Pass is one of only two train lines running from Alaska into Canada." He doesn't try to hide his interest, and his eyes burn with lust. No doubt he's hoping to find a bunkmate with whom to pass this cold winter night. "You're from Montreal?"

"I'm American," she answers, turning her gaze to the menu on the table.

It's the universal sign she's finished with us, but Aleister isn't done. "You're traveling to Whitehorse?"

The faintest hint of annoyance is in her blue eyes. It disappears when they meet mine. She smiles at me, and I fight the heat flooding my stomach, the tightness across my fly.

I'm not that easy.

It's been too long. I have too many questions.

"Just passing through," she says.

The girl across from her lifts a golden locket hanging from a long chain around her neck. It's chunky and stylish, not delicate, and the gold is dirty, like an heirloom.

When she speaks, her voice is soft and high, deceptively innocent. "It's almost eight, but it's still so bright outside."

"I wouldn't be so anxious to see the sun disappear," Aleister says. "At sundown, the weather turns brutal. It's a deadly night to be out in the wilds."

"Scaring the women, Fragonard? Hoping to lure one to your bed?" A loud authoritative voice breaks the hypnotic spell of the swirling snow, and Baron Robert Esterhaus pushes through the double doors with his valet Jeffrey following close behind. "Good evening, Fitz," he says to me. "I trust you're keeping this swindler on his toes."

"I am no swindler," Aleister growls, red rising around his collar. "The Yukon Territory is renowned for its dangers—"

"Keep your shirt on, I'm only yanking your chain." The older man takes a seat across from the two women and winks back at me. "Still, I left my wallet in my safe."

Aleister emits an insulted noise, and I break the tension. "I heard we might be in for some weather tonight."

"Yes, forecasters predict a blizzard, but these engineers know how to navigate it," Esterhaus says to the room.

Lara turns to the baron, and I'm not sure how she would know him. I remember him, of course. I've been following him these many years watching and waiting.

So far, he's walked a straight line.

"I haven't heard the weather report. Should we be concerned?" Lara asks.

"As long as this beast stays on the tracks, we aren't in any danger, despite what this Frenchman might tell you."

Aleister shifts in his chair, growing angrier by the syllable. Ustinov, our perky Russian porter, cuts off any further interaction as he enters the car.

"Limited choices on the dinner menu tonight, I'm afraid." He tugs on his starched white jacket and smiles. "We have Duck l'Orange or roast duck."

I'm turning back to the bar when I hear Molly whisper, "I don't care for duck."

"What comes on the side?" Lara asks.

"Ah, yes…" A wink is in Ustinov's tone. "We have a lovely roasted corn salad with avocado, or a risotto with exotic mushrooms and spinach."

"Avocado this far north?" Robert exclaims, his hearty voice loud in the small car.

"We received a special shipment from the California coast when we embarked at Juneau."

"We'll each have the roast duck with the risotto, please," Lara says.

The baron selects the l'Orange and corn salad, as do Aleister and I. Ustinov's mood seems to have assuaged my friend's irritation at our brash companion.

"Forgive me, I failed to introduce myself." Esterhaus turns to the women. "I'm Robert Esterhaus, and this is my valet Jeffrey. At the bar there are Detective Mark Fitzhugh, or Fitz as I call him, and Aleister Fragonard, The Grifter of Montreal."

Lara's eyes move to each of us as we're introduced, briefly widening when I'm introduced by my title. She never meets my gaze. *Does my profession bother you, beautiful?* They pause on a fuming Aleister, waiting for further explanation, which isn't forthcoming.

I know the baron despises him. They're still wrangling about a past business deal gone sour, but I've never dug deeper into that. I monitor these men once a year when I make the trip from the Yukon Territory to Juneau for my annual police association's conference. Aleister is returning from making purchases for his retail store, and Esterhaus is inspecting his holdings along the Alaskan coastline.

It's always the same… until now.

"How do you do," she says with a slight nod. "I'm Lia Hale, and this is my… sister. Molly."

It's a lie.

Perhaps that's too harsh.

Perhaps "Lia" has a sister named Molly.

Lara does not.

The younger girl's eyes stay on her plate, and her fingers return to her necklace.

"That's an interesting chain," the baron says to her. "It's early Romanov. Are you traveling from Russia?"

"How did you know that?" Lara's eyes fly to his, and she seems almost frightened. *Interesting.*

"I collect antiquities," Esterhaus explains. "It's one of my hobbies. Almost all of the Romanov collection was melted down following the revolution. Is it an imitation?"

"I don't know," Molly says without looking up. "It was a gift."

"I'd love to examine it further if possible. You might stop by my stateroom—"

Just then the doors open and another traveler joins us. He captures all of our attention, an African-American gentleman dressed in a dark plum coat with thin grey pinstripes. He doesn't speak to anyone, and goes to a table in the farthest corner of the room, turning his back on us.

I know Esterhaus well enough to know he won't let this behavior pass. He presides over the dining car like a lord in his castle, but before he can launch his investigation, Ustinov returns with several additional waiters carrying our dinner.

The young porter directs them on who gets which items before going to the new guest. They speak quietly, and he exits behind the bar, I assume to get another serving.

For a little while we don't speak. The Duck l'Orange is deliciously rich with a touch of sweetness. The dark-brown meat melts like butter in my mouth, and the corn and avocado provide the perfect accompaniment, crisp and fresh.

The bartender uncorks a bottle of Chardonnay and serves the baron and myself. The diners having the roast duck are given a light pinot. I notice Molly doesn't eat her meat, sticking instead to the risotto and mushroom side. She also isn't served wine.

Aleister is subdued, but I see him glancing at Lara. The women don't speak during the meal. Lara takes several bites of everything on her plate, but she finishes none of it. She does, however, have a second glass of wine.

Our new guest in the back places a tablet on the table and appears to read while having his own serving of the roast duck and red wine.

When Ustinov and his crew return to collect our plates, the baron stands and joins me at the bar, taking out a fat cigar and clipping the end. He holds the leather pouch toward me, but I wave him away.

"Every year I offer, and every year you decline," he chuckles.

"Never developed a taste for them." I lean back as the bartender pours the old man a scotch.

"You prefer a pipe," Esterhaus says, and I shake my head.

"No tobacco for me. Not worth the risk."

"Life is all about risk," the baron says.

"Life is about avoiding risk," Aleister argues. "Detecting it early and doing everything you can to get out of its way."

Ustinov returns for dessert orders. The other men and I decline. Lara holds up a hand in a *no* gesture, but indicates she'd like another glass of wine. Molly is the only one who does a little nod.

"I'd like the tiramisu," she says.

"An excellent choice!" Ustinov exclaims, pleased someone is taking his offer. "The lady fingers are imported from Vienna, the espresso is made fresh, and the mascarpone is light as air."

He oversells every item on the menu, but I don't comment. Aleister rises from his seat and gestures to Lara. "Would you join us at the bar?"

She shakes her head, causing her silky brown hair to shimmer in the light. It smells like springtime if I remember correctly, or perhaps *Lia* prefers another scent. "The smoke gets in my eyes."

"I'm so sorry," the baron moves his cigar further toward the end of the bar away from her table.

The bartender flips a switch hidden under the counter and a quiet whirring joins the background noise. "That should help," he says.

I see Robert preparing to address our strange companion, when the man rises and takes his tablet. He places a few dollars on the table and abruptly leaves the dining car, rendering us all momentarily silent in his wake.

I've decided it's time for coffee when Lara speaks. "You're from New Orleans, Baron?"

Her pointed question surprises me. Perhaps she does know him after all... But how?

Esterhaus straightens, seeming uncomfortable. "Why no. Calgary."

"But you spent time there," she insists.

"Many years ago." He clears his throat. "Many, many years ago. How do you know about that?"

"I'm from New Orleans," she says. "I thought I recognized your face. It just came to me."

The older man shifts on his stool, and I'm intrigued by this turn of events. I've never seen Esterhaus put on guard.

My skin prickles. Perhaps this is the trip I've been waiting for. I only need her.

I've always needed her.

He squints over his small glasses at Lara. "How would you recognize my face? Have we met?"

"When I was in the city, I worked at a theater. It operated a private club, which I believe you had an interest in."

The older man's expression goes from startled to stony in the flicker of an eyelash, and I shift forward in my seat. What she's saying is true, and I've often wondered how he doesn't recognize me from that... interest. I suppose he was drunk or stoned each time he visited the city. I wonder if tonight will be the night I place this gentleman under arrest...

"I was briefly involved in a nightclub establishment," he grumbles crossly. "I divested myself after a very short time."

"Is that so?" Lara's voice drips with innocence. "I can't understand why. It was such a vibrant and active place when I lived there."

"I was too far away to have an active hand in the business decisions. I didn't have a voice in what went on. I wasn't aware—"

His tone makes me think of a large snow crab backing up from a predator, front claws snapping. Lara is on her feet, sweeping toward him at once.

"I'm so sorry." Her voice is soft and endearing. "You must think I'm terribly rude to pry into your affairs. I simply love my hometown so much. So many years have passed since I was there. I enjoy finding others who can remember it with me."

Robert shifts on his leather stool, and I notice Molly has silently joined them. She stands at his arm, and holds out the chunky gold chain.

"You wanted to look at my necklace?" Her innocent tone seems to relax him further. "I've had it so long. It might be fun to learn about its history. Can you tell me?"

The cigar returns to his mouth, and Lara drifts away. I'm sure she would say it's to avoid the smoke, but my eyes follow her. My chest is tight, and a pain moves into my temple as Aleister acts quickly to provide her with company. I signal the bartender for another scotch and lean on my forearms, fixing my eyes on the glossy wood in front of me.

"A New Orleans lady…" I hear him say. I imagine his lips curling beneath his oily mustache to reveal his tobacco-stained teeth. "I detected your

French heritage the moment I saw you. The Acadian connection."

"I'm not Acadian," she says.

Aleister lights a cigarette, and my mind snaps back, across the miles, to a closet-sized room hidden down a dark passage in the back of an enormous theater.

Whispers in the shadows.

Cigarette smoke in velvet curtains.

Rooms covered in black wallpaper embossed with ornate velvet wreaths...

***

Five years ago...

I'm barely twenty-one. I'm not a policeman. I'm an errand boy, and tonight I'm running back to the theater from the drugstore on Rampart Street, a small white bag clutched in my fist. I say running, but I'm actually speeding in a borrowed Fiat, block after rain-soaked block.

A strawberry blonde named Tanya is the falling star of this burlesque show. On the posters she is Jezebel, Queen of the Angels, but behind the scenes, she spends her life strung out on fentanyl-laced heroin.

"Move..." Gavin's voice is stern. He stands over her with his hands on his hips. "Get up, I said!"

He's shouting, but Tanya only rolls onto her side.

I stand in the doorway behind Roland, who is also twenty-one. His hands are on his hips, and as I struggle to catch my breath, I look through the space between his arm and his lean torso.

"She's not coming out of it tonight," he says, taking a long draw from his ever-present cigarette. "She's done."

Gavin lets out a growl. As owner of the theater, he's responsible for ensuring the show goes on. He shoves meaty hands into his ginger hair and looks around the room.

Washed-out blue eyes land on me. "There you are! Where the fuck have you been? Give it to me!"

I rush forward and hand him the bag. It's Narcan, which he'll use to try and bring her around quickly. It's possible she could still perform tonight. I stand back, looking at her pale, clammy skin.

Her skeletal body is covered with a sheen of perspiration, and the hair on her head sticks to her face in stringy waves. She reminds me of a sick baby I saw in the street. Her pink lips are parted, and she makes gurgling sounds. Rosa, the costume mistress, holds her chin and slaps her, and she only does a little laugh.

It makes my stomach sick.

Roland, the pianist and conductor, makes a disgusted noise. "See if Larissa can perform."

"I'm not moving her to the lead yet," Gavin argues. "She's too young."

They continue to argue, but I back out of the stale, smoke-filled room and make my way down the narrow hall to another little closet. It's only big enough for a narrow cot, a changing screen, and a lighted makeup mirror. Still, she's lucky to have her own room.

"Can I come in?" My voice is soft. It's deep, but it doesn't have Gavin's edge yet. That won't come for another few years. I knock lightly.

The door falls open, and my body goes rigid. All the blood leaves my head, going straight to my cock, and I'm breathing faster.

Larisa stands in front of the mirror. Her long brown hair is pinned up on one side with a sparkling barrette, and a few pieces fall in waves around her face. With her olive complexion and bright blue eyes, she's dramatically beautiful. The Dark Angel.

A red robe hangs from her shoulders, and her waist is bound in a deep-red velvet corset. Skinny black straps hold up her thigh-high black fishnet stockings. Her legs are long and slender, and in her tall heels she is even taller, even more willowy.

Her beautiful breasts are bare, and even though I've seen her in this costume before, I get a hard-on every single fucking time.

I'm in love with her.

She's the rising star, and while she appears older than nineteen, she's not. She's innocent and sweet... and I should keep my hands off her.

I never do what I should.

"What's happening?" Her voice is soft, and smooth as silk.

She pulls the sides of the robe around her, and I tear my eyes off her body to meet her gaze.

"Tanya's not waking up." I step forward into her dressing room-slash-bedroom.

"Rosa is trying, but Roland thinks it's your night to take the lead."

"Fuck!" she hisses, and my cock jumps. I love when she swears. It makes her polished beauty edgy and raw.

"What's wrong?" I want to touch her, wrap my arms around her, and feel her warmth against my body.

Long lashes frame her cat-eyes. They blink rapidly, fanning my desire. Her lips are pale pink. She hasn't applied her lipstick, and it's how I like her. It's how I want to kiss her, bruise her pillow lips with my mouth.

"I don't know the choreography..."

"But you know all the songs."

She crosses the room to me and puts a hand on my chest. It's electric, and I wonder if she can feel my heart beating. We've been together a few times, and it's like a little piece of heaven, never enough.

"There's more to it than that. I can't just stand there singing."

Covering her slim hand, I close my fingers over her cool skin. "It's your big chance. Don't be afraid." I give her a warm smile, softening my tone and urging her. "Walk through the door and own it."

Her dark eyes rise to mine, and she looks at me with so much emotion. My chest swells at the sight. She looks at me as if she wants me to kiss her. My eyes go to her lips. They're full and slightly parted, dewy and soft. My own lips feel heavy with need. I'm leaning forward, a little closer...

Her door bursts open as if on cue, and we both jump apart. Roland stands in the empty space, and his dark eyes move back and forth over us rapidly. I can't help thinking he sees what I want.

"Tanya's awake," he says. "You're off the hook. Get dressed for your regular number. Come with me, boy."

I bristle at his words. I'm not a boy, and I don't like his proprietary attitude when it comes to Lara. Still, I'm the low man in this chain of command, and I have to do as I'm told for now.

I give her a tight smile. "Don't worry. Your time is coming."

I turn to follow Roland out, down the dark, narrow backstage corridors to whatever errand he has for me.

We run into Gavin in the hallway. "Where are you going?"

"Roland said—"

"I need you to go to Tanya's room and be sure she gets dressed and on that stage. If you see her even look at a drug, you'd better carry her out of there." He leans closer, furious eyes cutting into mine. "And don't come back."

"Yes, sir." I nod and change directions, heading to Tanya's dressing room.

I don't want to watch Tanya dress. Her body makes me ill. I can count her ribs through the skin stretched taut across her back. Her chest is flat as a boy's, and her hair is tissue thin and frizzled. Everything about her is like a toy doll left in the rain and snow, abandoned and forgotten.

"Out of the way, boy!" Rosa pushes past me. She's thick and bossy, and she has costumes over her arm.

I step back and hold the door, looking at my fingernails as the two of them wrap and fasten and tie and apply wigs and headdresses and fans. By the time the stocky woman is finished, Tanya is Jezebel. Up close she's clearly a malnourished drug addict, but from afar, she's pink cheeks and soft breasts pushed up into little peaks. She's a queen.

They pass me in a cloud of starchy powder and antique perfume, and I walk slowly after them, following the narrow hallway toward Lara's room. I'm sure she's gone as well, out to the wings to wait for her moment to descend to the stage as the dark angel. I need to head up as well.

These halls are deserted when they're performing. The skeleton crew is moving scenery and operating lights and equipment, and everyone else is standing in the darkness watching for anything that might go wrong. I'm surprised to see Gavin at her door. He's speaking softly, urgently, and she's blinking rapidly. I step to the side and creep closer hoping to overhear their conversation.

"I won't let that happen." Her voice is panicky. "I'll take her place."

The fear in Lara's voice shoots fire through my veins. *Why is she afraid?*

Gavin's voice is low. "I'll pass that along."

My fists clench, and I'm prepared to charge forward and slam one into his choleric nose. It's several days before I discover the bargain she made, before I chase after her down those dark halls…

That night I find her on her knees in one of the hidden rooms below the theater. The walls are papered in red velvet, and a row of doors lines the passage. It's like something out of a David Lynch film, surreal and unsettling.

I stop at the corner, carefully picking my way closer, looking for anyone who might be lurking in the shadows.

A knot of possessive anger is in my throat. I know what goes on down here. I'm ashamed that I've played a part in covering it up and allowing it to happen. That time I made a vow, I'll never Lara be hurt here.

I wait a bit longer to see if someone is planning to join us right away. After minutes that feel like hours,

I head around the corner and down the second red velvet hallway.

A diamond-studded crown embellishes the door, and a small black plaque reads *Private*. I reach forward and turn the handle, allowing it to fall open, allowing the narrow shaft of bright light from the hallway to illuminate the interior.

My voice catches, and my semi is back when I see her.

Lara kneels on the floor, her legs bent under her. Her palms are flat on her thighs, and her chin is down. A black satin mask is over her eyes, and she's breathing so fast, her full breasts rise and fall above the top of her corset.

"Lara?" I say softly, taking a step toward her.

She jumps and stretches her back toward me, but her movements are wrong. She seems fuzzy, drugged out somehow, and her neck is red like someone tried to strangle her.

I go to her and lift the mask off her eyes. "What are you doing? Why are you kneeling here?"

Her eyes widen and she reaches for me. "You're here!"

"What are you doing?" My hands are on her upper arms, and I attempt to lift her to her feet.

She struggles against me, raising her hands to slap mine away. "I have to do what he says... You have to go before he comes back."

"Who?" I look all around.

We're in an elaborate bedroom with mirrors on all the walls. A narrow fireplace is across from a single bed, and a red divan sits in the corner waiting. It's a boudoir.

"Are you..." I can't even say the words. "Why are you doing this? What's happening?"

"Give me the mask." She holds out her hand, but I swing the piece of silk behind my back.

Her chin trembles and she looks down at her lap. I wait, doing my best to swallow the pain in my throat, doing my best to keep breathing.

I'm on my feet, this time, pulling her up by the waist with me. "I'm getting you out of here."

"It's too late," she cries.

The words pull me up short. "What?"

She goes limp in my arms. "I thought I could keep her safe. I thought I could get her out of here, but it's too late now."

I've never cared about money, but for the first time in my life I'm confronted by what a necessary evil it is.

She reaches up and touches my face. "Sweet Mark. You want to help me?"

"More than anything," I say with all the conviction roiling my stomach.

A bitter smile crosses her face, and her eyes are full of so much sadness, it breaks my heart. "Then go."

"No," I say desperately. "I'm getting you out of here. I won't let anyone hurt you."

Thick lashes lower over dark eyes, and she shakes her head. "No one can save us now."

Pain flashes in my stomach. I'm ready to argue I can save her, and I will, when she rises onto her toes and places her parted lips against mine. Her cool hand cups my cheek, and her tongue touches mine.

It's a match to the desperate heat inside me. I grasp her body, pulling her closer. A noise comes from her throat as I consume her mouth, pulling her lips with mine, sliding my tongue to hers, stoking the flames higher with each pass.

My arms are around her, and I'm momentarily distracted by how she melts into me, gripping my shoulder with her free hand. Mine moves up her back into her hair. My fingers curl in her silky locks, and my cock stiffens in my jeans.

"Mark," she gasps, breaking her lips away, but I can't stop. I chase her mouth, covering it again with mine, drinking from her like a fountain in the desert. I want to take her away from here and keep her safe… I want to make love to her.

"You're coming with me," I whisper against her ear, overwhelmed by the passion coursing through my body. "You'll stay with me. You'll be mine, and I'll never let anyone hurt you."

My hand travels down the curve of her ass, and her fingers tighten on my shirt. "I want to go with you," she says in a voice that nearly slays me.

Stepping back, I'm ready to drag her to the nearest exit, leave this place, and never look back. I imagine days in the sun, a little white house with a picket fence and children playing in the yard. I imagine every corny thing a man ever imagines about the girl of his dreams when an iron hand slams down on my shoulder. I'm gripped in a vise-like metal claw, and our moment is shattered to little tiny pieces.

"Who the fuck are you?" A wolfish voice snarls loudly behind us.

I'm jerked around so fast, my grip on Lara slips. I reach for her again when a fist blasts pain through my entire face. White fills my eyes, and when I manage to shake the confusion away, I realize I'm on all fours on the floor.

"He's going to be a problem." Another man is in the room with us.

"Oh, no he's not," Wolf-voice replies. "I'll take care of this little fucker."

"No!" Lara screams, and I try to stop the room from spinning.

I try to get to my feet.

It's no use. A violent kick to my stomach sends me flying down onto my side, another blast of pain shatters through my body. More kicks, one after the other, and I'm coughing up blood. Still, they don't stop beating me.

The taste of copper fills my mouth, and I see the boot just before it flies at my face. I manage to get my arms up in time to block it from hitting my eyes, but my deflection only makes my attacker angrier.

"You want to be a hero?" the man shouts.

"Heroes don't last long in this place."

"Stop, please!" Lara's cry is more of a whimper now, and I look up to see her face shining and slick with tears. Her eyes are red and her nose is swollen.

Terror is on her face, and I try to reach for her. I try to say her name one last time. I'm sure the words are on my lips. I stretch out my hand. "Lara?"

It's the last thing I remember before another blast of pain hits my head, and everything goes black…

It's black as pitch when I open my eyes again.

Time has passed, but I don't know how much.

My entire body is a vessel of intense pain. The flavor of blood is still in my mouth. I try to move, but my wrists are tied to my ankles. I try to roll, but my shoulder collides with hard wood. I'm in some kind of box. I'm rocking side to side in a rhythm, and as I listen, I hear a familiar noise. I hear the sound of a train.

I'm tied up in the dark in a box on a train.

I didn't save Larissa.

I can't let myself think about how they might have hurt her.

I'll never see her again.

It's the end of my story…

* * *

Get "Sundown" on Amazon Today!

ACKNOWLEDGMENTS

The story behind this book is five years in the making. Maybe one day I'll share it, but for now I'll just say it's a story I've wanted to share with a large audience for a long time. I hope you loved it as much as I do. It's so special to me.

To get more specific, I have to thank the beta readers who helped me transform it into the version you're holding now—Ilona Townsel, Tina Morgan, LuLu Dumonceaux, and of course Mr. TL. I love you all!

HUGE thanks to my editor Tamara Mataya, and to my dear dear friends who always give me so much encouragement, Aleatha Romig and Ilsa Madden-Mills.

To all my amazing author-friends who made room in your crammed holiday schedules, THANK YOU so much!

Special thanks to Letitia Hasser for the gorgeous cover design, and Wander Aguiar for the perfect photograph! Thanks to Shannon for the gorgeous teasers and Nita Banks for the PERFECT book trailer. Love you, peeps!

Thanks to Jenn Watson, Lisa Hintz, and Brooke Nowiski for the tireless PR and marketing help! I appreciate you ladies more than I can ever say!

To my MERMAIDS, *Thank You* for giving me a place to relax and be silly. THANKS to ALL the bloggers who have made an art and a science of book loving. Sharing this book with the reading world would be impossible without you. I appreciate your help so much.

To everyone who picks up this book, reads it, loves it, and tells one person about it, you've made my day. I'm so grateful to you all. Without readers, there would be no writers.

So much love,
Stay sexy,
<3 *Tia*

About the Author

Tia Louise is the *USA Today* best-selling, award-winning author of *When We Touch*, the "One to Hold" and "Dirty Players" series, and co-author of the #4 Amazon bestseller *The Last Guy*.

She loves all the books (as long as they have romance), all the chocolate (as long as it's dark), strong coffee and sparkling wine.

After being a teacher, a book editor, a journalist, and finally a magazine editor, she started writing love stories and never stopped.

Louise lives in the Midwest with her trophy husband, two teenage geniuses, and one grumpy cat.

Keep up with Tia online:
www.AuthorTiaLouise.com

CPSIA information can be obtained
at www.ICGtesting.com
Printed in the USA
FSHW04n2252060318
45391FS